Little
Green

**Center Point
Large Print**

Also by Walter Mosley and available from
Center Point Large Print:

The Last Days of Ptolemy Grey

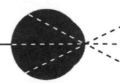

**This Large Print Book carries the
Seal of Approval of N.A.V.H.**

Little
Green

An Easy Rawlins Mystery

WALTER MOSLEY

CENTER POINT LARGE PRINT
THORNDIKE, MAINE

This Center Point Large Print edition is published in the year 2013 by arrangement with Doubleday, an imprint of The Knopf Doubleday Publishing Group, a division of Random House, Inc.

The text of this Large Print edition is unabridged. In other aspects, this book may vary from the original edition. Printed in the United States of America on permanent paper. Set in 16-point Times New Roman type.

ISBN: 978-1-61173-838-4

Library of Congress Cataloging-in-Publication Data

Mosley, Walter.
 Little green : an easy Rawlings mystery / Walter Mosley. — Center Point Large Print edition.
 pages ; cm.
 ISBN 978-1-61173-838-4 (library binding : alk. paper)
 1. Rawlins, Easy (Fictitious character)—Fiction.
  2. Private investigators—California—Los Angeles—Fiction.
  3. African American men—Fiction. 4. Los Angeles (Calif.)—Fiction.
  5. Large type books. I. Title.
 PS3563.O88456L44 2013b
 813'.54—dc23

                                                      2013014228

1

I came half-awake, dead and dreaming. My eyes were open but I couldn't focus on anything because I was still falling, as if the nightmare had followed me from sleep into the waking world. I didn't know where I was or where I'd come from. But the bed under me was turning and falling and I, I was sure, had perished. This sensation was so real, so palpable that I closed my eyes and moaned. The movement of the bed then took on a temporal quality; instead of falling I had become unmoored in time: traveling backward and then forward through a life that was mine and yet, at the same time, foreign to me.

I watched my mother dying in the bedroom of our shanty house in New Iberia, Louisiana. She was laid up in a feather bed, a big woman who was trying to catch her breath but couldn't inhale right. It sounded like she was drowning. She was so pretty, I thought. I had once loved her but could no longer raise this feeling in my heart. I might have even smiled as she shuddered under the labor of simple breathing.

Then I tumbled into a boxcar peopled by brooding and silent black men. They stared at the boy and he saw from their point of view a scared eight-year-old orphan child looking for companionship in those angry, bloodshot eyes. I was no longer that kid but had become those men who couldn't care about another defenseless child orphaned and destined, probably, to die. I saw myself and wondered, almost idly, if that young son would live to the end of the line.

I was surprised to see that he had made it to Fifth Ward, Houston, Texas. Stealing oranges, skulking in back-alley corners, asking everyone he met if they knew a name—Martin. "My grandfather," he said. He'd learned to speak up and stand straight. He already carried scars that would follow him through life but he found his grandfather: a hard man who allowed him to sleep on the outside front porch at night.

Time picked up speed after that. In an instant the boy, Ezekiel, was a young man, a fool who signed up for the army, for the war. He passed through North Africa, then Italy and France. He fought men and killed them out of reflex and fear. He *liberated* a concentration camp, a killer opening the gates for the dead and the dying and those left with the image of death permanently imprinted on their souls.

I was dying, no, had died.

Returning to Houston, the man, no longer weak or afraid, found that most of his friends in that part of town were deceased. Renfro had been slaughtered by a jealous woman named Theresa who in turn died from alcohol poisoning. Martin killed a white man and then shot himself in the burning shack where the boy had slept on the porch. Minna Rogers, Delphine Montesque, Michael Michaels, Big Boy Sanders, and dozens of others, all died while the boy-turned-man had survived the greatest war in history.

"Easy?"

There was a flood rising in the room that was swathed in darkness. My right ankle was shackled to the floor next to the bed, and the water was already up to my ears. I pulled against the chain but all that did was cause me pain. My ankle hurt like a motherfucker and the chain would not give. I tried to rise, hoping that I could float to the extent of the bond, that maybe I could keep my nose above water, but I knew somehow that my luck had run out, that Death had come in on me while I was distracted by the mountains of evil I had lived through. Just the fact that I could survive such terror made me guilty, and now he was coming up through the floorboards like he did for my mother.

Death. I had followed him through all the years of my life as he dropped bodies in my path as little reminders to me and others that the end of the road was no bed of roses, no kingdom come. It felt as if my whole life was an obstacle course, a slogging journey trying to catch up with Death, trying to get a good look at his face. . . .

"Easy."

And then, up ahead, on my journey through a past life that no longer belonged to me, I saw his back; the Reaper was right there in front of me, carelessly firing a pistol into the night. I could reach out and touch his shoulder. When I did this he grunted and turned and I realized that I knew this being, this deadly force that had dogged me from the earliest moments of my life.

He was well dressed for any occasion or epoch. Smiling with a gold tooth that had a diamond embedded in it, he was a colored man, not black but light-skinned and light-eyed. A brother who had littered the road I traveled with so many dead that even he had lost count.

"Easy."

His lips didn't move but I recognized my name, my true name, not the one my dead father gave me. Raymond Alexander, known as Mouse to his victims and friends alike, smiled at me and I shivered in pleasure and fear.

"Ray," I said, and his smile slowly diminished.

He stared at me and shook his head. I almost cried but then I remembered who I was and what I'd been through.

"No, man," I said. "You can't dismiss me like some schoolkid. You can't turn your back on me after all these years."

He smiled again, and even though I was dead I felt elation. This emotion was followed by the sense of

8

falling again. There was a broad ocean rippling gently under a partial moon and the execution of a perfect accelerating arc of plummeting downward. A shackle was affixed painfully to my right ankle but, impossibly, Mouse was still standing there in front of me, his expression daring me to do something about the fix I was in.

"You expect me to fly, motherfucker?" I yelled.

Mouse laughed without sound and nodded at me.

"Easy, wake up."

The command was feminine, a nuisance that somehow carried weight. The panorama of my hallucinatory journey called to me. I wanted to go off with Mouse, to follow the long line of dead black folks, soldiers, and Jews. I wanted to join the people I killed and the ones I couldn't save. I wanted to shed my scarred and pain-riddled body. One more breath seemed like too much to bear.

"Easy, it's time for you to wake up."

I tried to open my eyes but I was a child again, a slave to sleep, needing just two more minutes of rest. But a hand shook my shoulder and little aches came awake through my upper torso and down my spine.

It was this pain that opened my eyes.

I could see after a fashion but my vision wasn't proper yet. I couldn't get a bead on the room I was in, but the beautiful Asian woman sitting beside me on the bed was clear and present as a Catholic priest preparing to give last rites.

Instead of incense there was a mild floral scent of perfume.

"Lynne?" I said. My voice was hoarse and congested, cracking hard enough that I thought my throat might bleed.

"I didn't think you were ever going to wake up, Easy," the Chinese bit-part TV actress claimed.

"I died," I said.

She almost responded but then moved to a chair next to the head of my bed.

2

"I died, right?" I said, looking at the lovely Lynne Hua sitting in the off-white padded chair there next to me.

She was wearing a slight and short maroon dress made from fine silk. She crossed her olive legs as if to say, *If you don't respond to this you may very well be dead.*

"How are you feeling, Easy?" she asked.

My vision was still playing tricks on me. I could see the young woman but the room around her was blurred, without specific detail or spatial form.

"I . . ." I said.

Lynne smiled and moved toward the edge of the boxy chair.

"Do you remember what happened?" she asked.

The question almost brought me to tears. I concentrated so hard that I began to tremble.

Lynne took hold of my cold hand and squeezed.

"It's okay, baby, you had an accident," Lynne said. She smiled. Her teeth were perfect. "It was very bad, but you're pretty much all right. You've been coming in and out of consciousness for the last two months. Don't you remember?"

"No."

"You will."

"Is this a hospital?"

"No."

The nondescript room behind Lynne got lighter but I still couldn't make it out.

"Where?"

"It's the house that Jewelle MacDonald got you when you were trying to protect your family."

"How did I get here, Lynne? What happened?"

"I don't know the whole story, Easy."

"Tell me what you do know."

"The doctor said that when you came to and could talk we should make sure you stay calm."

"I'm calm. I need to know what happened."

"You were drunk, trying to pass a truck on Highway One."

"So you're saying that if I'm not dead I should be."

"Everybody thought you were," Lynne said. "Ray got the call from your son at four in the morning. They found your license on the beach and the registration in the glove compartment of your car. It had crashed into the surf."

"And I was in the water too?"

"Your body was lost. The driver's-side door was torn off. The police told us that you had probably floated out on the tide."

"So what happened?"

"I went up to the house with Raymond. Later in the morning after Christmas Black came to watch the kids, Ray and I drove over to Mama Jo's."

The image of the tall black witch-woman came up into my mind's eye. Just the thought of her power and magnetism anchored my floating thoughts.

"What did Jo have to do with it?" I was imagining some mystical rite where the witch had made a bargain with the Devil to raise the dead.

"Ray told her that you had died and that he wanted her to perform the funeral ceremony, especially since the body had been washed away."

"And did she agree?"

"She looked Raymond in the eye and grabbed him by both shoulders," Lynne said, still astonished by the act. "She even lifted him up on his toes. And all Ray did was stare back. After a minute or so she let him go and stood up so tall that her head almost touched the roof of the cottage and she said, 'Your friend is not dead, Raymond. While you're here feelin' sorry for yourself he's out there in pain, near death. Go back to where that accident happened and look for him. Look close.'

"I drove him up to the place you went off the cliff and he climbed down. He was gone for two hours searching through the hillside and bushes, between the big boulders and down along the beach. I just sat there and waited, thinking about how much Ray loved you and how sure Mama Jo was that you had survived. And then, after I knew there was no hope, Raymond came up the side of that mountain with you slung across his back. You know he's a small man, Ezekiel; you're almost twice his size, but he carried you halfway up that steep climb, brought you all the way to the car and laid you in the backseat like you were a child."

"Where was I?" I asked.

"Raymond said that when your car hit the first boulder the door flew off and you were probably thrown free. You fell into these thick bushes. They broke your fall but they also hid you from view. I guess the police just figured you were dead once they saw the car. You'd been there for almost a day and so were suffering from exposure as well as a bad concussion."

There came a ripple in the atmosphere between me and Lynne.

It felt as if an invisible wall had suddenly come down between us. She was still talking but I could no longer make out the words. I wanted to know everything about my death, but I couldn't speak or even gesture, and Lynne was slowly moving backward as if her chair was being drawn away by cables into the depths of the featureless room. As she moved off into the distance the light lowered and soon I was, once again, dead and dreaming.

3

The next thing I heard was the chirping of crickets. They cried out in the night like an orchestra of mad violinists playing what they really felt—not what anybody but their potential lovers wanted to hear. For long minutes there was just me under the covers surrounded by the love-hungry insects. I imagined that my bed had been dragged out of the room and I was now in a garden—the twittering chirps were that strong.

And there was something else. There was a breeze wafting over me: a chilly nighttime desert breeze that made me shiver and almost want to giggle. I was awake but my eyes were closed.

There was a scratchy striking sound and then a brief susurration. I smelled the sharp sulfuric odor of a struck match and then, five seconds later, there came the delicious scent of burning tobacco.

14

I took in a deep breath and then exhaled with a grunt of pure satisfaction.

One day cigarettes would kill me, but ten thousand days before that final hour they would be a balm, a medicine, and a doorway to a whole lifetime of memories, like Proust's fateful madeleine.

This last thought reminded me that I was, basically, an uneducated reader, a man who loved books beyond any other thing outside of family and close friends. André Malraux and Langston Hughes, Zora Neale Hurston and T. S. Eliot lived in me just as surely as backcountry lynchings and the scent of a lover's sex.

I opened my eyes and was not surprised to see Raymond Alexander sitting in the chair that Lynne Hua last inhabited. He was hatless in a glimmering, silver-colored suit and a muted red dress shirt with no tie, open at the collar. Smoke was wafting around his sharp features, and his smile seemed to move with the sinuous wisps.

"You shouldn't never take another drink as long as you live, man" were his first words to me.

We were good friends, old friends. Our camaraderie had worn down to a comfortable patter that we'd share standing next to each other in front of a firing squad or with one of us visiting the other on his deathbed.

"Lynne said that I almost died," I said by way of a thank-you for his mythic effort on my behalf.

"Almost?" Mouse replied, holding his hands a foot apart to show the enormity of my understatement. "You *was* dead, brother. I seen me a whole lotta dead men and you made half'a them look like they might get up and tap their toes. Shit. If Jo didn't tell me I was lookin' for a live man I might'a buried you right there under them bushes rather than strain my back."

He took a pack of Lucky Strikes from his breast pocket, teased out a cigarette, and lit it with the one he was smoking. He leaned over and placed the new cigarette between my lips. This intimate gesture reminded me of family. I inhaled deeply, grateful for that brief moment of feeling.

"Yeah, Easy," Mouse said. "You know I been dead before too. It wasn't only that time I was shot and Etta dragged my body off to Jo. Uh-uh. You know when you was off in the war me and this girl, Lorelle Pinchot Richards, started talkin' 'bout this rich white lady she worked for. Lorelle told me that Mrs. Lottie Montou had all kindsa gold and cash and jewels up in her house. I had told Lorelle that I was in with this bent white dude named Bill that was happy to take whatevah I stole and sell it in New Orleans or Atlanta. He was my fence and my front too. Anyway, Lorelle had this, what she called a first cousin named Vince, and she hinted that me and Vince could empty out the house after she drugged her mistress with a sleepin' powder.

"We did all that and then, when we was at Vince's cabin Lorelle held out her arms and said, 'Come here, baby; gimme some sugah.' I was young and stupid, and after I took one step Vince, who I later found out was not her cousin, shot me dead in the back. I pitched forward, missed Lorelle, and hit the wall.

"The next thing I knew I had dirt in my mouth and a knot in my back like a mothahfuckah. I sat up and the dirt from the shallow grave fell down around my shoulders. Doc Halberman said that the bullet must have had a weak charge and wedged in a bone, and I was just lucky that when I fell I hit my head and knocked myself out so they thought I was dead.

"Halberman told me to rest, but you know I had business to take care of, so I had him put a plaster patch on the wound and I went right out to Bill's little farm to warn him about Lorelle and Vince. You know when he come to the back door and saw me he turned another whole shade'a white.

" 'Are you a ghost?' he asted me, and I told him, 'Close, but not quite yet.'

"Then he give me a shot'a whiskey and took two for himself and led me down to the storm cellar. There was Vince's corpse and Lorelle all tied up like a turkey hen before you throw her in the oven. The minute Lorelle and Vince walked in on Bill he shot the boy and bound the girl. I had told him from the begin that I'd be the only one to bring him any loot. He told me that we had to kill her but that he didn't have the heart to shoot no woman, even if she was colored.

"You know I had got me some good pussy off that girl and I knew that it was Vince had pulled the trigger, so I just dragged Vince's body out to Bill's hog pen and let them get rid of the evidence, such as it was. Then I took Lorelle to this place I knew and told her that if she could bring a smile to my dead lips then maybe I'd just let her go."

I was at the butt end of my cigarette and so dropped it in a glass of water on the night table while Mouse lit me another. I took a deep draw and then asked, "So what happened?"

"You know, Easy, the threat of death has a miraculous effect on some poor souls. Lorelle loved me harder that night than any woman has ever done before or since. She had me strainin' so hard over that stuff that I give myself what they call a hemorrhoid. Shit, that thing hurt me longer than the bullet wound."

"And did you kill her?" I asked. Before that cricket night I wouldn't have dared ask Mouse a question like that, but right then I felt beyond petty fears of mortality or guilt.

"Naw, man," Mouse said. "She couldn't do nuthin' to me. She saw her boyfriend gunned down by a white man that she could never lay blame on and then I saved her. After that she joined Calvary Baptist in Galveston. You know she get down on her knees to thank God ever goddamned day. And me? I rose up out the grave a dead man among the livin'. And you know that wasn't the only time."

Mouse grinned, shook his head, and took another drag off his cigarette.

I smoked, slowly contemplating the man who had carried me out from my grave.

"Why are you here, Raymond?"

"What kinda question is that, Easy? You my friend, my best friend."

"That might be true, but Mama Jo already told you I'ma be okay, and Lynne must'a called you to say I was out of that coma. You runnin' over here in the middle'a the night when a sick man should be gettin' his rest mean that there's something you want, no . . . something you need from me."

Raymond Alexander sat back in the boxy padded chair and smiled, then grinned.

"They say Jackson Blue is some kinda genius, but there ain't a man I evah met knows people better than you, Ease. You read a man's face like a little kid readin' Dick and Jane."

"So what is Jane and her boyfriend up to?" I asked.

Mouse's good humor faded as it had in my dream. A serious look crossed his face, and he stubbed the cigarette out in an ashtray he had in his lap.

"There's a woman live two maybe three blocks

from your Genesee house named Timbale Noon. She got three kids. The oldest one, who she named Evander, is nineteen, twenty. He should be a man but he's immature for his age. You know that's a bad combination. He's gone missin'. I haven't talked to Timbale directly, but I heard from a friend'a hers that a few days ago Evander called his mama from up on the Sunset Strip and told her that he met this girl, that he might be late because they were goin' to listen to some music at a club up there.

"That was the last Timbale heard from Evander, and she is heartbroken. The police won't even take down a report. And you know a thirty-four-year-old black woman is not gonna get anything outta them hippies up there. I spent two days lookin' for him, but I couldn't turn up a damn thing. I mean, if I knew who to shoot it'd be different, but I need that Easy magic, that readin' faces like a child's primer."

I tried to imagine getting up out of the bed, putting on a pair of pants, and walking out of a door. Just thinking about it exhausted me.

"Can you do this for me, Easy?" Mouse asked.

If it was anyone else I would have said no. But Raymond had crawled out of a grave with a bullet in his back; he had shimmied up a seaside mountain with my body across his shoulders. And there were other, as yet unarticulated reasons too.

"I'll do it," I said, and then I passed out.

4

My next bout of consciousness was announced by sunlight battering up against my eyelids. It was warm and red. A breeze was still wafting but it wasn't chill. I opened my eyes and saw clearly the room I was in for the first time. It was quite large, with a cream-colored bureau against one wall and a solid oak desk next to an open sliding glass door. The bed I was in was king-size, and the chair next to it was ivory, not white. Dark blue carpeting covered the floor, and the ceiling was high and light blue enough to almost be a sky.

Inhaling, I picked up the sour smell coming from under the covers. The fresh morning breeze was the perfect counterpoint to the odor rising from my recently deceased and then partially resurrected body.

I lay still for a while, thinking about Lynne Hua and Mouse. Had they been there or were they phantoms my mind used while paving its way back to consciousness? I didn't remember much about the accident that Lynne had spoken of. I couldn't imagine little Raymond carrying my hundred and eighty-some pounds up a seaside cliff.

And when a man ran off the side of a mountain in a three-ton car he died. Didn't he?

These thoughts made the circuit of my mind six or seven times before I realized that I would never come up with the answer on my own. I decided then that I'd have to see what was outside of the well-appointed, unfamiliar blue bedroom.

I raised up on one elbow and fell back with a thump. The pain going through my head felt like a jagged lightning bolt come out of nowhere on a perfectly clear afternoon. That was okay. I'd had hangovers before that made rising a two-effort affair. I tried again, but this time I didn't make it as far up as on the first attempt. My next effort was more a thought than any kind of physical motion.

Finally I decided to roll to the edge of the bed and swing my legs over the side one at a time. The tug of gravity helped to pull my torso into a mostly upright position. The billowing curtains from the glass sliding doors seemed to be cheering me on.

The last thing I remembered I was a mature man with the sap still running, driving a car in the night. Now I was middle-aged and achy, dizzy too. It was a foregone conclusion that I would never be young again.

I took six deep breaths, tried to rise to my feet, failed, took another deep inhalation and succeeded. I was a bit wobbly but made it to the door without falling. It felt like victory just standing there holding on to the brass doorknob.

I don't know how long I lingered at the doorway, but at one point I leaned against the knob and rode the door out into the vestibule at the top of a white wood and blue carpeted stairway. The walls were white and hung with oil paintings of still lifes and of poor and rural black men and women. It struck me that I had rarely seen such intimate renditions of poor black folk. I wondered again where I was. Maybe I had died and gone to a kind of colored heaven, a big house on the edge of the estate where the white people went when they passed on.

There were three closed doors on that landing, but I didn't want to waste my strength investigating them. So, grasping the banister with both hands, I took the downward-cascading stairs one at a time, trying to keep from stumbling while studying the faces of sharecroppers and day laborers, laundresses and just folks at rest—most of them looking almost as tired as I felt.

One thing that kept me upright was a sharp pain in my right ankle. Every time that foot hit the floor, the shooting sensation would travel almost to the knee. Rather than resent this ache, I welcomed it, because with each second step I was shocked back to clarity. It was like a bright red spot on a fading gray plain, a distant sun—a jabbing reminder that my blood was still pumping, that life, if not a certainty, was at least a possibility.

I passed three floors and more than a dozen paintings before the staircase ended. On the first floor of the enormous house I felt a little lost. There were hallways with quite a few doors, a living room off to the right that had broad windows and was three steps lower than the floor on which I stood. There were no sounds, no indication of other human beings inhabiting this unlikely architecture.

I was wearing light blue pajamas. These too were unfamiliar to me. My dark brown hands reaching out from the pale sleeves seemed like they didn't belong in my clothes or that home. I stood there drifting through these aimless thoughts, waiting for a sign.

I didn't have the strength to go exploring. It felt as if I had a certain but undisclosed number of steps and breaths left in me. I had to husband these resources so as not to give out before reaching my goal—whatever that was.

A muted laugh came from somewhere. I looked around, but the white walls and pine flooring, the many doors and the awkward array of sunlight and shadows remained still and lifeless.

A louder laugh was emitted, and a direction suggested itself.

To my left, on the right half of a broad wall, was

an overwide pink door. It was from behind this portal, I was almost sure, that the laughter had come. I released the banister and staggered to a piece of wall next to the pink door. Leaning my head against the white plasterboard I heard speech that was muffled by the barrier. Then there was another high-pitched laugh—a female exhortation of near hilarity.

I hesitated.

This wasn't my house. This wasn't the home of any Negro I had ever known. It was familiar, but no more so than my body, which seemed to have aged a generation from the last time I knew myself.

After a moment of cracked logic I decided that I should go through the door and ask the white people on the other side why I was there in their house wearing somebody else's pajamas and staggering around like Max Schmeling after his first-round decimation by Joe Louis.

My decision made, I reached for the doorknob but realized that there was none. This simple detail flummoxed me. How could I get through a door if there was no way to open it? I stood there for well over a minute trying to think my way around the problem. I went over it again and again. Early on I thought that maybe I could just push against the pink panel, but for some reason I rejected this simple solution. I considered knocking, looking for another door around the corner, calling out for someone to come let me in, and simply giving up and sitting on the floor until somebody came out and found me. Only after deep consideration of each of these approaches did I finally decide to push the door.

It swung open as easily as the curtains blew inward in the upstairs bedroom.

Laughter and friendly talk were issuing from inside.

5

The door swung inward but didn't hit the wall, so no one turned my way. Revealed was a sunlit kitchen about twice the size of most houses I'd lived in. Two of the walls were floor-to-ceiling sliding glass doors and windows: One side looked out on a long swimming pool and the other onto a broad lawn lined by various citrus trees: grape-fruit, tangerine, lemon, lime, and navel orange.

To the right of the cavernous kitchen was a blond table, and on the other side was a built-in eight-foot-square stove that could be accessed from all four sides. Benita Flagg, a slight brown girl in a shapeless calico dress, was flipping pancakes with her profile turned toward me. She was concentrating on her task and so wasn't aware of my peripheral presence.

"I never said that," my adopted daughter, Feather, was saying. There was laughter in her young voice, nesting her words with warmth and feeling.

"Yes, you did," Benita said, still intent on her flapjacks.

Jesus, my other adopted child, now a young man, sat across from Feather, smiling silently as usual.

No one in the room had noticed me yet. This added to my feeling of being dead but not quite gone. I was like the ghosts that so many of my superstitious elders believed inhabited their homes and neighborhoods: blurry images down dark corridors, fleeting and semitransparent, morose, lost, and jealous of the living.

Then there came a yipping cry.

A chubby light brown baby in a pine crib was grinning through the slats, maybe at me. I thought it possible that only speechless infants could see the dead.

"I'm just telling you," Feather said, "that Aunt Jewelle said that Uncle JB wouldn't come over because he said that there must be some kind of voodoo curse here, and he's never going to go back where people practice things like that. But I never said I believed it."

Jesus began speaking in mellifluous Spanish, explaining something that I struggled to understand from his hand gestures, but failed. Feather answered in the same tongue. At twelve years old she already spoke three languages fluently.

"If you two are gonna start in talkin' like that I'ma take Essie upstairs and eat my pancakes with Jack LaLanne."

"I'm sorry, honey," Jesus apologized. He would have said more, but in turning toward his common-law wife he caught a glimpse of me.

"Dad," he said, frozen from the sight of me in the pink doorway.

"Daddy!" Feather cried. She leaped to her feet and ran toward me.

Essie began bawling. Jesus and Benita followed the fleet child in her collision course for my beleaguered body.

Watching the speed of Feather's approach, I girded myself.

The impact against my side made me feel like a matador when the torquing head of a bull hits its mark. I would have fallen over if Jesus hadn't rushed up and caught me by the arm. He was a small young man, but years of work on his little fishing boat had hardened his muscles and honed his coordination.

"Hold up, little sister," he said to Feather. "Dad's not a hundred percent yet."

"Not even fifty" were my first words.

"I'm so sorry, Daddy," Feather said while clinging to my other arm.

My back was against the doorjamb. Essie

hollered from her crib. Benita had stopped half-way between me and her frightened daughter.

There was life all around me, and I became aware of an ache on the inner side of my left forearm which at least gave me a semblance of living.

"How are you, Daddy?" Feather said.

"Come on, Dad," Jesus added, pulling me so that my right arm wrapped around his shoulders.

Leaning heavily on my son, I moved toward the sunlit table, taking deep breaths and wondering how sick I was. Jesus let me down on a hard wood chair, while Feather pulled her seat up next to mine. Benita had Essie in her arms, and Jesus stood over me, a son at least temporarily taking the headman's role.

I sat back and felt a knot in the left side of my back. This dull pain reminded me of Mouse being shot and buried alive. My friends and I had lived hard lives. I was happy that my children didn't have to go through that.

"How are you feeling, Daddy?" Feather asked.

She had light brown hair and café-au-lait skin, the daughter of a black man and a white woman, both murdered before she could utter a word.

Maybe, I thought, my life was easier than some of them coming up behind me.

"How long?" I asked.

"A little more than two months," Jesus said.

"The doctor said it wasn't a real coma, but you were unconscious and sleeping a lot."

I remembered then that Lynne had told me the same thing.

"I don't remember any of it."

"Doctor said it was the concussion combined with exposure," Benita said. The chubby brown baby in her arm was trying to stick her fingers up her mother's nose, but Bennie made her face a moving target while talking.

"So why am I not in a hospital bed?"

"Jo told Raymond that hospitals kill more poor people than they cure, and so he hired this nurse he knows and got Dr. Barstow to come by every few days."

Barstow was an army doctor I knew from the war. He took care of the children and most of my friends.

"But how did you feed me?"

Feather sidled up to my left side and rolled up my pajama sleeve. There was the needle of an IV taped to the center of my arm.

"It got infected once," she said, "but Dr. B gave you penicillin when it got too red."

"I smell like a whole barrel of sour pickles," I said.

"Antigone only gave you sponge baths every third day," Jesus told me. "And I turned you every six hours so you didn't get bedsores and the blood didn't settle."

"Antigone?"

"That's the nurse Raymond done hired," Benita said.

"So I've been up in that bed all this time?"

"Yes," Feather said, stroking my hand. "Except three days they had you in the hospital. Uncle Ray took you there first. But then we brought you here with Dr. B and Antigone. Everybody was really worried, Daddy."

Putting a hand on my daughter's shoulder, I said, "Can I get a half a pancake."

Eating was almost as difficult as coming downstairs. My stomach had shrunk to the size of a walnut, and it ached when just a teaspoon worth of pancake made its way down.

"Don't you like it, Mr. Rawlins?" Benita asked.

"My mouth thinks it's great, but the gut says that it's on strike."

At that moment I felt something wet and warm on the big toe of my left foot. Maybe if it was at some other time, when my senses were more acute, I would have kicked and jumped. But instead I simply leaned over and looked.

What I beheld was a minor miracle.

Frenchie, the little yellow dog that hated me more than bees hate bears, was licking away at my foot like it was fresh meat on a silver platter.

Feather noticed this too.

"Me and Frenchie would sit up with you at night

the first week you were home, Daddy. I was so sad that he started licking you to maybe help. I guess while he was doing that he started liking you too."

She giggled and I frowned.

The one thing I could always be sure of was that that little dog hated me, for good reason. That hatred was my barometer when I started to feel that maybe everything would be all right.

We settled into a breakfastlike routine. The kids were all talking, and Frenchie had curled up at my feet. I sipped at a cup of black coffee and thought about a young man named Evander, who was lost and needed to be found. I felt that if he was found, maybe the death sentence hanging over my head would be commuted for another few weeks, maybe even a month.

6

"I got to take Feather to school, Dad," Jesus said after washing the dishes, "and then I have to go to work."

"Kinda late to hit the fishin' boat, ain't it, boy?" I said in the language we'd used in his early years down around Watts.

"I'm working for Miss MacDonald."

"Jewelle?"

"They're building that big international hotel downtown and she got me a job on the crew. Said that she wanted me to keep an eye on things to make sure that the contractors weren't cheating or cutting corners."

The room began to shake slightly—an almost negligible shiver that came from my tentative hold on consciousness.

"So she got you workin' like a detective," I said. "Like me."

That got the boy smiling. He was pure Mexican, Indian at that. Two thousand years ago his direct ancestors were building pyramids and singing their praises of the sun.

"I get sixty-seven thirty-three a week from the job, and Miss MacDonald pays me another seventy-five to keep my eyes and ears open," he said. "You know I speak mostly Spanish to the other Mexicans they got working there. That way the bosses might let things slip if they don't think I understand English."

"Be careful, son," I told him. "People get a little irrational when they think they got a spy on 'em."

"I got a special number for Uncle Raymond if things get bad."

"The other thing you got to remember is that—"

"Mouse is only for if the house is burning down and the fire department is on strike," Jesus said, finishing a phrase that I'd used a hundred times in the past.

"Bye, Daddy," Feather said, rushing from somewhere and kissing me on the temple. She was wearing a shamrock green dress with yellow buttons down the front and gray sailor's shoes made from some rough material.

I smiled at her, and her happy face, for some reason, became somber.

"Do you need me to stay?"

"No, honey," I said. "But it's summer, right? I was just wondering what school you had to go to."

"I'm doing summer school French and algebra at Pasteur," she said, "advanced placement. I want to graduate from Hamilton High at least by seventeen so I can get away from these children."

Jesus and Feather left the house as they had for all the years they'd been together. He would walk her to elementary school before taking the bus to Hamilton High, and he brought her with him everywhere he went. His capacity for love, in spite of the hard knocks of his childhood before he came to me, was as great as any pyramid.

After my adopted family had gone I sat over a cup of coffee and stared out into the rich woman's yard. A hummingbird flitted from one citrus blossom to the next while Frenchie ran around under it, leaping now and then for practice.

I was trying to remember Evander's last name.

Noon, that's what it was—midday: the highest point of life and work. Looking for noon sounded like just the thing that a wreck like me needed.

"Mr. Rawlins?"

Benita was standing there with the freshly changed baby in her arms.

"Yeah, Bennie?"

"I have to go to work too. I got a practical nurse's trainee position down at Lance Holtz Medical Center in Santa Monica."

"What do you do with Essie?"

"I pay Antigone an extra six dollars to look after her while she's here with you. You know, all she had to do was change your IV and look in on you now and then."

"I guess that easy job is over," I said.

"Uh-huh."

"How are you, Benita?"

"I like livin' here wit' Juice and your family. Sometimes when Essie cries at night Feather gets up to walk with her. You know, it's kinda like what my mama used to say Alabama was like when she was a kid—everybody livin' together an' helpin' each other out. Only here we are in this big old house and everybody's got a job or school." Benita hesitated a few seconds, staring into my face. "You look tired, Mr. Rawlins, but at least you're awake again. I used to come in your room at night with Essie and just sit there, because you know you saved my life and brought Juice into it too. I know you coulda told him that I wasn't no good. I know you didn't have to let me in like you did, and I really appreciate it, and I'm very happy that you woke up."

We gazed at each other while Essie made soft cooing sounds.

When the doorbell rang I felt a sense of relief. The connection between Benita and me, at that moment, was beyond the limit of my emotional reserves.

The mother and child left the room and immediately I began thinking about a woman named Timbale and a son who had failed to come home. It was odd for Raymond to ask me for help, certainly for something as mundane as a young man going off into a dangerous world.

"People die," Mouse had said to me on many occasions. "They die and get born every second of every day. You know I can't be botherin' myself with all the people fallin' by the wayside. If I did that I wouldn't have enough time to pee."

I grinned at the memory and wondered again: What was Raymond's interest in Evander Noon?"

"Mr. Rawlins?" Benita said. "This is Antigone Fowler, RN."

I looked up to see a strawberry brown woman, maybe five-five, with hair tied tightly back, and businesslike efficiency about her like a ring around the sun.

"Pleased to meet you at last, sir," she said. She

36

wasn't from the South, but the accent was from somewhere in the U.S.

"Eyes open and everything," I agreed.

"Well," Benita said, "I'ma go put Essie in the crib in her room and then I'm gone."

When Benita came over and kissed my cheek I had the feeling that she got into that habit when I was comatose. She walked out of the swinging pink door.

I watched her go, feeling something like loss.

"Now let's get you upstairs to bed," the nurse said, her competence expressing itself with mechanical precision.

She came right up to me and took me by the arm. She tried to lift but I let the deadweight of my body resist.

"You have to help me, Mr. Rawlins."

"Have a seat, Nurse Fowler."

"I have to go take care of the baby, make lunch for you, check all your vitals, and call the doctor to get instructions on what to do now that you're awake," she said. "I don't have time to sit."

"Then you go do all those things and, just before the vitals check, you come back and have a seat."

"That's not how it's going to work," she replied sharply.

Sometimes you take a liking or a dislike to a person you meet—immediately. Just a few words pass between you, but you know everything you'll ever need to about how you are going to interact.

Nurse Fowler and I were not going to get along; that much was sure. What I had to do was to figure out how to settle our differences then and there so that I could get along with my resurrection or final rites.

"How much have my doctor and family told you about me, Nurse Fowler?"

"I'm not here for conversation," she said. It was clear that she was also trying to set the ground rules.

I took in a quick breath through my nostrils and rolled my shoulders forward.

"Fine," I said. "Then you can either listen or walk away."

I managed not to smile at her enraged stare.

"I almost died not too long ago, and for all I care I am dead. But in the life I lived before that, I have, for good and for bad, battled more men than I wish to remember. In the war I did it by rifle, pistol, bayonet, and hand-to-hand. With these hands," I said, holding up my dark brown mitts, "I bettered men younger, larger, and stronger than me. I am no child, Nurse Fowler, no senile old man that you can fold into whatever position you want. I am a man sittin' here, and I will not be disrespected by you or anyone else. So back the fuck up and do what I say or get your ass outta here. *Comprende*?"

Somewhere in the middle of that tirade Antigone Fowler saw something that she recognized. She was a tough woman—I could see that—and she was willing to tussle. But she could tell that there was no give in me either. She probably thought she would come out victorious if we struggled, but she heard my willingness to go down in the fight.

"What is it you want from me, Mr. Rawlins?"

7

While Antigone was upstairs taking care of the baby and doing whatever she had to do to prepare for an aware patient, I was involved with the monumental struggle of getting up out of the kitchen chair and then staggering to the section of wall next to the window that looked out on the pool. There was a baby blue wall phone there and a tall redwood stool, set in its own little corner, that I could prop myself on.

The phone number was a LUdlow exchange that I had been calling more than fifteen years. I could have dialed it in my sleep. I might have mumbled it in the grave.

"Hello?" a white man said, answering on the third ring.

"Peter?"

"Mr. Rawlins," the proper young man said. "How are you, sir?"

"Pretty good, Mr. Rhone. How are you?"

"Just about the same, I guess. Mr. Alexander said that you had regained consciousness. Everyone here is very happy about that."

Peter Rhone was a blond-haired, blue-eyed young man who, though he was married to a perfectly appropriate white wife, had fallen in love with a young black woman named Nola Payne. After Nola was murdered by a homicidal maniac during the Watts Riots of 1965, Peter suffered what can only be described as a dissolution of spirit. He left his wife and ended up living on the screened-in side porch of EttaMae Harris, one of my oldest friends and Raymond Alexander's wife. Peter was serving some kind of self-imposed penance, because he believed that he in some way shared the guilt for the racism and neglect that took his lover's life.

I was never sure if Etta kept him around because she liked having a man Friday to help her with chores and duties when Mouse was off who knows where, or if she felt his pain and was trying to help the poor white boy get up on his feet again.

"Mouse around?" I asked.

"No. Would you like to speak to EttaMae?"

"I'd always like to jaw with Etta, but it's Raymond that I need to speak to."

"Um . . ."

"It's important, Peter."

"Okay," he said, and then he whispered a number so softly that I had to ask him to repeat it—twice. I scrawled it down on a notepad that was on the counter under the phone.

I had to rest for a few minutes after the chat with Etta's manservant. Sitting there I realized how lucky I was that Antigone didn't decide to take up my gauntlet—she would have mopped the floor with me.

I tried the number that Peter gave. It rang a dozen times before someone answered.

"Yes?" She sounded put out by the intrusion.

"I'm lookin' for Mouse." I'm usually more civil. I use phrases like *excuse me* and *sorry to bother you,* but I just didn't have the wherewithal to exhibit good manners. "Who is this?" It was a white woman, I was almost sure. Maybe there was some kind of European accent.

"Ezekiel Rawlins," I said. "Easy."

"Why did you let the phone ring so many times?" she asked. "Don't you understand that if no one comes on the first few rings, they might not want to be bothered?"

"Is Raymond there or not?" I had certainly abandoned all etiquette.

There was a sharp intake of angry breath in my ear and then the banging of the receiver being thrown down. For a minute or two there was complete silence, and then came the sound of the angry woman ranting in the background.

"Hello?" Mouse said into the phone. "Who is this?"

"Me, Ray."

"Easy." I could almost hear his smile. Then, "Baby, baby, stop it. It's my man Easy. . . . No, I don't know why he's callin', but I do know we have to talk. So go make another drink and I'll be right in." Finishing with the woman's anger, Mouse turned his words back to me. "What you need, Easy?"

"Did you come see me up in my room last night?" I asked.

"Sure did."

"And there's some woman named Timbale Noon who has a son named Evander who has gone missing?"

"I know you didn't hit your head too hard, Easy, 'cause your memory is like a steel trap."

"Okay. Now let me ask you something."

"What's that?"

"Do you have any kind of grudge against that woman or her son?"

"No, sir."

"I'm not kiddin' now, Ray. I will not help you on some vendetta."

"Easy, you just saved my life from them police two months ago. Do you honestly think I would let a little revenge come between us?"

"So if I find this Evander it won't get him into trouble?"

"What I want is to get him out of trouble. Scout's honor."

"When were you ever a scout?"

"I had me enough onetime Girl Scouts to be an honorary member."

Mouse could always get me to smile.

"Okay, then," I said, feeling a little stronger. "I'll do it. Come on over here and pick me up."

"Now?"

"Now."

"But, Easy, you done just got out the sickbed."

"She can wait, Raymond. She sit on that passion a little bit and it might get better."

Mouse snickered and said, "It might at that."

I hung up the phone and stayed in place, leaning against the high stool. Antigone Fowler came in a few minutes later. She was surprised to see me standing almost upright. I got the feeling that she thought I might be asleep or at least a little more docile.

She walked up to me and wrinkled her nose.

"You need a bath," she said.

"I'll take a shower if you got one handy."

I wanted a shower because I knew that after lying down in a warm tub I wouldn't be able to get up again. We haggled a bit but I won the major points. Antigone told me that she wouldn't be being responsible if she left a man in my weakened condition standing alone in a tile shower.

"If you fell and broke your neck that would be on me," she said.

So we settled on me getting in the stall but leaving the door open for her to be there in case I slipped and fell.

I wasn't shy about taking off my clothes. I had been naked in front of enough strangers in my life. In North Africa I'd take showers with up to two dozen men, jostling over the soap and spray.

One thing I noticed was a nine-inch gash going down the front of my left thigh. It was partly healed and scabbed over, but I could see that it was a vicious wound, a scar that I could have to recall an accident which I no longer clearly remembered.

The shower was going pretty well. We didn't make the water too hot and so the spray refreshed me a little. Feeling the sourness wash away had a recuperative effect of its own. But we hadn't taken into account my many weeks of enforced celibacy. I don't think I could have managed a serious bout of kissing, but just a few minutes of standing naked next to that stern but handsome woman got me harder than I had been in years.

She was fully dressed in her short-sleeved white nurse's uniform, and about as erotic as a dead mackerel, but just her proximity had its impact on my long-dormant sexuality.

I didn't feel excitement. The insistence of the erection embarrassed me, but that didn't change a thing. I mean, I have never thought of myself as being exceptionally well-endowed, but it seemed like there were three of us in the bathroom—me, Nurse Fowler, and Hard John.

Antigone didn't remark on my condition. She just stood there, reaching in now and then if I moved too quickly or bent at all. She stayed with me when I got out, even helped me to dry off. The only thing I wanted was for my adolescent hard-on to go down, but it refused even after I pulled on the pajamas.

"Would you like to go up to your bed now?" she asked when we came out of the small first-floor bathroom.

"I guess I better, huh?"

That was the only time Antigone gave up a little smile. She looked me in the eye and shook her head about all men.

Looking back on it now I can see how the blood pumping helped to revive me even more than the shower. It was as if my body was using its natural wiles to prepare me for the trials I had yet to face.

I was about to allow myself to be herded up to bed, in order to hide my shame, when the doorbell sounded.

"Who could that be?" Antigone said to herself.

8

I waited by the bathroom door somewhere in the vastness of the first floor while Antigone went off to see who our visitor was. I remembered that the house was actually an estate with an electronic gate that kept out any but those that knew the proper codes or had a key.

I knew who was coming and so the erection flagged and finally failed.

He came smiling down the hall a minute later.

"Easy!" Mouse exclaimed. "It's a real pleasure to see you on your feet, brother."

"Ray," I said on an exhalation.

He was wearing dark blue work pants and an equally dark gray sweater. The blouse was cashmere, but most people couldn't tell that from a glance. The color scheme, or the darkness of it, told those in the know that Raymond was ready to do business: the kind of illegal business that he'd been practicing since childhood.

"Why don't you go upstairs and pull out Easy's tan suit, the linen one, a blue shirt, and his felt brown shoes," Mouse said to Antigone.

"Why?" the registered nurse asked, bureaucratic danger in her voice.

"Because me and Easy got to go out in the world and do some business."

"No," Antigone Fowler said.

Mouse looked at her and grinned.

"I mean it, Mr. Alexander," she continued. "Mr. Rawlins is not nearly strong enough to be out and active. He's suffered a terrible blow to his system. He needs rest."

"Listen, Annie," Mouse said in an almost sympathetic tone. "Either go upstairs and get Easy's things or go on home. I will send you the money I owe you by Friday next."

The anger and hardness in "Annie" Fowler's face spoke of her deep commitment to her profession. Raymond was her employer and he could dismiss her at any time. But I was her responsibility, her charge. She could leave—she wanted to—but that would be abandoning her duty, and that was something this woman would never do.

She nodded her reluctant assent.

"While you're at it," I said, "could you collect my wallet and keys and any loose change that I might have?"

"Anything else?" she asked.

"Yeah. What's the phone number here?"

"I can tell ya that, Ease," Mouse said.

Upon hearing this, Antigone Fowler walked away to reluctantly do our bidding.

"You got the new number memorized?" I asked my oldest friend.

"It was easy too," he said, "because it's the old number with a new exchange."

"How'd that happen?"

"Jewelle got an in with the phone company."

Twenty-five minutes later Mouse and I were driving off in his brand-new 1967 El Dorado. It was pink, as many of Mouse's cars were.

Nurse Fowler had removed the IV needle from my arm and put a bandage over the puncture.

Raymond drove down the curvy cobblestone path through the arboretum of a front yard until finally coming to a great iron gate in the middle of a fourteen-foot-high stone wall. Mouse got out and did something at the side of the gate and it slowly swung open. He drove us outside into the outer driveway, got out, and performed some other juju to close the entrance.

As we drove southward out of Bel-Air I sat back and began to fade from consciousness.

"You okay, Easy?" Mouse asked, causing my mind to blunder back toward awareness.

"You know, maybe Antigone was right," I said. "I mean, you even had to tie my shoes back there."

"Open up the glove compartment," he said as if in reply.

I did as he asked.

"Under the maps," Mouse urged.

There, beneath a folded map of Arkansas, was a

small crystal vial filled to its cork stopper with about an ounce and a half of lemon yellow liquid.

"Arkansas?" I said, picking up the vial.

"Did a little job out there a few weeks ago," he muttered. "Drink it down, man."

"What is it?"

"I can't tell ya what's in it. I just know what it does. Mama Jo give me twenty'a them li'l bottles for when I get hangovers. She said that when I need to be able to keep sharp this will do the trick. Go on, drink it."

I pulled out the stopper and downed the contents in one draft. It had the strong taste of fruit: not berry or citrus, apple or grape, but all of those flavors, highly concentrated—enough to make me pull my head back as if I had just slugged down an especially strong alcohol drink.

"Somethin', huh?" Mouse said.

"Wow." Within seconds I could feel the effects of the homemade medicine. It was like the sun rising in my chest and a clear sky blooming in my head. "What is that?"

"You know Jo," Raymond said. "She studied with every Chinese, Mexican, Indian, and savage tryin' to learn what she can. She does things make most doctors say, 'No, she did not.' "

I was coming awake for the first time since opening my eyes in the upstairs bedroom. I still felt like a dead man, but a dead man with a jig in his heart.

• • •

Mouse drove and I sat there next to him listening to radio station KGFJ. The song playing, I remember, was "Higher and Higher." *Your love keeps lifting me higher.* . . . Maybe it was the subject of the song that made Raymond decide to broach Bonnie Shay.

"You call her?" he asked. He didn't need to say who.

"I'll tell you what, Raymond."

"What's that?"

"You want me to go out looking for this boy, right?"

"Yes, I do."

"Then let's not talk about who I am and am not callin'."

"You got it, Easy."

Mouse was the most dangerous man I ever knew. He was deadly and criminal, vengeful and capable of taking matters into his own hands. But for all of that he appreciated the simple things in life: a well-told joke, a blunt statement of fact.

He wanted to talk about Bonnie and I didn't, so we sat there listening to Otis Redding, the Association, and the Fifth Dimension on L.A.'s premier soul station.

I was surprised at how clearheaded Jo's elixir had made me. My memory was still spotty, but my body felt like it belonged to me and would at least try to obey if I gave it a command.

50

When the news came on I turned the radio off.

"Did you really carry me all the way up half the side of that cliff?" I asked.

"Sure did," he said, shaking his head to emphasize the energy exerted.

"That's amazing."

"Not really."

"If you was a boxer you could hardly make lightweight, Ray. I'm a light-heavy at least."

"That's true. But you know I got this thing in my head."

"What thing?"

"When the need comes it just opens up and I'm like two people. I think twice as fast and I get stronger than a motherfucker. When I seen you lyin' there like that I just grabbed you and threw you 'cross my back. I didn't think that I couldn't do it. No, sir, not me. I do what has to be done. That's all there is to it."

We made it to Fairfax and drove down to Pico, turned left and cruised about five blocks, where we turned right on Stanley. Not four buildings south of Pico was a turquoise duplex. We pulled to the curb in front of this building.

"Timbale live here?" I asked.

"There's another duplex, exactly the same, right behind this one," he said. "She lives in the top unit."

"Is she home?"

51

"I think so."

"Didn't you call?"

Mouse shook his head.

"Why not?"

"Little Green was up on Sunset," he said instead of answering my question. "He met a white girl up there. I don't remember the name. Anyway, she had told him that they should go to this discotheque and he was all excited about it.

"Timbale is from the Deep South, and so she told him to come home. But he was stubborn and she said to be careful around those white people and spent the whole night waitin' up for him. But he didn't come home and he didn't call. And when the days went by she got desperate."

"That's when she called you?"

"She ain't call me, man. She got this friend named Lissa, who I know to talk to. Lissa called me and told me what I just told you."

"You called Evander Little Green," I said. "How come?"

"That's my nickname for him."

"So you are a friend of the family?"

"Not really."

"But even so we gonna go up there and talk to Timbale."

"You gonna have to go on up there by yourself, Easy."

"Why?"

"Me and Timbale don't really get along. I mean,

that woman hates the water I drink and the sun that shine on my back."

"But you're worried about her and her son?"

"There's many a time when Etta hate my guts. That don't mean I can't love her."

"Timbale was a girlfriend?"

"Never," he said with a curl to his lip.

"Can you give me any more than that?"

"Easy, I give ya what you need to know. A boy is missin'. His mother is on the top apartment behind this one. She's the last one that talked to him. It don't mattah what me and Timbale have between us."

It was perplexing, my friend's motivation, but it didn't seem to be all that important. He was right—the problem was before me, not in that car.

9

The first nine steps were a real pleasure. I was up on my feet and walking just as if I was a living man in the real world who knew about gravity but didn't worry about it bringing him down.

That got me to the concrete path at the side of the front apartment building. The concrete used to lay the path had been tinted a blue color that was meant to match with the turquoise plaster of the buildings—instead it clashed. When I noticed the discord of coloration my step began, ever so slightly, to falter.

All that means is that I'm still a little weak, I said to myself.

I was walking just as well as any other man: one step after another, evenly, in a forward motion.

But when I got to the little raised patio that served as a buffer between the two buildings I stopped before taking the step up. I was like a sentient gas engine that suspected that the fuel gauge was past empty. I was going just fine but at any moment the flow might begin to sputter.

I took the step up to the brick courtyard and strode in six paces to the bottom of the stairs. I estimated twenty-one white stonelike steps to the upper landing. Twenty-one.

Those stairs might have been one of the twelve trials of Hercules. Between the pain in my ankle, the dizziness, and the unfamiliar strain on the muscles pulling my body weight upward, I felt like a juggler forced to ply his trade just a few seconds after being shaken out of a deep sleep.

I also had the almost hallucinatory impression of leaving an image of myself on each passing stair. Every progressive Easy was a few years older and weaker than the last. When I made it to the small stone landing it felt like I had reached the century mark.

My lungs were working harder than a black-smith's bellows against white fire. I was sweating like a long-distance runner on the last leg of a losing race.

The turquoise door was open but the gray screen was closed. I put my hand against the doorjamb and counted out four deep breaths before pressing the ivory-colored plastic button next to my hand.

The ensuing bell was the two-tone economy brand, the kind of bell that a builder bought in bulk expecting to be asked to erect another building like the last and the one before that.

When there was no immediate answer my mind began making up things again. I imagined that I was almost a dead man and the bell was my request for eternal sleep. The reason for no answer was that my application had to be reviewed. I was being forced to hold on to the pain and exhaustion of life until the powers that be could make a judgment on the long list of things I'd done wrong.

The notion was ridiculous enough to get me to smile.

"Can I help you?" a woman asked.

She was dark-skinned and short, with hair cut closer than a marine recruit's. Her build, in the simple, short-sleeved olive-colored dress, was slender and yet brawny, like many a sharecropper I'd known in my days in the South. I noted that the dress had one big pocket on the left thigh. I knew she was in her mid-thirties but she could have passed for fifty easily. Her brutal face was softened by the roundness of her features and also by the slightly fearful tone under the anger in her voice.

She wasn't in any way pretty, but this woman was what the black sons of cotton pickers dreamed about when they had women in mind.

"Miss Noon?"

"Who's askin'?"

"My name is Easy Rawlins." Just saying these words dispelled the greater part of my exhaustion and banished pain to the outer regions of awareness. "I'm here because Ray Alexander asked me to come. He told me that your son, Evander, has gone missing and you might need someone to root him out."

The permanent scowl on Timbale's face hid any reaction she might have had to these words. But I didn't care. I was still tickled at the magic quality of speaking my name.

"You a preacher, Mr. Rawlins?"

"No, ma'am, a private detective."

"I never met a Negro detective before."

"We're a rare breed," I acknowledged. "But you know a black man has to be twice as good if he claims to be equal with a white."

The hardscrabble woman nodded against her will. When the truth is spoken among women and men like us there had to be an amen, had to be.

"You don't look like you could root out a radish

from sandy soil," she said, thick Mississippi in her words.

"If you're saying that I look tired, you're right," I said. "I wouldn't refuse a chair and some lemonade."

Asking a Southern woman for plain hospitality was like winking at a leprechaun: She had to give up her pot of gold no matter what.

"Come on in then," she said.

She unlatched the screen door, pulled it open, and, after a stutter of hesitation, moved to the side.

I entered the small and bare foyer. The floor was waxed pine and the wallpaper was light lime paper decorated with tiny cherry branches that were set in slanting lines. Timbale walked through to a slip of a room that ended, after only fifteen feet or so, at a glass door that opened up to a plant-filled terrace. It was a small veranda with room for just two iron chairs, painted white, and a low glass-topped cast-iron table.

We didn't go outside, however. Timbale had me sit on a backless couch in the den; then she went off to see to my refreshment.

"Excuse me a minute, Mr. Rawlins," she said as she went.

There were so many plants out on the platform that all I could see above them was the sky. Succulents, ferns, and a couple of potted pines made up most of the greenery. Plants that were simple to pot and grow.

A rattling from a distant place in the apartment caused me, for no identifiable reason, to wonder exactly what I was doing there. This inner question brought me to a memory of when I had been wounded six days after the Battle of the Bulge. A sniper had been aiming somewhere else, missed the mark, and the ricochet grazed my shoulder. . . .

"Here we go," Timbale said.

She came back into the room carrying a plastic tumbler in each fist. The liquid contained in the semiopaque containers was reddish in color.

"Don't have no fresh-squeezed lemonade," she said. "Kool-Aid will have to do."

She put the glass down on the TV stand next to me. I let my whole body list forward to pick up the plastic tumbler.

"What you got to do with Ray Alexander?" There was no give in her voice.

"He has retained me to help you find Evander, if that's what you want to do."

A spasm of anger went through her thin body. A little red sugar water sloshed out and down her knuckles.

"You really are a detective?" she asked.

I took out my wallet and showed her the license I'd procured after helping the police with a crime that they would have never solved on their own.

She read it, nodding her head angrily, and then passed the little card back.

"I was at work," she said. It was the beginning of a story that she had gone over again and again, hoping for a different ending. "At Proxy Nine, where I'm a nighttime security guard—"

"Proxy Nine?" I asked. "The French insurance company?"

"Yeah. Why?"

"Nothing. I mean, I got friend named Jackson Blue that works there."

"I never heard'a him. He work days?"

"Mostly."

"Anyway," Timbale said, "I was at work at a little after nine o'clock and Evander called me. He always calls around then. I could tell that he was outside, because I heard traffic, and so I asked him where he was. He didn't wanna say, but finally he told me that he had gone up to the Sunset Strip to see what all the hippies looked like and met up with these people that invited him to go to this club."

"Which club?"

"He didn't say."

"Mr. Alexander said that it was a girl that asked him."

"How he know that?"

I raised my palms and shrugged.

"It was a girl," Timbale agreed. "He didn't wanna tell me at first, but after I kept askin' he said. Her name was Ruby, but she was a white girl. I told him I didn't want him to go, but he wouldn't listen. He's almost twenty years old and got a job workin' for the Tolucca Mart grocery store on Robertson. At least, he did have that job. They told me that they had to fire him when I called to see if he had been there."

"Had he been there?"

"No. Nobody done seen him since he called that night."

Timbale Noon had cried all her tears in an earlier life. At this late stage the best she could do was frown and shake her head over one more blow to her attempt at happiness.

"Can you find him, Mr. Rawlins?" she asked, looking up.

"I can sure look."

The smile that crossed her lips and faded was like one of those rare flowers that blossom once a year for twenty-four hours and then wither.

Before I could ask another question the screen door flew open, followed by the clatter of feet. Two girls, a teenager and a younger one, burst into the den.

"Hi, Mom!" the younger girl exclaimed. "Did Evy call?"

"No, baby," Timbale said.

She reached out and pulled the child onto her lap. The girl was a little too old for this, maybe nine. She was lighter in color than her mother but still a strong brown.

The adolescent girl was probably thirteen. She

eyed me with some suspicion. She was already starting to have the hard visage of her mother.

Both children were clad in simple one-color dresses, red for the small one and ocher for the older. The hems on both came down below the knee. I thought they might have had different fathers, but the imprint of Timbale was strong on both of them.

"This is Mr. Rawlins, LaTonya," Timbale said to the girl on her lap. "What do you say?"

"Pleased to meet you, Mr. Rawlins."

"And this is Beatrix," Timbale said, introducing me to the older girl.

"Do you have a daughter named Feather?" Beatrix asked.

"Yes, I do."

"I thought so. She's gonna go to Louis Pasteur with me in the fall. I saw you with her once at the Christmas choral they had at Burnside Elementary."

"You two go on now," Timbale said. "Me and Mr. Rawlins have to finish talking and then I'll make you a snack."

LaTonya bounded off. Beatrix moved away more slowly, stopping at the doorway to the foyer, where she looked hard at me again.

"Beautiful children," I said when they were gone.

"I have made a whole lotta mistakes in my life, Mr. Rawlins, but I've had my share of blessings.

Evander was my biggest mistake and a godsend too."

"Does he have any good friends that might have an idea where he's gone?"

"He's a real bookish boy. Most'a my friends complain about their kids bein' on the phone day and night. Beatrix does a lotta that, but Evy ain't never on the phone."

"Maybe the girls know about people he knows," I suggested.

"I already talked to them about it. They said that he talked about the hippies sometimes but he never went up there."

It would have been better for me to question the girls myself, but I could see that Timbale would not let that happen.

I took a business card from the wallet that was still on my lap and handed it to her.

"Do you have a picture of Evander?"

The workingwoman put her hand in the solitary pocket and pulled out a three-by-five photograph. After gazing on it for a moment she handed the picture over to me. It was the color photo of a smiling broad-faced boy wearing a graduation cap and gown. There was something familiar about that face but I thought, at the time, it was the look that Timbale had stamped on all her kids.

"Isn't he handsome?"

"Yes, ma'am."

I took a deep breath and stood up with nary a waver.

"I'll go up to Sunset tonight and canvass the whole boulevard."

She winced at my vow. Maybe she worried that a dead man was only good for finding corpses.

At the door I stopped and asked her, "What's the trouble between you and Mr. Alexander?"

"No trouble. It's just if I ever see him I will send his narrow high-yellah ass to hell."

10

People have often told me that walking downhill is harder than climbing up. That might be true, but it felt a lot easier descending the stairway from Timbale Noon's second-floor apartment.

Before I got to the bottom I heard LaTonya laughing carelessly. I stopped for a few moments, listening to the squeals of childhood's abandon. It seemed very far away.

Maybe it was the sugar from the Kool-Aid and not the evocation of my name, but walking back to the car was easier than I expected. I jerked the handle to pull the car door open, then lowered into the passenger's seat with great concentration.

"Well?" Mouse asked.

"Why does that woman hate you, Raymond?"

"Lotsa people hate me. You think I know all their stories?"

"I think you know hers."

"It ain't nuthin', Easy, and it sure don't have to do with Little Gr—I mean Evander goin' missin'. You gonna close that door?"

"She corroborated everything that your friend Lissa told you."

"A carburetor?"

"She said that he went missing up on Sunset some days ago. Other than that all I got was a graduation photograph."

"Lemme see it," Mouse said, less a demand than a request.

I took the picture from my inside jacket pocket and passed it over.

He held it at a distance from his face great enough to show that his vision was deteriorating.

While he gazed intently at the photograph, his face gave up no inkling of what it was that he felt.

"Mind if I keep this, Easy?"

"I need it."

"You seen it already," he argued. "You not gonna forget."

"When I go around lookin' for him I'll need to show that picture to people."

"All right then," he said reluctantly. "Here you go. Now shut that door and let's get outta here."

"I'm walking," I said.

"Easy, we already in the car. I know you only a few blocks away but you been hurt, man."

"If I'm gonna do this for you I have to test my limits," I said. "Why don't you go down to Meaty Meatburgers on Fairfax and pick us up some food. I'll meet you at my place."

With that, using the full strength in both arms, I lifted myself out of the car. I leaned over to peer inside and said, "I'll see you in twenty minutes," then levered myself into an erect stance and slammed the door.

I knew that neighborhood quite well. A block west of the intersection of Pico and Stanley there was a huge metal structure, a hollow, nine-story-high building made from metal plating that had been painted dark yellow, almost the same color as Beatrix's dress. This was an oil well that plumbed the dark liquid out from under us.

There was no crossing light at the Stanley corner, so I walked past Spaulding down to my street, Genesee, where there was a light.

It was really only three blocks from Timbale's front door to mine, but the fact that I didn't know her was no surprise. Neighbors don't necessarily know one another that well in L.A. We spend most of our time in single homes and one-person cars. In the late sixties we moved as often as fleas leaping from one dog's head to another one's butt. There was no walking to or from parks or local bars where neighbors might hang out. If you went somewhere it was either to work or family. And if you partied it was rarely with neighbors.

By the time I made it to the southeast side of Genesee and Pico I was sorely challenged by the exercise. I could feel the exhaustion in the veins across my chest. A bead of sweat came down the side of my head, and I was happy that the traffic light was red. I leaned against the lamppost and sighed.

"Hey, you!" somebody said.

The voice came from behind me, but I didn't have to turn to know who it was.

I didn't have to turn, but I did so to greet the two dark blue–clad policemen who were coming at me like twin hyenas on a wounded wildebeest.

"Officers."

The luxury of fatigue left me. I was a soldier again and this was the enemy. The enemy doesn't ask you if you're too tired to stand your ground. The enemy has many wounds of his own and he hates you for every one.

"Let's see some ID," the one on the right said.

They were both young and white and male and had been after me as long as all three of us had lived.

I handed over my driver's license and said, "Name's Easy Rawlins. I live up here 'bout half a block on Genesee."

"Have you been drinking, Easy?" the cop on the

right asked. I could distinguish him by the mole on his right cheek and the ivory hue to his teeth, which he showed in a false smile.

"I have not."

"We're going to have to search you," the other cop said. "Put your arms straight out to your side."

"I thought you were asking if I was drunk?"

"You might have an open half-pint in one of your pockets."

I did as they told me. I didn't like it, but there was other, more pressing business on my mind.

They went through all my pockets and patted me down to the ankles. One of them, the one without the mole, had very bad halitosis. My walnut-sized stomach throbbed in anguish at the smell.

"Okay," the mole-festooned cop said when all they found was my wallet, the graduation photograph, seventy-nine cents, and some lint. "Now we're going to have you walk a straight line for us."

"Hey," a new voice proclaimed. "What you botherin' this man fo'?"

It was a light-colored black man who worked at the auto garage on the corner. He'd been watching, I supposed.

"This is none of your business," the unblemished cop informed the newcomer.

The mechanic was small, wearing gray overalls. He was the color of an old piece of vellum made from cowhide.

"He wasn't doin' nuthin'," my would-be defender

said. "He just walked up to the corner and rested against that pole. He ain't drivin' no car, so who cares if he had a drink?"

"I won't be warning you again," the mole-flecked cop said. He had unsheathed his baton.

"Yeah, nigger," the partner agreed.

I was getting worried about the well-being of my good-intentioned advocate when yet another voice joined our impromptu chorus.

"What did you say?" This from a tall white man, also in gray overalls stretched tight over his big belly. "What did you call my mechanic?"

"Hey, Sammy, what's goin' on out there?" yet another voice chimed in.

The garage was a low, whitewashed wood building that encompassed a big open space like a hangar for a small plane. Instead of a front wall the garage had a huge gate that was rolled up when the shop was open. I'd noticed the place when driving on Pico or Genesee but never patronized them. I took my car to my old friend Primo in East L.A.

"This cop just called Bertie a nigger," the boss man said. "Just like that. Maybe Bertie isn't as crazy as we said."

More men came out of the garage. Now there were nine of us standing on the corner.

"This guy was just walkin'," the man I now knew as Bertie said. "And then this one here up and calls me a niggah."

68

There were many fears registering in the white policemen's eyes: the fear of a complaint lodged against them; the fear of a small roust escalating into a minor riot; the fear of them losing control in a situation that they were not prepared for. But most of all they were afraid of their fellow white man. I didn't matter. Bertie didn't matter. But if a white business owner and his white employees stood up against the cops then they were transformed from law enforcement into what they really were—hired help.

"Why'd you call him a nigger?" the boss, Sammy, asked the clear-skinned cop.

"I didn't," he replied, gesturing vaguely at me.

"Not him," Sammy snapped. "Bertie."

Cars were slowing down on the street. A couple of them had pulled to the curb.

Sammy was angry and so was Bertie. The rest of the mechanics worked for Sammy and so felt that they had to stand behind him.

I suppressed a snicker. It wasn't so much a nervous laugh as an evil one: a chuckle spawned in the hell of my early life. Even though I couldn't have thrown a punch, I wanted to cut loose and fight.

Luckily for all of us, the policeman's radio started making noise. Mole Man went to the car and grabbed the microphone. He said something; something was garbled back.

"Hey, Jacob," he said. "Emergency on Olympic, an armed robbery. We gotta go."

And so they both jumped into the car and took off.

They didn't even leave us with a warning.

I had the definite feeling that while I was dead, the world had changed somewhat.

11

The policemen stopping me was wrong, but it most certainly saved me from more trouble up ahead.

I hung around the front of the garage for a few minutes thanking Bertie and Sammy for standing up on my behalf. Then I had to wait for another light. When I made it across the street I was bone-tired. So I sat down on a bus stop bench, breathing and wishing I had a cigarette. This was a desire and not a craving. The days of unconsciousness had weaned me off of the worst part of the smoking addiction. But the cigarettes I had with Mouse had reminded my system of their draw.

These thoughts blossomed into a full-fledged reexamination of waking up from death, not sleep, and now looking for a way back to what was before.

"Easy," Mouse called.

He had turned off of Pico and pulled to the curb so that his car was pointing north on Genesee— he'd even thrown the passenger's door open wide.

I went over to the car and got in without a word.

"You see?" he said jauntily. "I told you you shouldn'ta walked. I might've had to pick you up from the gutter."

"You mighta had to go my bail."

My place was just a few houses up from the corner. Mouse pulled into the driveway and jumped out faster than I was able. He was approaching the front door when I was just coming around the car.

"Do's open," he announced.

I remember wondering, inanely, if I had locked up when I'd last gone out—two months before.

A tall white man got to the door from inside at the same moment I came from up behind Mouse.

"Can I help you?" he asked.

He was lanky and courteous, wearing a gray, short-sleeved shirt with little dark blue dots all over and black buttons. He had on black trousers but no shoes or socks. It was the fact that this stranger was standing barefoot in my home that roused me from fatigue.

"You could tell us what you doin' in my friend's house," Mouse suggested.

"I don't understand," the white man said. "This is my house."

He had sandy brown hair that was in retreat

from his forehead, a jutting nose, and one pimple over the left side of his upper lip. His skin was the color of those white-sand beaches I saw along the West African coast. I didn't have time to register the color of his eyes right then because Mouse distracted me.

Raymond glanced quickly behind him. I mimicked the motion because I knew his next move: If there was no one there he intended some kind of violence.

The street was empty.

The next thing I knew there was that old long-barreled .41 in my friend's hand.

Before the white man could react Ray had hit him in the center of his vast forehead, knocking him into the living room and flat on his back.

Mouse stalked in over his victim, shouting to me, "Come on in and close that do', Easy!"

Once again, in greatly different circumstances, I did as I was told.

The white man was rising up on his right elbow when Mouse pushed him back with his foot.

"Stay down."

When the stunned man tried to get up again, Raymond leveled the muzzle of his gun and said once more, "Stay down."

The lights were on but the California sun outside had been much brighter. My eyes were as fatigued as the rest of me, and so I struggled to get my vision clear.

"What's yo' name, man?" Mouse said.

"Jeffrey."

"Well, Jeff, let me ask you again. What you doin' barefoot in Easy here's house?"

"I live here," he claimed indignantly. "The man who owned this place died and I . . . and I homesteaded it."

There was blood coming from Jeffrey's forehead, but we all knew that that was the least of his problems.

"It's my house," I said. "I had an accident but I didn't die. I'm back now and you should leave."

"Or I will kill you," Mouse agreed. "Right here, right now."

"I have to, have to put my things . . . I have to pack." Events were moving very fast for Jeff. One minute he was luxuriating in his home and the next he was homeless.

"What day is trash day, Easy?" Mouse asked.

"Tuesday."

"You could come by next Tuesday and pick what you want outta the trash."

"But that's—"

Mouse pulled back the hammer on his revolver to cut Jeffrey's complaint short.

As the squatter got to his feet I opened the door.

"What about my shoes," he whined. "I got to have my shoes."

In reply Mouse hit him on the side of his head with the pistol. The impact propelled Jeffrey out

73

the door and down to his knees on the front lawn. Mouse stood in the doorway waving his gun and said, "If I see you again I will kill you, Jeff. You don't know me, but believe it when I tell you I don't fuck around."

Mouse slammed the door and turned to me.

"Can you believe that shit? Mothahfuckah wanna come here and take your house. Claimin' to be some kinda homesteadah acting like he rolled up on the wagon train."

That's when I started to laugh. Between waking up from death, the acres of pain in Timbale Noon's eyes, the cops stopping me for walking, and now this squatter, I knew that, even if the whole world had changed, there was still a hard row to go and no hoe in sight.

Ray laughed with me. I lowered myself onto the sofa and he sat in the padded chair on the side.

I noticed then that he was carrying a grease-stained brown paper bag in his left hand.

It struck me as absurd that a man could exhibit such violence while holding on to a bag full of burgers and fries.

He placed the bag on the low coffee table and ripped it open. The strong smells made me realize how hungry I was and, at the same time, sickened me.

"They aksed me if I wanted chili and cheese on 'em, Easy," Mouse was saying as he tore the tawny paper wrapper off of his burger. "I said okay to the cheese but I thought chili might be too much for your gut."

I picked up my hefty sandwich and determined to swallow at least eight bites. It was my job to learn how to walk and eat and live like a man in a world where every step was a challenge.

"You seen Jackson Blue since the accident?" I asked Mouse some hours later.

I had already called the kids and talked to them. I told Feather that I was going to stay at the Genesee house because I was too tired to move around. She said that she loved me and that she was so happy that I was alive.

"Yeah," Mouse said in answer to the question about Jackson. "You know I got to like old Blue. He can do things that nobody else can, with them computers and telephone lines. I kinda collect special friends like that—especially if they black, but not only."

"You still hooked up with Lynne Hua?"

"Not really. She's gettin' married to this TV actor dude."

"And you don't mind that?"

"It's okay wit' me. I mean, she still gimme some'a that sweet thing if I want it. Woman need to be married. . . . Man too."

He was inviting me to talk about Bonnie Shay but I didn't take the bait.

"You wanna drink, Ray?" I asked instead. "I

think there might be a bottle in the kitchen closet if Jeff didn't get at it."

"No, thanks, Ease. I don't wanna send you down no wrong path."

I'd swallowed the eight bites and even had a few French fries. My stomach gave me serious grief but I rode that out.

By late afternoon the room seemed to be fading.

Mouse was telling the story of how I was the first one to bring him out to Los Angeles, when I called EttaMae down in Houston.

"Yo' ass was in serious trouble," he reminded me, "but I liked the weather."

He said more but I don't remember it. I leaned back and the room receded once more. I was falling for a moment and then there was sudden bliss.

In the dream I was sitting beside a flat boulder on a white beach. Black vultures hovered on the sea breeze just at the waterline, thousands of them. As far as the eye could see in either direction the scavengers floated. There was no escape and so I took a very deep, very satisfying breath and remained where I was.

There came a clattering. It didn't sound like a bird.

I looked around but there was no habitation, animal, or even any plant life to be seen. There was only me and those birds—and now the sound of . . . of hard surfaces clinking together: glass or metal.

I realized then that I had been sleeping, that sleep was much deeper after the accident. The dream was still there too. I was on that beach resting along with the carrion birds. It was a very peaceful feeling and I was loath to come back into the living world.

When I opened my eyes, the conscious awareness I had in the dream faltered. I saw a modern-looking blue-and-green lamp perched like a bird on the little table standing next to my padded chair. The room looked familiar, but where had that lamp come from? Where was I and where had I been?

More clattering sounds interrupted my bout of pedestrian existentialism.

Maybe it was the squatter making that noise. This thought came seemingly of its own accord, not mine. I wondered what was meant by a squatter. Then the memories came back in a rush: Timbale grief-stricken over her missing son, the police, Raymond . . . the squatter.

I sat up quickly and the room started to spin. Falling back on the sofa, I remembered that I'd been hurt. There was an intruder in my house and I was wounded and unarmed. The intruder had put a lamp on the table next to the chair. Why did he do that?

I closed my eyes and sat up slowly, thinking as I rose that it was probably better that I was unarmed. I wasn't strong enough to fire a pistol accurately.

After achieving an upright position on the sofa I opened my eyes. The coffee table was littered with the debris of the Meaty Meatburger feast. There was an ashtray filled with butts.

I hadn't quit smoking yet.

More rattling came from the kitchen and I began to believe that I wasn't under siege.

The dream, the fear, the weakness in every corner of my body came together to form the decision of what I had to do next.

I lurched up from the sofa and reeled toward the kitchen, expecting to see Mouse. But instead it was Feather standing at the sink; the tall-for-her-age biracial beauty whom I had stolen from a perilous fate.

"Hi, Daddy," she said, trying her best to sound like my little girl.

"How'd you get here?"

"Juice drove me."

"Why aren't you in school?"

"Because you drove off the side of a mountain and instead of letting people take care of you,

you're all the way over here all by yourself."

She was washing the dishes wearing jeans and a tight pink T-shirt. Her breasts were just beginning to form. She'd need looser clothes and a bra before long.

"Where's Raymond?"

"He wasn't here. This house is a mess. Has somebody been staying here? There were dirty dishes everywhere, and the sheets on your bed were so soiled that I threw them out."

"What time is it?"

"Ten thirty. Daddy, you should come back to the big house and rest until you get better. You look sick."

I put my hands on Feather's shoulders and stared her in the eye. She was maybe five-seven, but I still dwarfed her.

It was then that I smelled the coffee. The odor brought me unexpectedly back to the dream of the beach. I understood then that the coffee had been part of the dream but not in it. This seemed like a very important piece of information.

"You want some coffee, Daddy?"

"That'd be great."

"Sit down and I'll pour it for you."

We had a table that could squeeze in five at the bay window room attached to the kitchen. My little home was like a tinderbox compared to the big house in Bel-Air, but it was comfortable, and it was mine. Feather poured my coffee and sat down across from me. The morning sun fell on the light brown skin of her right arm.

"Daddy, you have to come home," she said.

I took her fingers and squeezed them lightly.

"I can't, baby girl."

"Why not?"

I looked into my daughter's face feeling all the fierce love that a father can know, imagining a young man falling for her the way I had been told I'd careened off that coastal cliff. These clashing images elated me.

"You know I come from a hard place," I said.

"I know," she replied in an exasperated tone. "Fifth Ward, Houston, Texas, where the police left on Friday afternoon and didn't come back till Sunday morning to count the bodies."

I laughed and said, "Am I that predictable?"

"I've been listening to you tell those stories my whole life. But you have to listen to me sometimes too."

These last words she learned from Bonnie Shay, I was sure.

"Okay," I said. "I'll listen, but I want to tell you something first."

"What?" I appreciated the petulance in her voice. I wanted my little girl to stay a child for a few years more.

"If you got sick," I said, "or Juice or Essie did, you'd do best to get in the bed until you were better. I'd take you to the doctor and hold your hand if you had to have a shot and I'd give you water with an eyedropper if you were too weak to hold the glass. That would be good for you, but I'm a different breed of fish."

"What's that supposed to mean?"

"Most fish can sleep after a fashion," I said. "They get under a rock on the ocean floor or float with a big school of their brethren with guards posted around the edges. But some fish, like the shark, can never stop moving forward. If a shark stops moving he will suffocate in his sleep.

"If I was to stay in the bed in that big house I'd perish just as sure as a shark would in a fish tank. I can feel it, Feather, in my chest and my heart. I was dying in that fancy bedroom until Uncle Ray came up there and held out his hand."

"But you're so weak," Feather protested. She had already been convinced, but this knowledge did not allay her fears.

"I know I am. But I think I can get around that. Yes, sir, I believe I can."

I sipped my coffee and felt at ease because I had spoken a truth to my daughter that I had not completely understood.

"Daddy?"

"Yeah?" I thought she would ask me about how I planned to regain my strength.

"You know when you had the accident and they called and said that you were dead."

"Uh-huh." I could hear the pain in her words.

"When I thought that you were . . . that you were gone, I started thinking about if I had a mother somewhere."

I held my breath, knowing what would come next.

"Juice told me that he remembered the day that you brought me home."

There's no rest for the weary, a woman, I forget her name, used to say when I lived in Texas. Six words with one contraction, and there was more truth in there than in the Christian Bible, *Das Kapital*, and *The Interpretation of Dreams* rolled up into one.

"Who was my mother?" Feather asked.

It was the question I most dreaded. I loved Feather, but the truth, I feared, would damage her more than all the love in the world could heal.

"Easy!"

Loud knocking came at the front door. I pushed up from the dinette table and moved toward the living room. I had never been happier to hear Mouse's bark.

13

He was standing on the front porch next to tall and flaxen Peter Rhone.

Peter was carrying a bag full of groceries. He wore faded jeans and a baby blue T-shirt. Mouse had on pearl gray pants and a square-cut green shirt that was short-sleeved and loose-fitting.

"Ray," I said, moving back to allow the two entrée. "Peter."

"Mr. Rawlins," Peter greeted me.

"Me and Pete brought you some food, Easy," Mouse said, making his way toward the kitchen.

Feather came out and smiled, as most women did, for the enigmatic killer.

"Hi, Uncle Ray."

"What you doin' here, Feather? I thought you was in summer school?"

He asked this question while pressing past my daughter into the kitchen.

The rest of us followed.

"I came to take care of Daddy."

Mouse just nodded while he took groceries from Peter's arms.

"I got breakfast here," he said. "Slab bacon, grits, and eggs. If that don't make him better I don't know what will."

"How's LaMarque?" Feather asked about Raymond's twenty-two-year-old son.

"Didn't I tell you? Oh, yeah, that was Juice. Etta send him down to Texas to stay with her brother and his wife. She said that a summer on the farm might firm him up some."

While he talked Mouse was taking the breakfast ingredients out of the bag and placing them on the counter. He had everything from eggs to butter to salt and pepper. He wasn't about to rely on any stores that the squatter Jeffrey kept.

"Sit down, you guys," he said. "I'll cook up everything. Feather?"

"Yes, Uncle Ray?"

"You clean up this kitchen? 'Cause you know it was a mess last night."

"Uh-huh."

While Mouse busied himself with cooking, Peter took a seat across from Feather and me.

"We came together because Mr. Alexander needed me to drive over from Primo's," the young man said.

Peter worked part-time for my friend Primo in a garage that the elder, Mexican-born mechanic managed.

"Why?" I asked.

"Bright red nineteen sixty-fi'e two-door Plymouth Barracuda," Mouse said excitedly. "Sittin' still that baby look like she goin' fast."

84

While Mouse opined, Peter put the keys down in front of me.

"What?" I said.

"Mr. Alexander said that you needed a car, and Primo had the Barracuda that he planned to sell in Mexico later this month. He and I were going to drive it down, but when he heard you needed a car he made what he called a permanent loan."

"Ray, you know I don't do my work in loud cars," I said.

"Loud car got it ovah a bus that never comes. You better believe that."

That was all the fight I had in me. I sat back while Mouse cooked breakfast and Peter talked to Feather about her algebra homework. I was floating, like one of those coastal vultures, enjoying a moment of rest on the long migration of life.

The four of us ate heartily, and my stomach hardly protested at all. Ray had some stories about small conflicts that he and Primo had gotten into when they went down to Tijuana once a few years back.

". . . mothahfuckahs didn't think I could talk Spanish," Ray was saying, "and so when I heard 'em say that they was gonna get the fat Southerner, I warned Primo and we got the hell outta there."

I could have objected to his language around my daughter, but she knew how I felt, and asking

Ray to edit his words was like requiring a porcupine to leave its quills at the door.

By the time breakfast was over I felt almost strong enough to do what I had to in order to keep moving forward.

"I told Primo that I'd have Peter back before the day was over," Mouse was saying as Feather washed dishes and Peter dried. "So we better be off."

"Take Feather back up to the Bel-Air house, will you, Ray?"

"I wanna stay here with you, Daddy."

"I have to do something for Uncle Ray," I said, "and there was this strange guy hanging around here. I'd feel safer if you were up in there."

"Okay. But are you coming back home tonight?"

"If I don't I will certainly call."

I saw my friends and family off at the front door. They cruised up Genesee in Raymond's pink Caddy. Feather was waving out the back window as they went.

Seeing them go I had to resist the impression that my lifeblood was draining away in their wake.

Back in the house I called Martin Martins, who was, for lack of a better term, a handyman.

Martins had moved to L.A. from Mississippi in the late forties like I had from Texas. He was a genius at anything mechanical or that had to do with building. Most of his leisure hours were spent studying machines and architectural design by looking at devices of all sorts and watching builders at work. I believe that he could have single-handedly built a skyscraper given enough time and resources—he was that good.

A few years earlier Martins was shot as he came out of a bar on Avalon at around midnight. The bullet, aimed at his heart, was true, but the shooter didn't know that the mechanic had an iron device, given to him by the bartender, in his left breast pocket. People were always giving Mr. Martins odd gadgets and tools because he loved to study any technology new to him. He liked to get just a piece or section of some larger device and try, from that one puzzle piece, to figure out the function of the machine it came from.

The .45 slug knocked Martin for a loop, and luckily for him, the shooter ran rather than check out his work.

At two that morning Jackson Blue called me asking for a late meeting with his friend Martins.

"Do you know who shot you?" I asked Martins at a few minutes shy of three a.m. We were sitting at a corner table in Cox Bar—an unlicensed establishment hidden off of an unnamed alley in the bowels of Watts.

"It looked like Bill Fern," the long-limbed master craftsman replied.

Martin was the color of a dark plum and formed from many angles. His face was nearly a perfect triangle set on the point of his chin. He had high cheekbones, long fingers, and a flat plane of chest that spoke of a day laborer's strength. "But I don't know why he wanna shoot at me. I mean, we hardly even know each other, and I can't think of one wrong I've done him."

"What's this Bill do for a living?" I asked.

"Work for the city, I think, collectin' trash. At least, that's what he used to do a few years ago."

"How'd you meet him?"

"My wife's coworker Nanette Yomen had a party for all the colored people she knew worked for the city."

"Did your wife know Bill?"

Even Martin's eyes were composed of angles. The orbital bones formed squares around the orbs. It's always a pleasure working with an intelligent man. He squeezed those squares down into thin quadrangles while peering inside his own mind.

After maybe two minutes he said, "I got twenty-one thousand dollars in the bank."

That's all he had to say. We—me, him, and Jackson Blue, who was there for the intro-duction—all understood what had transpired.

I knew a disbarred lawyer named Milo Sweet who wrote up the divorce agreement. They split everything minus five hundred dollars for expenses. Bill Fern was at the final meeting. He apologized to Martin and said that there was no reason to hold a grudge.

I gave the five hundred to Mouse and asked him to visit Bill at his apartment and impress upon him that if any violence happened to Martin that Ray had already been paid to take Bill's life.

I didn't charge a dime for that job. A good handyman in my corner outweighed any fee.

"Hello?" Hela Klineman answered.

Hela was a German woman who came to the U.S. after World War II. She'd been married to a black soldier named Mortimer Revert, but that union foundered at just about the time Martin's did. They got together but did not wed—both of them having serious reservations about the institution of marriage. They had a child, however, and seemed to be deeply in love.

"It's Easy, Hela."

"Hold on."

"Hey, Easy, how are you?" Martin said when he got on the line. That man loved me.

"I need some help."

"Name it."

"Could you install bars on all my windows and new locks, good locks, on the doors?"

"How soon?"

"The sooner the better."

"I'll be over there in an hour then."

"How much?" I asked.

"Materials," he said. "And I'll get you my builder's discount."

I might have died but the world still remembered me.

After making sure of the security of my home I went out the front door. I made it to the sidewalk, where I stopped and remembered that I had forgotten something, not knowing exactly what that something was. I went back into the house and stood in the front room waiting for insight. Then I smiled.

In the bedroom closet, on the shelf above the hangers, was a little door that was not immediately obvious in the gloom. On the other side of that door sat a .22-caliber pistol and a box of shells. I loaded the gun and spent a few moments reacquainting my hand with its weight.

After that I left the house again.

The Barracuda looked like a bloody wound on the street. I climbed in, though, and drove off just like it was the most natural thing in the world.

14

It was on Central Avenue that the memories started coming back.

I was smoking a Camel cigarette from a new pack that I picked up at a liquor store along the way. The window was open and the air whipped around the inside of that Barracuda like a man-made tornado.

Aretha Franklin was belting out Otis Redding's song "Respect" on the radio, and I was feeling only slightly anchored to the world that I had left behind.

Down Tucker Street, in the heart of Compton, if you drive far enough, you come to a dead end. The asphalt turns to hard yellow soil. Thirty feet after that a seemingly impenetrable stand of avocado and eucalyptus trees blocks the way. Through and beyond the trees are dense bushes, many of them with thorns. If you push past the bushes you come to an unexpected door that seems like just another part of the forest, a yellow door with green lichen growing on it.

I stopped there to consider my actions. This was not a threshold that one, even a man in my condition, crossed lightly.

I waited a moment and the door opened of its own accord.

Jo was taller and darker and more substantial than I was even before the accident. She was in her sixties but might have been forty except for the heavy toll experience had left on her dark eyes.

"I wondered when you was gonna get here, Easy," she said in a strong tenor voice that man or woman would have been proud of.

I inhaled, taking in the strange odors of the backwoods alchemist's lair. The smells were sweet and bitter, vegetable and mammal, fish and also the deep, rich odor of the earth in its various refined guises.

I exhaled, feeling that the breath coming out of me carried an imprint of my soul that the house itself would study and pass judgment on.

"Come on in, Easy," Mama Jo offered. "Take a weight off them shaky legs."

Mama Jo's home was like no other in Southern California: one generous room that performed every function of a house and a backwoods clinic. The floor was packed earth and the furniture could have been built by peasant hands in Europe's Dark Ages. There was a hearth with a mantelpiece that had thirteen skulls on it. Twelve were armadillo heads and one was Domaque, the father of Jo's only child, and the one true love of her life.

She had a pet raven moving back and forth on its

T-shaped oak stand, and two live armadillos that stayed to the corners of the wide room. I saw something else move in the shadow under her long worktable but failed to make out the species.

"Sit down ovah here, baby," she said.

I lowered myself into a chair made from arm-thick branches and animal hide. It was the chair I most often used at Jo's house.

Jo sat down on the bench placed at her work-table. Behind her were dozens of crocks and jars, hanging bunches of dried leaves and branches, and more than a few hand-bound volumes.

There was barely six inches of space between our knees. Jo reached out for my hands and I gave them willingly, focusing my eyes on her bare feet.

"Easy," she said, and I looked up.

We sat there for an interminable period, passing breath and feeling between us. My hands began to sweat and that was just another form of communication.

After a long time Jo blinked twice and let me go.

"It's like you was dead out there in them bushes, Easy," she said.

I nodded and sighed.

"You were down there in the pit and it was Raymond's love that dragged you out. You two is just like chirren on a seesaw. One'a you is up and the other one down. That's how it goes."

I grinned but had no words to say.

"Man is a animal, Easy," Jo continued on her impromptu and yet ready sermon. "Bobcat can have the biggest fight of his life on a Tuesday noon. And win or lose, either way, on Wednesday, if he still alive, he'll need water and meat to survive.

"It's a good thing that you run up off'a that cliff. A good thing. Because when you hit the bottom there is only one place left for you to go. You know that, don't ya?"

"I don't know a goddamned thing, Jo," I said, unable to keep my anger in check. "Not a fuckin' thing."

"You know you tried to kill yourself and that Death threw you back. He held you in his hand a minute and then said, 'Maybe.'"

I laughed deeply in spite of the pains in my chest and back. The idea of the Absolute looking at life and tossing it aside sounded so right that it was almost unbearable.

"I'm lookin' for somebody for Raymond," I said when the laughter subsided. "Evander Noon."

"That's just the seesaw action," Jo replied. "You lookin' for yourself."

"I'm not sure if it's for Evander or me," I said, knowing that there was no arguing metaphysics with her. "All I do know is that I walked a block and a half yesterday and nearly collapsed. And here I got miles up ahead of me."

"And that's why you come here?"

"You gave Mouse this little vial for hangovers," I said.

"Hangovah ain't like dyin'," she replied. "That's just a little pick-me-up after a night out."

"You got somethin' stronger?" I asked.

"There's health in your body, sugah, and death in your soul. I can give ya somethin' help to see you through this thing, but I can't tell whether you gonna come back alive or not."

"All I know is if I stop right now I will be dead in a week. I know it."

Jo's hard black face cracked into a girlish grin.

"I knew when you was just a teenager that you were gonna be one helluva man, Mr. Rawlins. You look at the world and see what's there. You know there ain't one person outta three hundred could lay claim to half"a that."

Jo got up and turned around to reach for something on a high shelf above the long and deep worktable. I had been looking almost only into her eyes since entering the cottage—either that or her workwoman's feet and near-feral pets. Jo had the kind of will that kept you engaged. But when she turned I noted that she was wearing an almost festive yellow dress that came down to the middle of her calves. She had dressed for company. She had dressed for me.

"Here we go," she said.

She handed me a wooden crate divided into

eight three-inch-square sections. In each slatted section was nestled a little green bottle—all of them stoppered with hand-cut cork plugs. The liquid inside the bottles was dark and thick.

"I call this here Gator's Blood," Jo said as she regained her seat. "That there is some powerful juju. You take yourself a nap and then if you feelin' weak you drink down one bottle. After that you'll be good to go for whatever time your condition will allow. When you get tired again don't take another bottle until you done falled asleep and woke up naturally. It's some powerful shit, Easy, so don't think you can break them rules. . . . But if you do what I say, not only will this medicine give you strength but it will help you heal."

"This is great, Jo," I said, "just what I wanted. I was wonderin' if you had some tar balls too?"

"What for?"

"I don't have any trouble falling asleep, but the dreams I've been having are sometimes too strong. And if I remember right, those tar balls cut down the strength of dreams."

"They up on the shelf. But lemme make you some tea right now. I think that would be the right thing."

Jo sat me on her hemp-padded sleeping cot and pulled the chair I'd been sitting in up next to it. She served me a sour-smelling sweet-tasting tea in an earthenware cup that might have been a century old. I took a sip and yawned.

"It's good to see you, Easy," Jo whispered.

"It's good to be here."

I took another sip and my eyes felt like they needed to close.

"You can't fight with Death," she said. "All you can do is stand your ground and hope that the foundation don't fall out from under you."

"Can you get word to Juice and Feather that I'm here and that I'm all right?" I said as she took the cup from my hand.

"I'll tell 'em that you're here," she said, and I fell on my side, sleep coming up around me like high tide.

15

I came awake alone in Jo's Compton cottage. She was nowhere to be seen. I didn't know if it was day or night, because Jo's place had no windows and it was always lit by oil lanterns and candles. Breezes came through the walls and ceilings to ventilate the place, but I never knew how this process was achieved.

On the worktable there was a plate of food under a flat-topped crystal cover. Standing on this glass protector stood a cat that had pointed ears like a lynx but weighed no more than five or six pounds. The feline hissed at me and I laughed.

I really enjoyed the soul food repast: pig tails, dirty rice, and collard greens cooked with ham hocks and finished with white vinegar. My stomach hardly complained. There was a cola bottle with a bottle opener next to the plate. Next to the meal sat the wooden tray of Gator's Blood bottles with five rice paper–wrapped lumps, which looked like tar balls, wedged in between them.

I took one of the bottles, teased out the cork plug, and drank the contents, five or six ounces, in one draft. The concoction tasted like equal parts hard cider and swamp mud. The medicine was astringent against my tongue and throat. It felt like acid burning away the lining down to my stomach. This burning, which was at first painful, quickly spread through my chest, out along my arms, and finally up into my head. I broke out into a sweat and stood up because I had to.

I rose to my full height in the middle of Jo's place shivering, witnessed by the avian, feline, and rodent roommates of the absent Southern witch. The heat in my chest turned to hilarity and the being in my soul was momentarily transformed into a hyena when the moon is full and the hunt is on.

After thirty minutes or so I was feeling better than I had in years. It was nighttime outside. There was a warm breeze blowing and the sky was both clear and black, except for a few stars.

I put the remaining Gator's Blood bottles and tar balls in the trunk of the red Barracuda and then attended to the sky for a minute or two more.

I drove until coming to a World gas station, where I used the pay phone to call the Bel-Air house.

"Hello?" Feather answered.

"Hey, baby girl."

"Daddy?"

"How are you?" I asked my daughter.

"Fine. Mama Jo called and said that you were taking a nap at her house. Are you okay?"

"Sure. Why?"

"Why? Because you had that accident. You just got out of the bed yesterday morning."

It hadn't yet been two days, but it felt like there were months between me and the partial coma.

"I'm going up to the Sunset Strip to do something for Uncle Ray," I said. "Don't worry about me. Jo gave me some of her special medicine and I'm as strong as a bull."

"You sound funny, Daddy."

"That's the medicine working. It makes me feel good."

"You should come home," Feather said.

"And I will just as soon as I finish this job for Ray. Don't worry, Feather; I will come back to you and I will answer every question you have about where you came from before you came to us."

After that I jumped into the borrowed car and blazed my way toward the future.

L.A. at night, back in the sixties, was a wonderful place to drive. There were lots of people but it wasn't overcrowded. The avenues and boulevards were wide and open to free-flowing traffic. I felt great with Jo's concoction in my system and the desert wind coming in through the windows. The Temptations were singing "My Girl" on the radio, and people seemed happy and alive in their cars.

I wore Death on my shoulders like a superhero's cape, but that didn't matter. I was going to fight the good fight and, win or lose, I'd be counted as a man who struggled against his own fate.

I parked on San Vicente, five or six blocks down from the Strip, and walked from there because my legs needed stretching. The energy thrumming in my body had to be burned off some before I started talking to people about Evander "Little Green" Noon. In the state I was in I might have started off by yelling and grabbing strangers by their lapels.

Just down from the corner of San Vicente and Sunset there was a small liquor store done up in yellow plaster and red neon. When I walked in the diminutive white clerk stuck his hand down under the counter. I had the pistol in my belt, but the few blocks of fast walking saved that man from getting his face perforated.

Lifting my hands to shoulder level I said, "Just here for a carton of Camels, my man. I already done robbed my quota of liquor stores this month."

There were three men and one woman customer in the place, wandering up and down the aisles looking for potato chips, candy, and other sundries that California liquor stores sold. They looked at me oddly, wondering.

The little clerk frowned, which struck me as funny, because he had very thick and black eyebrows like Groucho. His right hand was still out of sight. I suppose that even a Marx Brother didn't get every joke. No one else in the store was laughing, so I allowed my own smile to fade.

"Look, man," I said. "I'm gonna put my hand in my back pocket and come out with a wallet. I'm gonna take five dollars from that and put it down in front of you. Then you're gonna give me a carton of Camels in one'a those long paper bags you got on the shelf next to that gun you're holding. . . ."

"I don't have Camels in cartons," he said. It was almost a plea.

"Lucky Strikes?"

"Yeah, yeah, I got them in cartons."

"I'm easy," I said.

It still took a moment for the clerk to move to my demands. He was so scared that he trembled a bit.

That's what the Watts Riots did for L.A. For the first time West Coast Caucasians were frightened of almost any black face that loomed before them. We had proved that we were willing to fight, but most white people didn't understand our complaints and so were afraid of almost anything we did.

Armed with my bag of two hundred cigarettes I made my way west on Sunset.

It was about ten p.m. and the sidewalks were crowded with literally thousands of long-haired, barefoot, dope-smoking, acid-tripping, free-loving hippies. There were rock clubs and head shops, Hare Krishnas chanting joyously, and a whole host of policemen in uniform and not. You could identify the plainclothes cops by their leather shoes and the telltale creases in their trousers.

The hippies were not just white people either. They made up a rainbow of black, white, brown, yellow, and red. There were runaways, throwaways, and some no-way-at-all youngsters traveling in the company of older hipsters. They were talking mind-altering chemistry, philosophy, music, and religion. They carried guitars, harmonicas, and, hidden in their pockets, homemade pipes constructed of anything from durable aluminum foil to fragile handblown glass.

Music blared from clubs like Whiskey a Go Go and also from passing automobiles. One young black man who wore farmer's jeans and a shirt made from chains carried a huge radio on his shoulder playing the Chambers Brothers.

I felt at home for the first time since regaining consciousness. This was like a primal purgatory where transient human spirits stopped to party until the final decision was laid upon their brows. I was just another soul passing through, making believe that the illusion of my life had substance.

I handed out cigarettes and showed Evander's graduation photograph to anyone who'd talk to me: longhairs, militants, and lay monks of many stripes.

"His mother just wants to know if he's alive," I'd say, or, "Want a cigarette? I'm looking for somebody," or, "He's my brother and he's got an asthma condition."

I'd handed out over half of my supply of cigarettes and got nothing but shrugs, frowns, and maybes. But that didn't stop me.

I even asked a policeman. I figured if something happened to Evander, maybe an official would know.

"Haven't seen him," the rangy cop said. He was studying me closely. "Your son?"

"My friend's boy. He's down lookin' for him at the beach."

At the corner of Doheny and Sunset I saw a pretty blond teenager and three young longhairs talking. I was on the job, so I stopped to jaw with them.

"You want some cigarettes?" I asked.

"Who are you, Straight?" an auburn-haired skinny guy asked.

I didn't understand the word, so I took out a pack of Luckies and shook some butts out for him to choose from—he took all four.

"My name's Easy," I said. "I'm from down around Fairfax and Pico and I'm looking for the son of one of my friends."

"Who's that?" the pretty girl asked as she took one of the cigarettes from the young man.

I took out Evander's picture and showed her. She gave the photo a milky frown and shook her head.

Two of her other friends also shook their heads. But this one raven-haired young man, who was a head taller than the rest, said, "I don't squeal to the pig."

"You think I'm a cop, man?" I asked, Gator's

Blood rousing in my system like its namesake on an unsuspecting doe. "How many times you been busted, beat up, or betrayed by a black man? When's the last time you saw a brother on TV tellin' you that hippies are communists?"

I suppose I was a little more aggressive than I intended, because the tall young man blanched behind his black beard and mustache. He backed away and I had to concentrate not to advance on him.

The power of Jo's medicine had made itself evident. It released some kind of demon force in my heart and soul. I actually wanted to beat that boy just because that's what he expected.

"Excuse me," a small voice said.

The quartet I'd been talking to was moving away, and I was consciously hanging back. I turned and saw this smallish brunette girl, maybe twenty, maybe not. She was wearing a white dress and blue socks in red Keds tennis shoes. She had on pink lipstick and violet eye shadow.

There were as many kinds of hippies on Sunset as there were definitions of snow in native Alaska.

"Yes?" I said.

"I heard what they said to you," she told me. "Some people just don't get it that it's a class, race, and culture war all rolled up into one. They don't know that they're guilty of the same thing the Man is if they judge you by how you look."

She certainly got my attention. Her patter was intelligent but peculiar to that street, those people, and an era that had seemingly popped up out of the ground, or maybe out of the radio.

"Have you seen this guy?" I asked, showing her Evander's photo.

Immediately a light of recognition showed on the young half hippie's face. This illumination was immediately followed by another, less identifiable reaction. She looked up at me and said, "Maybe."

"Maybe?"

"I mean, um, I think he's this guy we been callin' Evy. He gets high in this little alley up above Sunset."

"Is he there right now?"

"He's been there all week."

"I'd really like to see him," I said. "I have a message from his mother. Will you show me where he is?"

"Okay."

The white girl in white led me down three blocks of Sunset. There we moved shoulder to shoulder with unwashed humanity from every state and city in the country. It was a profound experience for a black man like me to walk along with so many white people and them not having any kind of revulsion, fear, or disgust. That night, on Sunset Boulevard, the playing field was even, but that hardly mattered, because there was no competition.

If I didn't have a life somewhere else I might have stayed right there for a good long time—until I got the rancid taste of my own particular history off my tongue and out from my nose.

"This way," the girl in white said.

She led me up a side street and then turned at the block. Walking a few houses over, we came to a lane that led down to an alley behind a block of Sunset businesses.

"Over there," she said, pointing at the back door of some building.

At that very moment something hard hit me on the back of the head. The blow hurt but did not debilitate me. I understood then that Mama Jo's medicine had somehow strengthened my awareness and speeded up my reaction time.

While allowing my body to lurch forward I realized that the girl had set me up to be mugged. Why not? There had to be criminal hippies along with those involved in flower power. I let my left knee go all the way to the ground and then genuflected beyond that. Above my head a man grunted and the slight breeze of a heavy object passed overhead. My right hand reached under my jacket, behind my back, and grasped the .22 I'd brought from the secret chamber in my closet. I fell on my left side and looked up to see two scruffy men with longish, but not hippie-long, hair. They wore black leather jackets, angry beards, and had, respectively, red and blue bandannas tied around their throats.

Time was moving at a normal rate, but I felt like three different men watching various sections of the action as it unfolded.

"Stomp 'im, Jess!" one of the beards ejaculated.

I saw the girl in white behind me while the two men were rushing up from my feet. One of the guys raised his metal-rimmed boot, intending, no doubt, to bring the heel down on my forehead. But I shot right through the leather toward the toe and he screamed so high that I actually wondered if he was descended from swine.

"He shot me! He's got a gun!" the wounded mugger yelled.

His friend caught him around the waist and they hurried away at a surprising speed. The girl tried to join them, but I caught her by the ankle and she went down.

"Jess! Tony! Help!" she cried, but her friends knew that they couldn't do anything against a man that could and would shoot.

17

The girl shouted, "Let me go!" and I slapped her.

I didn't feel bad about hitting a woman in those circumstances. After all, she had just set me up to get mugged and beaten. Also, I didn't hit her very hard, just enough sting to get her attention and to keep the police from coming.

"Shut up. I'm not gonna hurt you, girl."

Her wild eyes were a sight in themselves. I could see in them a great deal of suffering and pain that lived inside her like a parasite that had been in her gut since childhood.

"Then let me go," she said at a half shout.

"I'll do you one better," I said. "I'll let you go and give you twenty dollars if you tell me where I can find this Evy. That really is his nickname and you couldn't know that unless you met him."

Money means freedom; that was what people in the white America thought then. Citizens like me knew that whatever you had could be taken away in an instant. We knew that value was first and foremost defined by the hand that offered it. Those on the receiving end were one-legged tightrope walkers.

But for the white girl in the white dress and blue socks, money would open a door that she could pass through; at least, that was what she believed.

"He was talking to a girl named Ruby down by the Blues Hut near Fairfax," she said.

"Where can I find Ruby?"

"She's always down there this time of night. She sells flowers that she steals from people's gardens in Beverly Hills."

I still had the pistol in my hand. I had a carry permit granted me by one of the assistant chiefs of police who hated my guts but also needed my help from time to time.

I put the gun back under my jacket and took a twenty from my front pocket.

Before handing the money to the girl I said, "You know there's a whole lotta men would kill you for what you tried to do to me."

She stared into my eyes, looking for that death blow.

I handed her the bill and let go of her arm. She ran so fast that it was comical.

I laughed and started walking.

I had made it all the way to the mouth of the little lane before my next trial.

A flashlight winked and then shone in my face. I winced but remained otherwise still.

"Stop right there," a man's voice said. "Let's see some ID."

I didn't move.

The policemen phased into sight from the

darkness and the partial blindness imparted by the flashlight. Both men had pistols in their hands.

"I said," the man said, "show me some ID."

"I will certainly do that, Officer," I replied in a jaunty voice. "But I just wanted to tell you that my wallet is in my back pocket."

"Move slowly," the other man said.

I was thinking that I had a good chance of killing those two men. It was merely supposition, but a frightening thought still and all. I took out my driver's license and private investigator's ticket and handed them to the second man.

"Look at this, Leon," the cop said after shining his light on my proofs.

"Private dick?" Leon said incredulously.

I thought about nodding but didn't.

Leon moved closer to get a better look at me.

"This is you?" he asked.

"Yes, sir."

"I never met a colored private dick before."

"We're a rare breed."

"What are you doing up here?"

"May I take something out of my inside breast pocket?"

"What?"

"The picture of the young man I'm looking for."

"Okay," he said, leveling the pistol at my chest.

I showed him and his partner Evander's picture and told them pretty much the truth about my intentions.

"So what are you doin' up here?" the cop who was not Leon asked.

"I met a girl down on Sunset who said that Evander would sleep behind a Dumpster in the alley back there. I came up to look but instead I see these biker guys fighting."

"Did one of them fire a gun?" Leon wanted to know.

"No gun that I saw, but they made one helluva racket pushing and fighting around those big Dumpster cans. I called out, thinking that maybe one of them was Evander, but when they ran I saw it wasn't him."

The officer-not-Leon handed me my identification and said, "You have to be careful up around here, Mr. Rawlins. A lot of these kids hate the establishment and they sometimes rob men and women dressed like you."

"I'm beginning to see that. You know, I believe that if those guys weren't fighting each other they might have attacked me."

The police left soon after that, looking for bikers that had been fighting in the dark.

I made my way back to Sunset. Somewhere along the way I'd dropped the carton of Lucky Strikes, but I still had Evander's photograph.

Walking down streets so dense with humanity you don't really move in a straight line or very fast. All you have is a general forward motion shoved around by couples, corpulence, and unexpected pirouettes of ecstasy. Hiking eastward toward Fairfax felt like a fragrant dance in itself, all the bodies and faces, odors and sounds.

"Hey, man, that's a groove," a patchouli-scented white face said.

"Three dollars a lid, I swear," a marijuana-eyed black hippie announced.

After a while I felt like I was part of a flood, not a singular man at all. It reminded me of outlying Negro towns in Louisiana and Mississippi on Saturday nights, when the workers all hung around the juke joints drinking homemade liquor and dancing. Back then we laughed and cried because we were down under the thumb of racism so strong that there was no escape.

These hippies felt under the gun too. They were ostracized because of their clothes and habits, outraged by the war in Vietnam—but unlike my people in the old days, these young men and women believed that they could change the world that tried to hold them down. They believed that they were part of a revolution.

You could feel the hope coming off of them in waves.

After six or seven blocks I believed it too.

On the southeast corner of Fairfax and Sunset sat a slender white girl on an upside-down red plastic bucket. She wore a tie-dyed yellow-and-violet dress that hugged her figure and went all the way down to her ankles. Her face was long and would become homely as she aged, but that year she had a particular beauty brought out by the mostly peaceful mutiny of people in the street.

As I approached she looked up and smiled. Her eyes were amber. Her hair was long and brown. At her bare feet sat a white plastic bucket with roses, dahlias, small sunflowers, poppies, and maybe half a dozen other flowers arranged at random.

"How much?" I asked.

"Whatever you can give," she said.

"What if I don't have anything?"

"Then that's what you can give."

"But aren't you here to make money?"

"I'll get enough for some bread and honey whether you pay me or not." Her eyes went a little out of focus. "One time a guy gave me some French bread and strawberry jam and only took one little snapdragon."

"Are you Ruby?"

"Yes."

I held out a hand and she rose to shake it.

"What's your name?"

"Easy."

"Wow."

She was standing very close to me. I could smell rose attar and human sweat. People were moving around us, but there was an aura of stillness in the little patch of sidewalk that we occupied.

"Do I know you, Easy?"

I took out the graduation picture and showed it to her.

"Evander," she said.

"He hasn't been home in four or five days and his mother wants to make sure he's okay."

"Maybe he doesn't want to go home," she suggested.

"I just need to see him breathing, that's all."

Ruby considered me for a moment, came to a decision, and said, "Come on."

"What about your flowers?"

"Somebody'll take them."

She took me by the hand and we waded into the throng. For a brief moment there I felt alive and that something great awaited me.

Holding hands with a stranger, walking down the boulevard, I was unmoored and somewhat grateful for the warm night and its surprises.

Ruby's gaze was restless. Moving her head from left to right and back again she was looking for something that had yet to be defined. Her smile was alive and anticipatory.

She let go of my palm to grasp my index and middle fingers.

"I met him when I was selling flowers, the way

I met you," she nearly shouted. "He said that he wanted to go to a disco."

Her head bobbed so close to mine that I could feel the breath of her words on my cheek. This sensation was all the more intimate because we were in the middle of a moving mob.

"Evander?" I asked.

"We dropped some orange-speckled barrel and went out to get something to eat."

"Dropped?"

"Took acid."

"LSD?"

"Yeah. He said that he never did it before, and somebody gave me a two-way hit for some roses."

"That stuff is dangerous, isn't it?"

"So's deep water, but people still go swimming in it."

That's when I began to like Ruby.

"So what happened after the club?" I asked.

"We never went, because I had to go up behind the Shangri-La to give some of the girls up there their makeup."

"Another club?"

"Yeah," Ruby said with a one-shoulder shrug and a little frown, "but no. I mean, Lula's place is up behind the club. It's there for, you know . . . sex. I go up sometimes and Lula lets a couple of the girls pay me to make them look like hippies. Some'a the guys want to ball a hippie chick and I give 'em the look."

"There's a whorehouse on the Strip?"

"It's work," the girl said, gesturing with her free hand at the sky. "I mean, it's really no different than sellin' your body to a production line or a coal mine."

Or the cotton fields, I thought.

"Did Evander go there with you?"

"Yeah. I thought we'd leave together, but he met this guy and they cooked up something. I don't know what, but when I finished workin' he was gone."

"What was this guy's name?"

"I don't know. I've seen him before. A white guy who likes to wear all green—shirt, tie, everything."

"Like a straight guy?" I asked, experimenting with the language.

"He wasn't a hippie, but he wasn't straight either," she said. "I didn't know his name, but he was a pimp."

The Shangri-La discotheque was vibrating from an overactive electric bass. We took an alley down the side of the blocky three-story building and ended up in a dark parking lot behind.

Across the lot was another three-story building. There were wooden stairs with no railing that went from the lower right corner of the building to the upper left, making a stop along the way for the door to the second floor. The only light was at a small deck at the summit of the stairs. On this upper platform was a yellow chair with an occupant who seemed large even from that distance.

"That's Lula's up there," Ruby said.

"Let's go."

"I don't wanna," she said. "I mean, I go when they pay me, but it smells bad and the men look at you like you were meat . . . the women too."

"I thought it was just another job?" I said.

"I'll stick to my flowers. You want me to wait?"

"If you'd like."

"Would you like?"

I nodded and touched a tress of her hair. She put three fingers on my left elbow. After that communication I headed for the long stairway.

Walking up that precarious flight of steps sticks out in my memory of that night. Jo's Gator's Blood was still roiling in my system, but it had waned appreciably since my fracas with the bikers. The stairs were wide enough for two lanes of foot traffic, but the feeling that there was no bannister to grab onto seemed to focus the insecurity of an entire generation on that climb.

I listed toward the wall, reaching out now and then for its solidity, and climbed with great concentration.

About halfway up I saw that the man sitting in the chair was broad, black, and bald.

When I was only three steps down he bellowed, "What you want?"

"I'm here lookin' for the son of a friend'a mine," I said in our common patois.

"You ain't got no friends up here, mister."

I took two more steps and the big black man stood up from his comfortably padded seat.

"You best to turn your ass around," he advised.

I took the last step.

"I seen dudes in parachute school make a two-story jump," he said. "Hit and roll, they said. You think you could do that?"

I turned my head to look down on the parking lot. I could see Ruby standing at the outer edge, looking up at me.

"Three nights ago," the Gator's Blood said with my lips, "a young man named Evander Noon came here. That was the last time anyone saw him. I've come to find out where he went next."

"Niggah, didn't you hear me?" Big Boy said.

"Evander is a young brother," my voice continued. "Maybe twenty. I have a picture."

"One more word and I'ma throw you down on the asphalt."

"Okay," I said, suddenly relenting. I even took half a step down. "He's not my friend anyway. I came here for somebody else—Raymond Alexander. Maybe you heard'a him. People like to call him Mouse."

That was cheating. I didn't usually use

Raymond's name to get into, or out of, trouble. But the fact was that I'd have to call Ray if the bouncer didn't let me in. And then Big Boy would have been the one who plummeted down to the ground.

"Say what?" the man asked.

"No lie, man. Ray called me to go find his friend's son. I'm a detective."

"Shit."

I handed him my ID.

"Raymond paid me to find out where the boy was last. Now, if you don't let me in then I'll have to tell him that the trail ends right up here—at your big toe."

He studied the picture and pondered the ramifications. Then he handed the ID back.

"Mouse, huh?"

Ray was known in every illegal corner of Los Angeles, and most of the rest of Southern California.

"Wait here," the man I dubbed Big Boy said at last.

He went through a red door beyond the yellow chair and closed it behind him. I heard a bolt being thrown and smiled, because that meant he was taking me seriously.

I couldn't see Ruby anymore. I wondered if she decided to leave. Her unexpected absence got me thinking about Bonnie Shay. She was getting married. She was with her man. I wasn't devastated or heartbroken because of my close encounter with death, but there was still sadness there, a melancholy that said no matter how hard I tried I'd never be able to hold on to the happiness I craved.

"Come on," Big Boy said at the door.

I hadn't even heard it open.

A black woman in a green-and-gold kimono sat behind an ivory-colored table in the small reception area. Looking down, I could see her well-formed breasts. Her eyes were dead but she smiled pleasantly enough.

This emotional juxtaposition made me feel right at home.

"Come on," Big Boy said again.

He led me down a long hallway with open doors on either side.

In most of the rooms men and women were having commercialized sex. Nothing looked good or fun. There was a lot of grunting and pounding, urging and gyration. The whorehouse was in full swing while free love raged in the street below.

We came at last to a closed door. This Big Boy threw open. He stepped to the side, but the hall was so narrow that I had to squeeze by him. As I passed I could feel his hot breath. This made me think of Ruby talking to me on the Strip. I hoped that she'd be out there when I left.

There were three lamps on in the low room, but mere electric light had failed to illuminate the darkness. The office was furnished with a desk, two thin-legged doelike chairs, and a soiled tan sofa.

Big Boy took one of the chairs and placed it in a corner, where he sat down to keep an eye on me. A white woman, naked except for a turquoise feather boa around her neck, lounged on the vinyl couch. When I came in she lifted her left foot up on the cushion, displaying her pubic area like a beggar exposing his war wound.

Behind the desk sat a well-worn, fortyish white woman with dyed red hair and two blue eyes, one wandering and the other fastened on me.

"Lula Success," she said, not rising, not holding out a hand.

"Easy Rawlins," I said.

"That your real name?"

"Can I have a seat?"

She smiled a crooked smile. I took this as an invitation.

The room felt cramped but it was large enough. It was hot in there. The madam's smile was like that of the alligator at home in the warm waters of my blood.

"Ezekiel," I said.

"Come again?" Lula said.

"Easy. It comes from Ezekiel."

For some reason this delighted Lula.

"Do they call you that because things always go your way?" she asked.

"Just the opposite."

"You're not here for pussy, are you, Mr. Easy?"

"Not right now. You see, a few nights ago a young man named Evander Noon came here on an acid trip with a girl named Ruby—"

"The makeup hippie girl," Lula interjected.

"—and he, Evander, left with a man dressed all in green—I'm told."

"Maurice," Lula said to Big Boy. "I should have known."

"Known what?" I asked.

"Are you here for Haman Rose?"

"Never heard of him. My friend Mouse sent me."

"Oh, yeah, Arthur said something about him."

I supposed Arthur was the name Big Boy went by at this job. It probably wasn't his real name. You only gave people your real name if they paid you with a check.

"Who's Haman Rose?" I asked.

"The kind of guy you don't want looking for you."

"Neither is Mouse," I said, and Arthur Big Boy grunted.

Lula frowned at her employee.

"I don't want any trouble, Easy," she said. "I remember the young man. He was flying pretty high. Maurice was here that night. But I don't remember if he had anything to do with your friend . . . do you, Sparkle?"

"Uh-uh," the naked couch ornament murmured.

"They left together," Arthur said.

"When?" I asked.

"Maybe around ten. Maurice said that he had a new girl for us, but when he met the kid he forgot all about that and they split."

"Where?"

"I'ont know."

"And this Haman Rose has been looking for him?"

"Keith Handel was," Big Boy said. "But everybody knows that Keith works for Rose."

I turned back to Lula.

"You know where I can find any of those men?"

"We aren't that close. I do business with Maurice from time to time, but I've never kissed him on the lips."

All the forward motion of that night came to a halt then. I wasn't weak, but the strength Jo's medicine had given me was gone. I sat there a few seconds too long without speaking.

"You disapprove of prostitution, Mr. Easy?" Lula asked, maybe just to fill in the silence.

"Not at all. I'm just a little surprised to find it here, with all the free love out there in the street."

Lula's sneer seemed to be accented by her wandering eye.

124

"Nothing's free," she said. "Free sex is like a pusher giving you a sample of his heroin. Once you get a taste you start paying."

"For everything except air," I agreed.

"Except that."

19

Walking down the stairs I felt the strain in my thighs. I was getting weaker by the moment, and there was a long road left yet to travel. I took my time, because thinking and walking had started to vie for my attention. I'd take two steps and then stop, wondering where Evander was and what he had to do with a man in green that bad men were looking for. Then two more steps . . .

The parking lot was empty of life. The cars looked so settled and secure that I considered climbing into one and taking a brief eight- or nine-hour nap.

"Hi," she said, giving the word two syllables.

Ruby had come from behind a slender pine at the edge of the lot.

"I was smoking this joint," she said.

"That someone gave you for flowers," I added.

She smiled. "Want some?"

"You hungry?"

"Like a beast," she said.

• • •

Down near La Cienega was a disheveled little diner called Holly Heron's All-Night Chili Palace. Ruby and I crowded in at the counter.

There was a jukebox playing from the corner.

That was the first time I ever heard the song "Somebody to Love" by the Jefferson Airplane. I liked the moodiness of the lead singer's voice. I also liked it later on when I found out that they took their name from the bluesman Blind Lemon Jefferson.

Ruby wanted chili and I ordered a hamburger, even though I knew it would make my gut ache. I wasn't bothered by pain that much in those days after coming to from the accident. Feeling anything, even if I didn't enjoy the sensation, was like a little blessing.

"You got a girlfriend?" someone asked. I was unsure of who it was because the diner was packed and everybody was talking and the music was playing and my thoughts seemed to have sounds of their own.

Ruby pulled on my jacket sleeve.

"Hey, Easy," she said.

"What?"

"Do you have a girlfriend?"

"I was in love with a woman named Bonnie," I said, though I hadn't meant to. It was as if the words had a will of their own and decided to come and play. "We lived together, and when my little

126

girl got sick she took her to Europe and got a cure. Feather is alive because of Bonnie."

"Your daughter's name is Feather?"

"Yeah."

"That's cool."

"In order to help her Bonnie reconnected with an old boyfriend. They got close there for a while and when she came back I couldn't stand it and threw her out of my house."

"It's the pigs, man!" someone shouted, and the noisy restaurant went silent.

The only sound was the Rolling Stones' "Ruby Tuesday."

In the mirror on the other side of the counter I could see through the glass behind me. Four uniformed cops were passing by, looking into the restaurant for misdemeanors or worse.

When they were gone the din wound up again.

"Wow," Ruby said. "And you never asked her to come back?"

"I did but it was too late."

"So what did you do?"

"Drove my car off a cliff up on Pacific Coast Highway."

The food came then. A wild-eyed freckled white woman with a strawberry blond Afro put the plates down in front of us.

"Peace," the waitress said.

Instead of taking up her spoon Ruby put her

hand on mine. I was deeply grateful for the gesture and not sure why.

"I'm from Ohio," she said. "My folks were born again. I never did anything they said and they hated me. Really they did. My mother told me that I was the devil and their burden. My father said that everybody'd be better off if I was dead.

"On my sixteenth birthday I balled my civics teacher and we ran away in his Pinto to L.A. We had this nice little apartment down on Venice Beach, but then one night he brings home this chick named Sandy. He said she needed a place to crash, but before a week they moved me out in the street. Then they went up to Berkeley and had a baby. They invited me to the wedding."

"Did you go?"

"No."

"Well," I opined, "at least he got you away from parents who wanted you to die."

Ruby thought about this a moment and then smiled brightly.

"I like you, Easy."

These words seemed to bring on the exhaustion that was hovering over me. I tried to answer Ruby, but all I could do was sigh.

"You look beat," she said.

"Still recuperating from the crash. I'm okay for a while, but then the legs are cut out right from under me."

"Can you make it home?"

I shook my head, realizing that this motion took more energy than saying no.

"I could drive your car," she suggested.

"It's down on San Vicente. I couldn't walk that far."

Ruby had a young face, its emotions transparent like a child's. She took a deep breath, held it while concentrating, and then said, "I know. Do you have a dime?"

I handed her the coin and she ran to a phone booth set against the far wall of the diner.

I considered putting my head down on the counter, next to the uneaten hamburger. But I worried that something bad might happen while I dozed. So instead I looked around the long room at the mostly white crowd. That place reminded me of the colored joints I'd frequented in my younger years.

When the Watts Riots had ended I saw the divisions form among the nonwhite races of L.A. I'd also seen a split in our own community, where brother turned against brother and corrupt city officials stepped in to take their revenge. But in that hippie diner there was the hint of something hopeful. There were white people realizing for the first time what it was like to be shunned and segregated, fired for no reason and arrested because of the way they looked.

"He's on his way," Ruby said. She took me by

the elbow, and I followed her as if she was my mother or some trusted neighbor on the dirt road of my childhood.

"I have to pay," I said.

Ruby steered me to the cash register, where I gave the freckled waitress seven dollars.

Outside I leaned against a wooden telephone pole, hoping that the police had better things to do than to roust me again.

Life in the form of lights swirled around me, and for a while time passed without my direct involvement. Ruby was standing next to me, but she also was distracted by the gaudy pinwheel of Sunset.

"You Ruby?" a man said.

Looking down I saw an electric blue mid-fifties Chrysler. There was a furry-faced guy leaning out from the driver's-side window.

"Yeah," she said. "My friend here and me need a ride just up on Ozeta Terrace a few blocks north."

"Is he sick?" Furface asked. "You know it's a bitch cleaning the vomit out from between the cushions and the carpet."

"He's just tired. He was in an accident," Ruby assured him.

The next thing I knew I was being poured into the backseat of the car. Coming to rest was almost a spiritual delight.

"This a taxi?" I asked as the car pulled out into Sunset traffic.

"It's the Blue Tortoise," the driver said, "a hippie cab. You got money? Dope?"

"Six dollars?" I said.

"That'll be fine."

I don't remember the ride or getting out of the cab. The next thing I knew I was standing, propped up by Ruby, before a large door in a dark courtyard. This door was the portal to a mansion that loomed above us.

"Where are we?" I asked my new friend.

"A place where I crash sometimes," she said. "I keep my makeup box here."

"Oh," I replied, thinking that I could go to sleep right there, standing outside.

"Here you go, Easy," Ruby said. "Lean against the wall while I get the key."

Time passed, crickets sang, now and again a car would drive by beyond the tall hedge that separated the courtyard from the street.

The next thing I knew I was on my back and someone was pulling down my pants. My shirt and jacket were already off, socks and shoes too.

I kind of wanted to resist, but then the final wave of sleep rolled in and dragged me out to unconsciousness on a tranquil and moonlit sea.

20

Given enough time I can recall each and every sexual encounter I've ever had—in some detail; that is, except for that night.

At one point I came halfway to consciousness thinking that I was holding my erection, masturbating on the floor in a strange dark room. But when I willed my hand to stop I realized that someone else was stroking me slowly.

I tried to rise but a hand pushed me back down.

"Sh," she said, and things went blank again for a while.

The orgasm brought me nearly all the way awake, but just for a moment. Drifting back into sleep I felt a kiss on my lips and a weight being taken off my chest.

"You're beautiful," she said, and I luxuriated in the compliment and the slow descent into blissful darkness.

Then there was light, sunlight coming through a tiny window high up on the wall of a room no larger than a long broom closet. I was naked and Ruby was too. There was a blanket draped around both our legs and coming up to her shoulder. She was on her side with her right arm thrown across my chest. I tried to remember what my hands had been doing with the girl, but I couldn't conjure an image or even a sense memory. This failure made me feel incompetent.

There was something moving. That's what had awakened me, not the light. On my left side my pants were sliding toward the door, slowly, maybe even stealthily. I watched the maroon leather belt in the straw-colored trousers move past my elbow down to hip level before I understood what was going on.

"Hey!" I shouted, and then jumped up.

I lunged at the partially open door of the tiny room and grabbed a scruffy-looking guy by the arm.

"Let go!" he yelled back.

His right hand was gripping my suit pants.

"Then let go'a my clothes!" I told him.

"Yancy!" Ruby screamed. "Get the fuck outta here! What's wrong with you?"

The little hippie guy was pulling on my pants. He was shorter than Ruby and rail thin, but I was still weak and found myself losing the tug-of-war with a ruddy little white guy with shoulder-length black hair and a beard.

"Yancy!" a youngish male voice declared.

The little guy let go of my pants and fell backward on his butt. There was a wacky element to his tumble, like in an Abbott and Costello skit.

133

Yancy had deep green eyes that opened wide to take in the newcomer.

This was a tall late adolescent with very long and stringy dirty blond hair, bad skin, and a nose that was bulbous and in poor contrast to his long face.

"Terry," Yancy said. "Hey, man, listen . . ."

"This motherfucker was tryin' to steal Easy's pants," Ruby said before Yancy could concoct some lie. "We were sleepin' in the little room and he tried to pull his pants out from under us."

"I just wanted to borrow a few dollars," Yancy said. "You guys were sleepin'. I didn't want to bother you. I just needed some breakfast."

"There's food in the kitchen," Terry said. He looked nineteen, but I would have bet he was younger. Ugliness just piled the years on him.

"I . . . I . . . I didn't know," Yancy was saying.

"The fuck you didn't, thief," Ruby spat.

"You got to go, Yancy," Terry said as he pushed a lock of moplike hair from his face. "I can't have people stealing from each other in my house. That's bad karma, man."

Yancy got to his feet and focused his angry green eyes on me. His hair was neither straight nor curly; it was more crinkled, like pubic hair.

"Nigger," he said.

"Oh, no," Terry said. "Go, go on."

The tall hippie boy waved his hand in a way that seemed truly regal. Yancy stooped under the weight of this gesture and then scuttled down the stairs.

The fact that there was a downstairs told me that I was above the first floor of the big house. I wondered how Ruby got me to climb in my weakened condition. Reflecting on this thought, I wondered if I was still suffering from concussion. My mind seemed flighty, easily led down any tangent. I should have been angry by the attempted theft; there was anger there, but I couldn't hold on to it.

"I'm so sorry, Easy," Terry said, turning to me. "I try to keep my house open to anyone who needs a place to crash, but some people just can't throw off the straight world."

"You think the straight world is full of thieves?" I asked.

"It is based on theft."

Ruby and I were naked. Terry noticed Ruby's body with some interest. She saw his look and smiled. I experienced a rush of jealousy before remembering where I was and why I was there.

"Come on downstairs and I'll make you guys breakfast," Terry said to Ruby.

The girl and I showered together. It was almost platonic except for a kiss or two.

While we were dressing she said, "You're a surprise, Easy."

"In what way?"

"Usually when I ball a straight guy he wants to talk about it afterward. You know, to apologize for something or say that he likes me or some lie."

"To tell you the truth, girl, I was so out of it last night that I don't remember what it is I should be sorry for."

Ruby laughed, and I wondered if we would know each other after that morning.

Terry was cracking enormous eggs into a big white ceramic bowl in the kitchen. It wasn't as big as the kitchen of the place where my family was staying, but there was an eight-burner stove and a table big enough for twelve. The room only had one window, but there was also a door that was open wide, letting in the sunlight that California is famous for.

"Those are some big eggs," I said, coming up to him at the cream-and-maroon-tiled counter.

"Duck eggs," the ugly young man said. "I get them from a woman named Nugent. She's an organic farmer from up around Isla Vista."

"Never had a duck egg."

"They taste like chicken eggs should."

He made cheddar cheese omelets and bacon, buttered toast with apple butter, and fresh squeezed orange juice. He had an electric machine where all you did was drop the orange through a hole in the top and the juice came out of a spout on the side.

He was right about the eggs. They reminded me of the ones I ate when I was a child in Louisiana and my mother's smile met me every morning at the breakfast table.

"You live here with your family, Terry?" I asked.

"My dad lives back east," he said. "My mom is dead."

"And this is your house?"

"When Mom died Dad decided to move back to New York, but I wanted to finish high school, so he let me stay here. He gives me money in a bank account and I let anybody stay who wants to crash for at least a few nights. . . ." He glanced over at Ruby. "Or more if they want."

Ruby was sitting next to me, but she was leaning toward him.

"I haven't seen you for a long time," she said to the young master of the crash-pad mansion.

"I was up in San Francisco for three weeks. I just got back day before yesterday. You want to go down to the beach today?"

"Yeah."

I must have made a sound or moved in some way. Ruby looked at me with the slightest hint of guilt on her face.

"Easy's looking for the son of a friend'a his that I did acid with the other night."

"You mean Evander?"

"How did you know that?"

137

"You brought him here, didn't you?" Terry asked.

"Yeah, we came over to get my makeup kit after we dropped that acid. But you were up north."

"He came by right after I got back. He was looking for you. He was scared and kinda nervous. He said he didn't remember what had happened and wanted to ask you something. I didn't talk to him much. I was going to the movies when he got here."

"Where did he go?" I asked.

"He started talkin' to Coco. I haven't seen him since then."

"What about Coco?"

"She almost always sleeps on the third-floor roof outside the White Rabbit room."

21

Terry told me that it would be easy to find the White Rabbit room, and I, in my addled state, recast the words: *Easy would find the White Rabbit room*. It didn't make sense, what I thought I heard, but Terry was right.

The first door I came to on the manor's middle floor was black with a crude image of a bunny painted with white slashes for its body and bright red for its disconcerting eyes.

138

There were five or six beds lined up side by side against the wall of the large room. At least nine naked and nearly naked bodies sprawled on and across the mattresses. A young woman wearing big square-framed glasses was reading a hardback book that had a bright blue cover. As I moved past her, headed for the window in the far wall, she looked up, dug in her nose with a finger, and then went back to her book.

I wanted to ask her what she was reading but managed to squelch that question. Then I wondered what time it was, but said to myself, *It's right now, man. Now move on.*

I climbed through the window thinking about Alice through the looking glass.

Outside the big bedroom was a triangular red gravel-and-tarpaper roof—maybe sixteen feet at its widest point. There was a ten-inch-high ledge along the outer edge. Behind me, above the window, was the domed structure of the upper floors. The outside roof on which I stood was cut out of floors three, four, and five. I had never seen a house like that. It must have, I thought, been built up slowly over time. Maybe it started out as a normal two-story home and had been added on to until it became this patchwork novelty.

I shook my head to clear out the errant thoughts and concentrated on the sleeping bag that was up against the ledge at the outer edge of the roof.

Next to the occupied bedroll was a thick pile of heavy rope.

The color of the synthetic fabric that covered the sleeping bag was drab green. The only life visible was a thatch of brown hair that was so full and healthy that in other circumstances I might have thought it was an animal pelt—maybe even with a live creature under it.

I hesitated then. Coco, whoever that was, didn't know me, and even though we were outside this was still a bedroom of sorts. The morning air was fresh with just a slight chill to it. I squatted to sit down, but the pain in my ankle betrayed me and I fell with a thump.

The vibration roused the head of hair. It turned and rose up on both elbows.

Coco was most definitely a young woman. A very beautiful young woman with eyes to match her hair and skin that had absorbed a lot of sun. She sat up. This alone wouldn't have meant much, but she was naked, and it was hard for me, in that frame of mind, not to allow myself to get distracted by her well-formed charms.

"Who the hell are you?" Coco asked.

I put up my hands in surrender and said, "No disrespect, lady. Ruby and Terry downstairs told me that a woman named Coco was up here and that she might know where I could find Evander Noon."

Words could be either glue or acid, an old man

140

named Tyner once told me. I was fourteen and staying on his three-acre farm ten miles outside of Houston. I helped him with the chickens and gardening and he let me sleep in the basement, where it remained cool on the hot summer nights. *Words are the finest invention that human beings have ever made. They build bridges and burn 'em down. Glue or acid, that's what the words you say will be. But you got to be careful. Sometimes you might have both parts at the same time. You got to watch out, because some words will at first pull somebody close and then turn him against you in time.*

"You're looking at my tits," the beauty said. It was hardly an indictment, more like an argument against my claim.

"Um . . ."

She brought a pink T-shirt out from the sleeping bag and pulled it on.

"I'm not turning in nobody to the cops," she said. The words came naturally, but her elocution told me that this dialect was a learned language. I wondered where she was from.

"Well?" she asked when I didn't respond.

"I'm not a cop." I took the picture of Evander out and handed it to her. "Evander's mother, Timbale, gave me this and told me that he had gone missing. She's scared sick. I know that Evander loves his mother and would at least want her to know that he was okay."

Coco winced at me. There was something in what I said that resonated with her. But she didn't know me, and I wasn't dressed, coiffed like, or the right age of the people she trusted. Then again, I was black and Evander was too.

The young woman—I figured her to be around twenty-two—seemed to come to some decision. She stood up from the sleeping bag, unconcerned with the fact that she was nude from the waist down.

In another frame of mind I would have looked away from what my Christian brothers and sisters would have called her shame. But she wasn't ashamed and neither was I. I had driven my Pontiac off of a cliff and crash-landed in a new world where women like Coco lived according to a whole new set of laws and beliefs.

So I watched while she rooted around for a pair of black sweatpants shoved down into the sleeping bag. I lit a cigarette as she pulled them up and drew the waist string tight. It wasn't like the shower with Antigone or when I had sex in my sleep with Ruby; I wasn't aroused. I was just a witness to the new world, like a failed Magellan or Columbus that had been shipwrecked and beached among an unfamiliar people. My job was to take on the local customs or get thrown back into the sea.

"Why do you sleep out here on the roof?" I asked as she went about the task of gathering her other possessions.

142

"I don't like most men," she said as if in answer.

"So it's just that you want to be alone?"

"Not only." She took a pair of red sandals, three books, a wallet, a plastic semiopaque golden box, and a see-through blue plastic pouch that had everything from bandages to Q-tips to loose change in it. These things, except for the sandals, she put in a purple velvet bag that was her purse. "I like being outside up here. Even when it rains sometimes I put up a tent."

I smiled.

"What?" she said in challenge.

"I don't know," I said. "It's funny to think of pitching a tent right outside the window."

"You think it's stupid."

"Only if you get wet."

Coco went about rolling up her sleeping bag and binding it.

After waiting a bit I asked, "Do you have disdain for all men?"

I think it was the use of the word *disdain* that raised her head. She pondered a moment and said, "No. I just don't waste time with them unless they're cool."

She threw the bundle into the corner that cut deepest into the dome of the upper floors and then started pulling on her footwear. She did this standing up. I was impressed by her steadiness.

"Was Evander cool?"

"He was all freaked out," she said. "Ruby had given him some acid and he had a bad trip that lasted for days. He came here a couple of days ago asking everybody where Ruby was. He was asking if we knew some guy but didn't know his name. He said that he met him at Lula's cathouse and that he wore all green. I didn't know who he was talking about.

"Evander was going around asking everybody his question and crying a little, and this asshole named Yancy got mad and picked a fight with him. Yancy slapped Evander like people do in the movies to stop them from being so scared, but everybody knows that you can't pull somebody out of a flashback by hitting them. Evander pushed Yancy and Yancy pulled out a knife . . ."

I wondered if Yancy had that knife on him when we tussled. Terry might have saved my life.

". . . so," Coco continued, "I got between them and told Yancy to fuck off. A couple of other people crashing said he should take a time-out and he split. After Yancy left, me and this girl named Vixie tried to calm Evander down."

"Did he tell you where he'd been or where he was going?"

"You hungry?" she asked.

"Sure," I said. Then I made the mistake of standing up.

The first pain was in my right ankle—I expected that—but then there was a stitch that felt like a tear running up my left side, and my neck refused to straighten out.

I must have grunted from the pain, because Coco asked, "Are you okay?"

"Fine. Just a cramp."

"We could go get a good breakfast at a place I know for three bucks each," she said.

"Sounds good to me. I only want coffee anyway."

"You got the money?"

"If you got the time."

Coco smiled at the phrase, went to the pile of rope, and heaved it off the roof. I went to see why she'd done that and saw that the rope had unfurled into a ladder like the ones they use on big sailing ships. It was hooked to two metal bolts that were sunk into the ledge.

"You want me to go first?" she asked.

"We can't just use the window?"

"I like to stay outside as much as possible."

"After you," I said, bobbing my head lightly.

I waited until Coco had made it down to the lawn before clambering over the side.

It was a foolish thing for me to scramble down that shaky ladder. With each step the ladder's swing became more pronounced, the bodily pains increased, and my sense of balance flailed from side to side. But this was all of a piece, because everything I was doing right then was foolish; just the fact that I was out in the world rather than at home in the bosom of my family seemed like a fatal gaffe.

Chuckling at my own reckless nature made the netting wobble more, but I couldn't stop laughing.

"Watch it!" Coco called. She steadied the rope and I took the last half dozen rungs with hardly a misstep.

On the lawn I was exhilarated, like a child who had successfully taken his first ride on the slide under his own power.

"You almost fell," Coco said.

"*Almost* being the operant word."

Once again my use of language gave her pause.

Since she was just standing there, looking at me, I asked, "Where's the breakfast place?"

"Down on Pico. You got a car?"

"Ten or eleven blocks from here."

Sunset was almost empty at that time of day. As much as I'd enjoyed the throngs of the night before, I was grateful for the silence that accompanied the early morning. Coco and I had made it to San Vicente before we started talking again.

"So what was Evander so freaked out about?" I asked.

146

"He kept saying that he forgot almost everything over the last few days, but then there was something about blood and money that he didn't understand. He wanted to ask Ruby what had happened, but neither me nor Vixie knew where she was. Vix said that Ruby was bound to come back, but that Evander should get his head together first. So she told him that maybe they should go up to Caller's Creek, up above Malibu, to let the trip wear off. You know, Ruby and your friend's son did this acid that people call STP. It lasts a lot longer."

"What's this Vixie like?" I asked.

"I don't really know her. She crashes at Terry's sometimes. I mean, Terry's cool, but he likes to have sex, and the girls know it and so sometimes they come up and ball him and he lets them hang around for a few days or whatever."

"And you?"

"What about me?"

"Are you friends with Terry like that?"

"No. Of course not. I like that roof 'cause I can sleep out there alone. I'm almost like part of the family at Terry's."

"Ruby too?"

"She could be, but Ruby's all over the place. She sells her flowers and goes off any way the wind blows. I like her."

"Here," I said. "Let me make a stop at this phone booth."

It was a free-standing booth on the corner. I closeted myself inside and dropped the dime.

"Hello?" Feather answered after quite some time.

"Hey, girl. You sleep okay?"

"Uh-huh. Where are you, Daddy?"

"Up in Hollywood, near there. I think I might be going down to the beach looking for that guy Uncle Ray wanted me to find."

"He said that he was going to be staying at our Genesee house the next few days."

"Ray did?"

"Uh-huh. When are you coming home?"

"Pretty soon. Um, tell me something, Feather."

"What?"

"Did you know an older girl who used to go to Burnside named Beatrix Noon?"

"Yes. She was one of the nice girls. I taught her a nursery rhyme in French. What about her?"

"Did you ever meet her mother or her brother?"

"She has a little sister named LaTonya. She's still at Burnside. And . . . and her brother—I don't remember his name—he would meet her after school sometimes and walk her home. He worked at this supermarket that made their own buttermilk doughnuts. Beatrix gave me half of one one time. Why?"

"It's Beatrix's brother, Evander, that I'm looking for."

"How come?"

"He went off and his mother's worried."

"I hope you find him then. He was really nice to me. He said that he wanted to go to the University of California at Berkeley."

"He didn't seem strange or anything?"

"Nuh-uh. He was just serious like."

"Is Jesus there?"

"He's asleep. You wanna talk to him?"

"No. But tell him that I'd like it if he and Benita stay with you until I'm back."

"Okay."

"Okay, baby, I gotta go. Have fun at summer school."

"Okay."

Coco and I walked on. My gait, I noticed, was oddly light. It was as if I was sneaking down the street, avoiding being noticed by some greater power that preyed on flesh like mine. I wasn't exactly weak, but the gas tank, once again, was near empty.

When we reached the Barracuda I went right to the trunk, took out one of Mama Jo's bottles, and drained it in one gulp. The heat was there almost immediately, but it would be a while before the fire ignited.

"What's that?" Coco asked.

"For all I know it's voodoo," I said. "I don't even believe in it, but it still has faith in me."

Coco's beautiful face broke out into a resplendent smile.

When we were in the car, driving south toward Pico, she said, "You're a very unusual man, Easy."

"In what way?"

"How you talk, this crazy low-rider car—the way you almost fell coming down that ladder. It's kind of like you're coming from four different directions at once."

I laughed heartily in reply. This humor rose from the anticipation of the minor resurrection Jo's medicine would have on my body, and the recognition of the actual definition of a black man's life from that white girl's lips.

Not long after that we came to Pete and Petra's Diner, a little bit west of Sepulveda on Pico. It was a ramshackle barnlike building with a huge blacktop parking lot for a yard. There were lots of cars parked there in the early morning. This was a weekday workingman and workingwoman's joint. A place where three dollars would keep you stoked until it was time for the brown-bag lunch in the backseat.

The morning restaurant was vast and crowded. With not much natural light there were fluorescent fixtures hung in random fashion above the diners. There must have been sixty people eating their eggs and bacon, pancakes and ham. Most of them were white, but there were some blacks and Asians, even a Mexican here and there.

A man in a light blue suit brought Coco and me to a booth made for two at a rare small window. He left us with menus and muttered something that I didn't catch. The Gator's Blood was gaining strength, and I was distracted by the internal physical changes caused by the elixir.

"What can I get you?" a middle-aged and portly waitress with bottle-black hair and cornflower blue eyes asked us.

I gestured at Coco and she said, "Coffee, hot chocolate, pecan pancakes, a side of bacon, and a side of ham."

"Toast?" the jolly woman asked, and I smiled.

"No, thanks."

"What can I get for you, Bright Eyes?" the waitress asked me.

Her name tag read HARA.

"Well, Hara . . ." I began, but then I noticed a man sitting at a booth with five other men, staring at me—or at least he was looking in my direction. "Well, Hara, I already had something to eat, so if you just bring me a coffee I'll be doing fine."

"Regular?"

"Black." Back in those days regular meant with cream and sugar.

Hara left me with the notion of being called Bright Eyes. The medicine was coming up to the surface—I could feel it and the waitress could see it; the curious white guy in the dark blue work shirt maybe could sense it from his table of friends.

"So tell me about yourself, Coco," I said, sitting back and letting the world flow around me.

"Why?"

"Why? Because we're sitting here on a beautiful clear morning with food on the way and nobody after us. Because you're a young white woman and I'm a middle-aged black man, and a waitress just took our order without even a second look."

I was beginning to experience Coco's smiles as little gifts.

"I was born in Dearborn," she said.

"Near Detroit?"

"You been there?"

"No. But I read about the Detroit riots."

"We lived in a big house," she continued, "and went to church. I was gonna go to college back east and then one day the police came and arrested my father."

"For what?" I looked up and saw the white workman staring me in the eye.

"He had robbed a bank before he met my mother, used the money to start a ball-bearing business for the car companies."

"Wow."

"Two weeks after he was put in prison my mom comes home with this guy named Lawrence and says that they were getting married and we were moving to Spokane. She said that we were gonna start goin' to Catholic mass because Larry was a Catholic. I never liked it, and so one day I hitched to the coast and then down to L.A. And here I am."

By then the Gator's Blood had seeped all the way to my fingertips. I was ready for anything. Life stopped being normal and it was more like I was living in a movie. And then I thought about my life like it was one of those 3-D tableaus the architects make to represent their projects. I saw that there was never anything natural about my life in the first place: not my being orphaned, black, a soldier in World War II, or my life of found children and detective work that was more like a secret war where you fought on both sides at once.

"Well?" Coco asked.

"Did you ask me something?"

"Yes. I asked, do you think I'm weird?"

"Not at all," I said. "As far as I'm concerned you're the most interesting woman in the room."

"Excuse me," a man's voice said.

I wasn't surprised to see the white man in the blue work shirt standing on the exact spot where Hara had taken our orders.

I looked at him but didn't say anything. There was nothing for us to say to each other; I knew that but he did not.

"Let me ask you something," he said to me.

I glanced over at the table he'd come from. I wanted to see if the men were smiling or in any other way anticipatory. They were not, which was a relief. I moved my hand away from the pistol in my belt.

Coco was looking up at the man now.

"I just wonder," the man continued, "why a nigger needs to take up with a white chick when there's so many colored gals walkin' the streets."

It was the second time that morning I'd been called a nigger by a white man, and still it came as a surprise.

"Who the hell do you think you are?" Coco said loudly, and then she stood up from the stumpy little booth. "We aren't messing with you. We weren't talking to you. All we're doing is sitting here and trying to get some food and some coffee like everybody else. And you come over here with this fucking shit about niggers and chicks and gals in the street. Just who the fuck do you think you are, anyway?"

"Listen, girl," the man said.

He was a few years my junior, early forties. I would have been happy to let him go on talking, but he held out a hand as if he might have wanted to lay it on her.

So I stood up. My right hand turned into a fist and my left shoulder slanted forward so I could pull it back, adding to the force of the blow that by now was a foregone conclusion.

But there's one thing I've learned about inevitability—it never is.

Before I could execute my punch the other guys from our detractor's table came up in a group and grabbed hold of him.

"Come on, Lucas; let's get out of here," one of them said.

Lucas made a rather weak attempt at shaking his friends off and then allowed them to pull him away.

Coco and I were standing there. Everyone in the room was looking either at us or at the men as they piled out the door.

Hara came up with Coco's breakfast and my coffee on a perfectly balanced, very large cork-lined resin tray.

"Sit down," she urged. "Sit down. Don't worry about some fool like him."

We did sit. After a while Coco started eating. I leaned back in silence, thinking about the disjointed movie in which I was an unknown bit actor: like Lynne Hua—exotic yet forgettable.

"That was fucked-up," Coco said after a few minutes had passed.

I smiled.

"Why are you laughing?" she asked.

"I used to know these two brothers," I said. "Romulus and Remus, I kid you not. That's what their mother named them. Anyway, the wolf brothers were rough-and-tumble. They'd go to some restaurant or diner or what have you in a part of town where people didn't know 'em. They'd sit apart and order two big-ass meals. And just when they were almost through one would say something to the other and they'd commence to fight. Now, they'd fight for fun anyway, but the people in the restaurant didn't know that. After they crashed around a few minutes or so the owners would throw them out, not even thinkin' about them payin' for the meals."

Coco's anger turned quizzical and she asked, "Are you really that thick-skinned?"

"My mother could have named me Rhino and she wouldn't have been half-wrong."

23

The drive down to Santa Monica was uneventful and blissfully quiet. The radio stayed off and there was no chatter about things that didn't matter, or that did matter but we couldn't change. There was a certain comfortableness between the young white woman and me that I wouldn't understand for many years to come.

"Just follow the coast highway up," she said when we got down to the beach.

I wasn't expecting the drive to have any kind of

emotional effect on me. After all, I had taken that ride a hundred times since moving to L.A. in 1946. But the last time I'd cruised up that highway, in the wee hours, I was barefoot, drunk, and heartbroken.

As I passed Sunset Boulevard where it ran into the highway, my breath was loud in my ears like a bellows, and my hands were shaking nervously on the wheel.

"What's wrong, Easy?" Coco asked. It's a good thing she did, because I might have become the man I had been when I drove headlong off the road otherwise.

"I was just remembering the accident."

"What accident?"

I told her about the last night before I awoke from my partial coma.

"Sounds more like a suicide attempt than an accident," the clear-eyed, overly blunt young woman said.

This straight talk made me smile and relax.

"Yeah, it does," I said. "I learned back in the army that when a man's at war his impending death has no more hold on him than a drink of water or the need for a nap."

"What war?" she asked, looking around at the road in front of us.

"We're always at war," I said, not really thinking about the words I spoke. "Vietnam is a war we're in. But not only that—the Strip is a war of the new

157

against the old, my skin is a war not of my making, and love . . . love is a war too."

"That's very romantic, Mr. Rawlins," Coco said. I think she meant it as a compliment.

After that we drove for over an hour. Coco took one of the three books from her velvet bag and began reading. I didn't mind the silence.

My mind was filled with images and imaginings about life before and after the car crash. I was thinking about sharecroppers again: those small-bodied, powerful men and women who dragged bulging sacks up to five times their size across fields of cotton. This image seemed the appropriate metaphor for my life. That huge sack was my house, my car, my job hunting down a boy I never met. Rather than a burden, this weight, this millstone was my chance at deliverance. If I could survive that labor then my rest would be deserved.

We'd passed through Oxnard and Ventura and were well on our way to Santa Barbara and Isla Vista when Coco said, "You see that sign that says Caller's?"

Up ahead was an unofficial little white sign, like a flag of surrender on a green pole that had the name rudely painted on it.

"Yeah. That's not a regular highway sign."

"There's an action group called Puck and His Magic Tricksters that puts up signs like that for hippie folk. It tells us where the magic is at.

"About a mile up is this dirt turnoff to the right. You can tell because there'll be just a green stick to mark it. You go in and there's an underpass to the beach. That's where you can get in to hike up to Caller's."

I followed her directions, making it down to a leveled lot where there was nary a car. I parked and got out. The salt air was lovely. I breathed it in, hardly thinking of the night when I followed that scent over the side of a mountain.

"Come on," she said. "The path is back this way across that little stream."

The stream was just a trickle and the dense foliage beyond might have daunted me except for the Gator's Blood. I was at full tilt at that moment, ready for anything—at least, that's what I thought.

"It just looks impassable," the educated hippie said, "but after about twenty feet of bush there's a little trail."

This was true. The trail was actually a creek bed that had gone dry. It was rocky and uneven, but I welcomed the irregular pace, because this was all a part of my rejuvenation. It was my Yellow Brick Road. This was the path Mouse had set me on, that Mama Jo medicated me for, that I had to travel if I was going to make it home in one living piece.

As I walked I felt that something was missing. After a while it came to me that it was the pain in my ankle that was absent. I wondered at the power of Jo's elixir. She was a backwoods genius and I was the nonbelieving beneficiary of her craft.

We hiked up a pretty steep incline for twenty minutes or so. Coco was breathing hard, but I fell into my role as a GI in the Italian Alps and the walk was like nothing to me.

When we got to the clearing the young woman sat down on a fallen tree and I squatted next to her.

"Is this it?" I asked.

"I don't get it, man," she said. "This morning you could hardly climb down a ladder but now you run up this hill like you were a mountain goat or somethin'."

"I just needed to get warmed up. Is this it?"

"It's what most people call Caller's Creek, but it's not where we're going. Across the way there's an old oak tree and behind that are these two big boulders. If you go between them for thirty feet or so there's another path that leads down into Rev's Commune."

I stood up to look around.

"I think you've ruined your suit," Coco said.

She was right. The cuffs of my pants were stained beyond cleaning, and there were spots of tree sap on my jacket, but I didn't care.

"Pretty silly for me to be dressed like this," I said.

"You didn't know." Coco got up and marched us

to the oak tree and then around to the close-standing sandstone boulders.

It was a tight fit for me down the corridor of stone, but I made it through.

On the other side was a proper trail under the sun-dappled shade of various trees leading downward. This decline was a relief for Coco.

The pace was faster and we reached a turn in the path in less than fifteen minutes. Instead of continuing on, Coco studied the bushes to our right and spread them apart.

"What are you doing?" I asked.

"Terry has these friends up here who keep to themselves. It's like a commune but not every-body is invited to stay. I'm pretty sure that's where Vixie took your friend."

"Lead on."

The tiny zigzag path beyond the wall of bushes brought us to a stone ledge that looked down upon a crude campsite which seemed empty except for one occupant—a bare-chested black man with his arms bound behind him, around a pretty thick sapling elm. His head was bowed as if in sleep or defeat, and my heart sang an unbidden, bitter song of revenge.

"Is that him?" I asked.

"You don't know what he looks like?"

"All I've seen is the picture, and his head is hanging down."

"That's Evander."

"How many people live here?"

"It's usually just four guys. I don't know their names. There used to be a street preacher named Rev that lived here, but after these guys moved in he went up north."

"I don't have to know their names," I said, needing to challenge something.

"These guys get grass off a boat that comes up from Mexico every two weeks or so. Terry buys a few keys from them now and then. But he doesn't like them too much."

Just then three long-haired men came out from behind a tree at the far end of the camp. I laced my fingers together so that I wouldn't grab my pistol and go down there shooting.

The men spoke to each other but we were too far away to make out what they were saying. One of them, sporting dirty blond hair and wearing a dark red shirt, nudged Evander with his foot and the young man jolted awake.

"I don't remember," the prisoner said loud and clear.

Redshirt leaned down and slapped him.

"We should go get the cops," Coco said.

"What's on the other side of that tree where they came from?"

"It's a shed they built to hold the dope until they move it."

"Come on."

162

• • •

I was a sergeant again, in the army again, waging war on the Germans—the absolute white men of the twentieth century—again. My army was a brown-haired white girl who fell into line behind my command.

We worked our way through the wilderness around the smugglers' camp. When we got to the storage shed I went inside and found it vacant. Maybe the fourth man had joined his friends. That was a stroke of luck for him, because I would have certainly strangled him as I had done to five Germans during my brief tenure as defender of the American way.

There was a kerosene lantern and a cheap pine table in the room that was piled high with plastic bundles of marijuana. I took the glass guard off the lantern, lit the wick, turned the flame up high, and placed it directly under the table. Then I hurried out and gestured for Coco to head back the way we'd come.

"What did you do?" she asked as we went.

"Made a diversion."

"A diversion for what?"

"For I don't kill them hippies like I want to do."

Back at the ledge I could see that all four hippie men were having a meal around their prisoner. Evander was wild-eyed, looking back and forth between his captors. I studied my breathing and waited for my moment.

"What did you do back there?" Coco asked after a minute or so.

And, as if in answer, Redshirt yelled, "Smoke!"

He pointed at the air above the trees. Their stash was on fire and so the whole tribe rushed to put it out.

"Come on," I said again to Coco.

We ran down to the campsite and I used a knife from one of the tin plates to cut Evander's bonds.

His hands were swollen and he cried out when the rope was cut.

"Who are you?" he asked.

"Friends of your mother, Evander," I said. "Now get up, because we got to run."

24

The young man had a thick build and was quite strong, though not from exercise. When I mentioned his mother he jumped to his feet and we began the long trek, the hazardous escape from his captors.

Coco ran in front of us, Evander staggered behind her, and I took up the rear, making sure that the man we were saving didn't tumble to the creek bed or run into a tree. Every third or fourth step that Evander took was precarious. It was as if, during his time of captivity, he'd lost his sense of equilibrium. He'd veer off to the side, lower to his knees now and then, as if the chase was over and now we might stop for a catnap.

Coco paused whenever Evander did.

"Keep on going," I said the last time she did this. "Just keep on running till you're back at the car." I threw her the keys and she caught them, just barely. "Unlock it and start it up. That way we'll be ready to go when I get him there."

The young woman, whom I hadn't known six hours before, nodded and took off with our hope in her hands. I believed in her, but at the back of my mind I was well aware that I could have been wrong. What if she was so scared that she drove off before I could get Evander to the beach?

I shrugged at the possibility and pulled the boy up by his arm.

"Come on, Evander," I said. "There's bad men after us and I'd like not to have to kill them if possible."

Pushing him forward I saw the burns on his shoulders and back. Those thick welts would leave scars like the bullwhips made on our slave ancestors. I forced myself to go on, not backward—toward liberation rather than retribution.

Evander cried out in pain as we passed through the sandstone corridor. The rough rock scraped against his wounds. I would have given him my shirt but I didn't feel we had the time. The smugglers would realize soon enough that their prisoner was gone. They might very well come after us.

Evander fell flat on his face in the dry creek bed when the scent of salt air was strong. He tried to rise but failed. I could see that he was exhausted and defeated by our run, so I put his left arm around my shoulders and brought him to a standing position. His weight didn't feel like anything. I didn't know if it was Gator's Blood or adrenaline, but I made the last three hundred feet dragging that bulky kid along like one of those sacks of cotton on a Mississippi sharecropper's farm.

The red Barracuda was still there, with Coco sitting behind the wheel.

This was another moment in the development of a friendship that I would come to value over time.

She jumped out of the car to help me pile the nearly unconscious bare-chested boy into the backseat.

"Easy!" she cried as I was folding Evander's legs up on the cushions.

I pulled my pistol for the first time and turned to study the coastal foliage from which we had come.

Four long-haired white men, two of them with

pistols of their own, came out from the leaves. There was a great plume of white smoke in the sky behind them. The color of this plume told me that they had managed to extinguish the fire.

Redshirt pointed at us, making a guttural sound that had meaning without linguistic articulation. He wanted us dead and there was no argument that would dissuade him.

The man's yowl seemed to go on beyond his breath. It came to me that a nearby siren had extended his promise and threat.

Redshirt heard the fire engine too. Or maybe it was the police.

"Get back behind the wheel," I said to Coco.

She didn't argue.

Redshirt pointed his pistol at me and the far-off wail got closer. He lowered the gun, wishing with his gaze that I was close enough for him to strike me. Then all four men faded back into the coastal trees—wild-eyed primitives retreating to their primordial home.

I went to the driver's-side door.

"Get in the backseat with Evander," I said. "I'll drive."

She hopped over the seat and I put the red Barracuda in gear.

"Is there another way out of here?"

"If you drive north along the beach about half a mile there's a regular turnoff."

She didn't have to tell me twice.

"He's got a fever, Easy," Coco said two hours later, when we were on the Santa Monica Freeway headed east for L.A. proper.

We had passed six fire trucks headed north toward Caller's Creek. I could only hope that Redshirt and his crew were caught, or at least that they didn't recognize Coco sitting in the car.

"I don't know where the money is!" the boy shouted. "I don't know where the blood came from!"

He had been calling out now and then, delirious after the ordeal.

I stopped at a gas station that had a sign for ice. I got fifteen pounds and took a couple of extra plastic bags. These I gave to Coco to apply to Evander's head and shoulders.

"We have to take him to a hospital," she said.

"I got a better place in mind."

Coco argued the whole way.

"This man is sick and wounded," she said. "He's been tied to a tree and beaten. He needs a doctor."

"You already said that, girl. I'm just askin' for you to help me bring him to this woman I know. If, after we get there, you think he needs a doctor, I will be happy to oblige."

"But that could be too late."

"Honey, I have carried wounded men across

battlefields. I have been too late more than once. Evander is hurt but he's not dyin'. Not yet."

When we got to Mama Jo's it was midafternoon.

Coco helped me carry Evander through the trees to Jo's yellow door. We passed through, and when Coco laid eyes on Jo all the complaints stopped.

I put the boy on Jo's visitor's cot and without introduction she began to work on his wounds, burns, and bruises.

"Hand me that white pottery jug," she said to Coco. "And gimme that glass jar . . . the square one. Okay now, take three white buds off'a that hangin' bunch'a herbs on the far right and . . ."

Coco did everything Jo said without error or complaint. She didn't ask questions; nor did she make any objection.

I sat back in my regular chair and the last iota of strength fled from my limbs. I could watch but that was all. My job, for the moment, was over. After a while my eyes started to close. I fought sleep, because I knew that it would lead either to death or nightmare—neither of which I was prepared for.

"Do you want some more soup?" Jo asked on the other side of closed eyelids.

"Yes, ma'am," a young man replied.

"This is delicious," a woman added.

"Thank you, Coco."

"My real name is Helen Ray," the woman I knew as Coco said.

"I like your nickname." There was something odd in Jo's voice, but I was too out of it to try to figure out what that something was.

My purpose in life right then was to open my eyes and sit up from wherever it was that I had been laid down. I was on my side and decided visual reconnaissance should be my first act.

Jo, Evander, and Helen "Coco" Ray were sitting at the medieval table, sharing a meal.

I wondered about that table. Maybe it had been constructed in some ancient Spanish canton in the twelfth or thirteenth century, moved from place to place until it found its way aboard a galleon bound for the New World. It had come to Louisiana and finally to Jo's country fortress. Now that same table, so well built that it had outlasted its own history, was in a California home that conformed to its forgotten origins.

"Easy," Jo said, and I focused, as well as I could, on her. "Evander, go help Easy up."

The young man that I virtually carried through the coastal woods now pulled me up from a straw bundle on the floor.

The house raven squalled and the armadillos wrestled in their corner. The lynx-cat was nowhere to be seen.

Jo served me oxtail stew over yellow rice, and for the first time since my revivification the food didn't hurt my stomach.

"How are you, Easy?" Jo asked.

Upon hearing Jo's tone, Coco looked at me as if for the first time.

"Like a bleeding, wounded shark among his brother sharks," I said.

"You saved Evander here."

"Those men had him tied to a tree," I answered.

"Coco says that she wanted to run and call the cops, but you planned the whole escape in just one minute and didn't even have to kill nobody." There was pride in Jo's voice.

"I thought there mighta been a guy out back of the camp. If there was I woulda killed him," I promised.

"I know," said Jo. "I know that you a man do what he have to."

Now Evander was looking at me.

"Did my mother really send you?" he asked.

"Her, LaTonya, and Beatrix too."

"Well, thank you," said the young man that Mouse called Little Green. "I don't know for sure, but I think those guys mighta killed me." He was wearing a loose gray shirt that was three or four sizes too big even for his large frame.

"Is that shirt Domaque Junior's?" I asked the air.

"Uh-huh," Jo grunted.

"How is your son?"

"Him and that girl he was livin' wit' on the commune, Loretta, have moved up to north Alaska and got themselves a fishin' boat."

"Damn."

"Do you need an assistant or something, Miss Jo?" Coco asked.

Jo turned to the beautiful white girl and stared. Raymond had told me that she had what was known as second sight that she used now and then when the truth was there but unspoken. I never believed any tales like that except when I was actually in Jo's physical presence.

"You go on with Easy," Jo said after a minute or two. "If you still interested after ten days' time, call him and he will bring you here to me."

"What time is it?" I asked Jo.

"I don't have no clock," she said. "Maybe nine, ten."

"How long was I out?"

"A few hours," she said. "You should get a better rest before you take any more'a that elixir."

"Then it's time to go, Evander," I said, a little

loudly for the small space. "You too, Coco Helen Ray."

Now both youngsters were looking at me. Leaving that medieval cottage was the last thing on their minds.

"Easy's right," Jo said, adding her authority to mine. "You children got business to take care on."

Evander had gone through the yellow door, and Coco was just about to follow when she turned and gave Jo a serious kiss on the lips. Their embrace ended when Jo gently shoved the girl on.

Then Jo kissed me lightly and said, "Watch that medicine, Easy. It will push you further along than you used to goin'."

"That's okay, Jo. I got a long way to go."

She smiled and kissed me again.

The next thing I knew I was driving through Watts. There were still lots of boarded-up, burned-out buildings that indicated the businesses that had yet to return to the 'hood after the devastating riots. My community had suffered decimation as I had. It was trying to come back, but there was no promise that it would rise again either.

It was not yet ten p.m. when we reached Terry's Hollywood mansion. Coco, Evander, and I had said fewer than a dozen words on the long drive. I was exhausted but not as depleted as I had been the day before. Evander was in a nightmare that he could not decipher. And Coco had met her first muse, a black witch-woman from a place most men had never even dreamed of.

Coco climbed out from the backseat, came around to the driver's window, and kissed me on the lips.

"Maybe not all men are so bad," she said.

"It took Jo sayin' it to make you know it."

"She's an amazing woman."

"It's an amazing world out there if you give it half a chance."

I watched Coco until she was in the front door and then I went around the driveway back to the street.

Three blocks away I started talking.

"A man named Raymond Alexander hired me to go to your mother and ask her if she wanted me to go looking for you."

"That can't be," he said definitively.

"What? You don't think your mother would send a stranger out looking for you?"

"I don't think she'd talk to you if you came from Mr. Alexander."

"Why not?"

"When I was a kid," he said, "maybe ten or so, it was my birthday and I was playin' in the front yard. This fancy man came up and gave me a toy pistol that made a sound like a ricochet. He patted my head and called me Little Green. I asked him who he was and he said Ray Alexander. And when I went back to the house Mama threw away my toy and then that night she called somebody on the phone and started cursin' at him. I never heard my mother curse before or since.

"But the funny thing is that she gets these envelopes once a month with money in 'em. One time she threw one away and the return address had the name Alexander written on it."

I pulled to the curb near La Cienega and Pico. It was a few minutes before eleven.

"Evander."

"Yes, Mr. Rawlins?"

"I don't know what it is between Raymond and your mother, but she did tell me about your call from the Strip, and she gave me this picture to help look for you."

He took the graduation photo, looked at it, and then handed it back.

"I live about three blocks away from your house. I can either take you home the way you are or you can come to my house and get yourself a little more together to keep Timbale from distress. I mean, Jo has tended to your bruises and burns, but you need maybe a day for the swelling on your face to go down."

"Okay," he said. "Let's go to your house."

"Raymond might be there."

"Good."

26

The porch light was shining above my front door.

I wasn't exactly surprised to see an ounce or so of what looked like partially dried blood on the top stair of the entrance to my house. There wasn't enough to assume that someone had died, at least not then and there. The dollop had a bright red eye at the very center and had dried to black around the edges.

I was confounded when my key didn't fit the lock. For a moment I wondered if, in my tired state, I had come to the wrong house. But then Martin Martins came to mind. He must have changed the locks as he promised to do. I reached up into the brass lanternlike light fixture above the door and found the right key. It was silver and quite long. I used the new key and pushed the door open, going in before Evander. On the first step into the house a man rushed out from the kitchen. He was a crazy-looking gray-brown Negro with dark topaz eyes and curly, not kinky hair. Only five-ten and a hundred and seventy tops, he had huge fists that rivaled those of Sonny Liston.

"Niggah . . ." he said, as if I had somehow insulted him. "What you doin' in my house?"

The third man to call me nigger in less than

twenty-four hours, but this was a black man and the term, though not friendly, wasn't actually disparaging either.

"Your house?" Another squatter? Was that Raymond's blood on the porch? Had the previous trespasser hired this guy to push me out?

"What is it, Mr. Rawlins?" Evander asked from behind me.

I didn't need Gator's Blood to push my mind into coming up with an immediate plan that included the intruder and my young guest.

The strategy was simple: I'd stammer something unintelligible and vaguely apologetic, back out of the door as if retreating, pushing Evander as I went. The angry man would follow me, feeling that he had the upper hand. While moving I'd pull out my pistol. He'd be halfway out the front door when I shot him—first in the knee and then, if he reached for a weapon, somewhere in the head.

I wasn't worried about the police. Even a black man could protect his home from intruders—if those intruders were also black.

"S-s-s-sorry," I stuttered.

My back pressed Evander off the front steps.

"Where you think you goin'?" the home invader said in the same insulted tone.

"Mister!" another voice yelled from somewhere in the house.

Mouse came out from the hall that led to our bedrooms.

The gray-brown Negro hesitated.

"Ray?" I said, coming back into the house.

Mouse was wearing a loose-fitting royal blue shirt and red-brown silk pants. He had on black shoes that looked like shiny bullets. His expression was casual; he looked unconcerned about the violence about to blossom in front of him.

As I came in Evander followed. When Mouse saw the young man his expression changed. There was a new emotion in his gaze. A look I had never seen in my friend's mien.

"You go on, Mister," Raymond said to the madman. "This here's Easy Rawlins. This his house."

"He the one gonna pay me?" Mister said, every bit as angry and outraged as when he thought I was an intruder.

"Go on, man," Raymond said. "I'll drop by in the morning and settle up."

"Why not right now?"

Mouse turned his head to look at his temporary henchman, and the aggression drained right out of the man named Mister's bearing.

"I ain't gonna tell you again," Mouse said. "Go on now. I'll give you your money tomorrow."

Mister hesitated maybe two seconds, then ducked his head and brushed past me and Evander without another word.

"Some niggahs just don't know how to act,"

Mouse said as he closed the door behind the disgruntled Mister.

Ray parted the closed drapes and watched the nighttime street until we heard an engine turn over and a car drive off.

Ray then turned to Evander and said, "Boy, you look like you been through a meat grinder."

"Why is there blood on my front porch, Ray?"

"Jeffrey come back with these two fat dudes this evenin'. I figured he might. You need somethin' to drink, Evander?"

"No, I-I mean, no, thank you."

"Have a seat, boy," Ray said.

The boy sat on the sofa and Mouse perched next to him.

I took the chair and said, "The blood on my porch?"

"I figure you was helpin' me, and so I aksed Mister to come play some penny-ante blackjack while we waited to see if Jeffrey needed some more explainin'.

"First Martin Martins come by to put up bars and new locks on the doors and windows. He had a helper and they did the job in under three hours. You know, I like Martin. The way his mind works is a mystery to me.

"Then later on Jeffrey come up with these two fat dudes. I stabbed one'a them in the leg and Mister used his big fists on the other guy. They lit out. Pretty sure they ain't comin' back."

Raymond shrugged and gave me his innocent look.

"How you doin', Li'l Green?" he asked Evander.

"I'm okay. I'm all right." Just then the boy flinched and jerked his head to see what might be happening in the corner.

"You want a beer?" Mouse asked.

"Okay."

Ray got up, went into the kitchen, and came back with three bottles of Pabst Blue Ribbon.

"So what happened to your face?" Raymond asked Evander.

"He was tied to a tree by a gang of dope-smugglin' hippies and they were torturing him," I said.

Raymond stood up and I held out a hand.

"Sit down, Ray. This isn't any simple thing here."

"No?"

"Evander," I said.

"Yeah?" He was still glancing into the empty corner as if some threat were crouching there.

"Why did those men have you tied to that tree?"

"They wanted the money."

"What money?"

Mouse sat down again.

"The money that was in the bed next to me at the Flamingo Motel on Hollywood Boulevard when I woke up."

"Was there anybody else there?"

"No. But there was a lotta blood and I wasn't hurt yet."

"And where's the money now?" I asked.

"I don't know."

"Did you leave it in the motel?"

"I don't think so. But I don't remember too much after that acid trip."

"Acid?" Mouse said. "Why the fuck you wanna fool around with that shit?"

"I met this girl named Ruby. She just put it on my tongue . . . with hers. And I swallowed it. After that I only remember things here and there. I was in this place and there was a naked woman on a couch smiling at me. And then there was this guy dressed all in green."

"Maurice?" I asked.

"Yeah," he said in revelation. "That was his name. Me and him drove off in his convertible Cadillac and we went . . . we went . . . to do something. At least, I think that was with him."

"And then you woke up in a motel with money," I said.

"Pretty much."

"How much money?"

"A whole helluva lot. I mean, it was hundred-dollar bills and fifties and everything. It was a whole lot."

"And you don't remember anything else?"

"There was a fight and people were yellin' and I

think somebody got shot . . . maybe more than one person did."

I looked over at Raymond. He was taking the ad hoc deposition very seriously.

"Are you my father?" Evander asked Mouse.

"No. I am not your father."

"Do you know who my father is?"

"Yes. I do know. Hasn't your mother ever told you about your old man?"

"She says that she didn't even know his name."

"Is that so? Hm. I don't mean to say nuthin' bad about your mother, boy, but she knows his name. She might wanna forget, but she knows his name."

"Who is he?"

That question was a signal for thoughtful silence.

Then: "A son deserves to know who his father is," Raymond said in his most serious voice. "It don't matter who he was or what he'd done. A son deserves to know and make up his own mind what to do and who to be.

"But it's a mother's job to give her boy that information."

"LaTonya and Beatrix got different fathers but they know both'a them," Evander said, regressing into childhood as he spoke. "Louis Champagne ain't no good. That's LaTonya's father. Bigger Lewis and Mama just don't get along, but he still loves Beatrix. He comes over and takes her out for ice cream on her birthday."

"I hear ya, boy," Mouse said. "I hear ya. I'll tell you what—I want you to go to your mother and tell her that I said, that Raymond Alexander said if she doesn't tell you who your real father is then I will. You got to give her the chance to do the right thing, but if she don't I will."

Evander, in spite of the bad shape he was in, looked hopeful. All he had to do was follow the bread crumbs and he would arrive at a place that maybe he should never, ever go.

27

"We got right now to worry about before we have the luxury of revisiting the past," I said.

Evander turned to me, but Mouse was still studying him.

"The first thing we need to know is why those men had you tied to that tree," I continued.

Evander's round face scrunched up, giving him the appearance of a much older man—the man he'd grow to be if he was lucky. He shook his head three or four times, throwing off one remembrance after another.

"I . . . I . . . I met a girl name of Vixie," he said. "It was after I took the acid. I think it was after I woke up in the motel. Yeah, that's it. I went to this house where I thought Ruby lived at because I didn't remember where the naked lady was and I wanted Ruby to tell me where I could find Maurice . . . but . . . but . . . but I couldn't even remember his name."

Evander stopped there, feeling that he'd answered the question.

"And what happened with you and Vixie?" I asked, seeking substantiation of Coco's story.

"I was still kinda trippin', but I knew I had to do somethin'. I asked that girl Coco—"

"What girl Coco?" Raymond asked, showing that he was paying attention.

"She was at the house."

"What house?"

"I don't remember. I just went there . . . you know, like it was in my head, but it didn't have a street or number or anything."

"Vixie was there with Coco?" I asked to push the story along.

"She was there. I don't think Coco liked her much. But this little dude slapped me and Coco told him to go on. That's when Vixie sat down with us. She told me she knew a place where I could get my head together. She and I hitchhiked up north on the ocean road until we got to this green stick and then we walked a really long time until there was this commune with these guys livin' outta tents and sleepin' bags. Vixie told 'em I had a bad trip and could I stay out there a few days. They said yeah and made chili and beans from a can and poured it over tortilla chips. When I ate it, it sounded like a waterfall in my head."

While Evander was remembering the crashing waters, I was making a checklist that told me at least Coco had been telling the truth.

"Then this guy handed me a joint," Evander said, as if the conversation going on in his head broke the surface of that water like a shark's fin. "I never smoked before, but I just took it and inhaled like I'd seen people do with cigarettes. Vixie showed me how to hold the smoke in, and all of a sudden I was trippin' hard again.

"After that I don't remember."

"Do you remember having your hands tied behind that tree?" I asked.

"Yeah."

"Do you remember when that happened?"

After a moment of serious thought he said, "No."

"Did they hit you?"

"This one guy they called Haskell took a burning stick and laid it on my shoulder."

"Easy," Mouse said, "tell me where these motherfuckers is at."

"Did Haskell ask you anything when he burned you?" I asked, ignoring Mouse.

" 'Where is the money? Where is the money?' " He was mimicking the men that tormented him.

"Did Vixie tell them about the money?"

"I don't know."

"Did you tell them?"

"Maybe. Maybe I did. . . ." Evander's eyes latched onto a tableau outside the confines of my small TV room. "It was like I was trippin' again and I was doin' all the same things I done before. . . ."

Raymond was about to ask something else, but I put a hand on his shoulder and shook my head.

"I woke up to blood and money," Evander continued. "I washed off as much of the blood as I could. The money was in these burlap sacks that were covered with blood too. It felt like I shoulda known where the money come from, but it's like when you forget somebody you know's name. So I wrapped the sacks of money in a sheet and took it down to the . . . to the . . . to the bus station and put it in a locker. Yeah, that's what I did. I remember that it took me a long time, because I kept seein' things like snakes and lynchers. I took a lotta buses."

"Is that what you told those men?"

"I don't remember, but Haskell kept hittin' me and askin' me what was the locker number and where was the key. And then . . ."

"Then what?" I said. It was more a suggestion than a question.

"It was cold," Evander said with a shiver in his voice. "I was tied to the tree and there was six devils on my back prickin' me with their pitchforks. I counted 'em. It was like my eyes

186

floated up behind my back like Dr. Strange does in the comic books. And then Vixie come up and say that they was gonna kill me if I told where the money was. I told her I didn't remember. And she said that even if I do I shouldn't say.

"She told me that I should tell her where the key was, but I couldn't say even if I wanted to, because every time they had hit me or burnt me the memory just went deeper. It was the acid. It made my mind like a deep dark hole.

"Vixie left that night. Haskell thought I told her sumpin' but I didn't. He hit me and I still didn't. Then he hit me again and I was a black crow in a blue sky bein' attacked by blackbirds protectin' their nests."

"Where's the key, Evander?" I asked.

The kid turned to me, his face like a fallow field in the late fall under the first frost of the season to come.

I cut my eyes to see what was up with Raymond. He usually got very excited when the question of money came up. But that night on the comfortable sofa, on the other side of the door from a blood-spattered porch, Raymond seemed more interested in the boy than the story being told.

"What happened after you put the money in the bus depot locker?" I asked.

"I went to the house to find Ruby."

"In the morning?"

"Uh-uh, I don't think so."

"What time did you wake up in the motel?"

"Mornin' time."

"So what did you do between the bus depot and the house where Ruby was supposed to be at?"

The thaw was slow and ponderous. He closed his eyes and shook his head slowly. He looked up at Raymond. I thought he might ask again if Ray was his father, but he seemed to go through that discussion in his head—silently.

"I went to see Esther," Evander said, surprised and delighted by the memory.

"Esther who?"

"Corey. Esther Corey."

"Angeline Corey's daughter?"

"Yeah."

"How you know her?" Mouse asked.

"We went to L.A. High together. We sat three seats apart at the graduation."

"You went to her house . . ." I primed.

"And she kissed me . . . on the lips."

I heard Mouse sigh. I knew exactly what he was thinking.

Angeline Brown had been married to a man named Charles Corey. Charles was a straight-up fence who moved stolen merchandise at a low profit margin but also at a prodigious rate. He had outlets from Redondo Beach to Beverly Hills.

His business was so good, as a matter of fact, that a fellow named Cool Louie, a white guy from the gambling mob downtown, decided to take Charles out and assume the business.

Louie managed the hit but he couldn't run the business, because he didn't have the kind of infrastructure that could maintain the low profit margin.

In the meanwhile Angeline took up with a man named Ashton Burnet. Burnet killed Louie and his three top lieutenants, thus returning the business to Angeline.

But Angeline, being smarter than Louie, her dead husband, or Ashton, turned the business into a request company. People came to her when they needed some commodity or other and she would assign the job to any of dozens of free-lance operatives. Everybody worked for Angeline, be they white, black, or Spanish-speaking. There were even a few Koreans in her stable.

Combining Angeline's fearlessness and smarts with Ashton's violent tendencies, you had one serious, very formidable threat.

"Did you give Esther the key?" I asked Evander.

"Yes, sir. I sure did. I told her about the blood and money and she wasn't bothered at all. She washed my face and kissed my mouth. She said that she always liked me. And you know, that felt good."

28

I had more questions, lots of them, but it was late and Evander's mind stopped at the oasis of Esther Corey. He couldn't remember anything else, and that was fine—for the moment.

Mouse said, "I gotta get outta here, Easy."

"Evander's gonna stay with me tonight," I replied, "until we get him presentable enough that his mother doesn't lose her mind."

"Okay, then." Mouse rose to his feet. "You take care'a yourself, Li'l Green."

"I'ma call you after I told Mama what you said," the boy replied.

"That's fine. Just ask Easy. He always knows how to get in touch with me."

"I'll walk you to the car, Ray," I said.

Mouse's pink Cadillac was in my driveway. It was after midnight and the stronger stars were glistening in the sky.

"How much for findin' the boy?" he asked.

"Nuthin'."

He smiled and opened the driver's-side door. For some reason this reminded me of him as Death in my waking dream.

"Well, let me say thanks then." He held out a hand and I grasped it.

"You the only real friend I evah had, Easy."

"Don't I know it."

After Ray drove off I backed the Barracuda all the way up into the driveway so that no one would see me take two bottles from the rude crate of Mama Jo's medicines into the side door to my house. I don't know why I felt so secretive about Jo's elixir; I guess it was because she never really cared if her ingredients were legal or not.

When I returned to the front room Evander was standing with his back to the northwest corner, looking up at the ceiling.

"What you doin', son?" I asked.

"Um, uh . . . I got a little jumpy and had to get to my feet. You know . . . the acid makes it like things are movin' around the edges. I think it might be a rat or sumpin', so I got up. And then there's voices and sounds sometimes too."

I took the boy by the elbow and led him to the chair.

"Sit down," I said.

"What?"

"Sit down."

When we were both seated I handed him one of Mama Jo's tar balls.

"Eat this," I said.

It was the size of a large jawbreaker, but

Evander put the whole thing in his mouth. He chewed at it a minute or so before saying in a garbled voice, "This taste like it comes from Mama Jo."

I got him to his feet and led him down the hallway to my bedroom. On the way I pointed out the bathroom.

By the time he stepped out of Domaque's oversize old shoes he was drifting.

"I'm sleepy," he said from a seated position at the side of my bed.

"That tar ball will put away all the dreams and nightmares," I said, but I don't think he heard me.

Evander slumped down on the bedspread.

Looking at him lying there, I felt exhaustion rest a heavy arm on me like a Santa Ana wind descending on Southern California.

I literally staggered back to the couch in the front room and then collapsed on the cushions as Evander had done on my bed.

I think I went to sleep, but it didn't feel like it at the time.

With my skull wedged against the armrest, it came to me that I had died and was resurrected by a smiling devil dispatched on a witch's errand from her hut in the woods. Sunset Boulevard and Caller's Creek were all part of a limbo that I was passing through on my way—maybe to life or possibly some eternity that was beyond any value system I could apply. The sofa was like a piece of turf where I was forced by fatigue to rest before continuing the unlikely journey.

I was asleep or maybe just half the way to that blissful state. I wasn't sure, because I heard breathing as if it came from someone next to me, but I knew that I was the only person in the room. It's possible that sleep for me in that brief period was death, and the manifestation of life—my breath—kept rousing me like Lynne Hua had done when I emerged from the semicoma.

The knocking came after many, many breaths. In my sleep state I was trying to justify the hard sound with the repetitive and slow susurration of respiration. But the rapping, like a foreign language, insisted that it was something different, something indecipherable that still needed to be heeded.

When I opened my eyes the room was dark except for a weak glow that came from the hallway that led to the bedrooms. I remembered leaving the forty-watt hall light on so that Evander could find his way if he awoke in the night.

The knocking sounded again, rousing me to a higher state of consciousness. It felt like every time I woke up I was a different man. Instead of the one man I had been when I drove off that cliff I was now a series of men, each being born out of the husk of the last.

Knocking.

I smiled at the concussion or the existential

reaction of a mind that had given up to death only to find that it was a feint. I sat up and the soft rapping came again. I pulled the pistol from my jacket pocket and took the two steps to the door.

After flipping the light switch on the wall I yanked the door wide with my left hand while halfway lifting the pistol in my right. I was ready for anything—almost. It could have been Jeffrey, a red-shirted hippie, or even my mother come to ask when was I going to give up the mortal coil and come to spend eternity with her. It could have been anyone or anything.

Anything or anyone but Bonnie Shay decked out in her Air France flight attendant uniform.

"What happened to your suit?" she asked.

Putting the gun back in my pocket I said, "I went on a hike in the woods to find a lost boy."

"Did you find him?" Her smile lit up the question.

I fell in love all over again, even with one foot planted solidly in another world.

"He's asleep in my bed."

"That's good."

"What time is it?" I asked.

"Almost three." Her Guyanese lilt thrilled me.

"Why are you here?"

"It's cold out here, Ezekiel."

"Yeah, yeah, right, come on in."

We went into the kitchen, where I brewed English breakfast. I was happy that Jeffrey hadn't used my honey, because Bonnie had to have honey in her tea. She liked to have a lemon wedge too, but that wasn't essential. She needed honey and I had it right there.

We settled across from each other at the dinette table. We hadn't spoken hardly at all since she'd come in.

I wanted to say something, many things, but looking at her was overwhelming. I still loved her, and that love was the same as it had been, but in the interim I had changed. Seeing Bonnie I knew that she was lost to me: like the old country to an émigré; like a dead parent buried in another state decades ago in a grave I never visited, in an abandoned graveyard that I wouldn't be able to find.

"Feather called me when your car was found in the ocean," Bonnie said. "I was at the Bel-Air house when Raymond called to say that he'd found you alive. That was eighteen hours later. Not even a day, but my feelings settled and set. I realized when I thought you were dead that you were my man. You saved my life and you forgave me later on."

"Too late," I said, repeating the last words I remembered her saying to me before I went to drive off the side of a mountain.

"No," Bonnie said, "not too late. You brought Jesus and Feather into my life, and when you lost your mind over me and Joguye I should have

195

understood. I should have called you and asked you to forgive me. I should have known that a real man can't stand by and watch his woman . . . his woman being loved by another man."

"I should have asked you to come back," I said.

"Maybe."

"And now I've died and everything that was fell away like snakeskin."

"Before Raymond called I told Joguye that it was over, that I would not marry him."

"What did he say?" I asked, wondering why I cared.

"He didn't understand. He is royalty and rich, a part of a world that no black American or Caribbean could ever really understand or imagine. But I told him that you were my man, dead or alive."

We finished our tea and repaired to the sleeping couch of the front room. I was sitting side by side with the woman I loved as much as I had my Big Mama, who died of pneumonia when I was too young to fully understand death. I was there but still mostly silent.

"Easy."

"I was in a semicoma," I said to the floor. "That's what they told me. Part of me feels like I still am. It's just Jo's chemistry experiments keepin' me goin'."

"Feather says that you're on a case."

"Yeah."

"What is it?"

"It was finding the boy in the back room. But now it might be something else."

She put a hand on my knee. I liked Bonnie's long brown fingers and her sensibly trimmed nails.

"When it's over call me," she said. "We can go out for dinner and talk."

"Like a date?"

Instead of answering she leaned over and kissed me. The force of that contact made me lean back. Bonnie followed, kissing me all the way down. When I was prone again I started counting osculations: One, two, three, and I was asleep again. This time it was a deep rest with no breaths or knocking or questions about the road between here and there.

There was sunlight blooming at the periphery of my closed eyes. It wasn't shining directly into the shuttered living room but glowing out from the kitchen, from the unshaded window there.

I took in a deep breath that seemed to fill my entire body. Exhaling, I sat up. I was weak but no longer dizzy. Instead of dithering I got right up and opened the drapes.

The sun almost bowled me over. It was so bright that I had to get back to the couch. Sitting there, garnering my strength, breath was like a playful carp swimming in and out of my body, strengthening me with each visit, bringing the light in small parcels that my living carcass could absorb.

After a while, I have no idea how long, I got up and went down the short bedroom hallway.

First I looked in on Evander. He was half under the blankets, having thrown two of the three pillows on the floor. He had taken off the borrowed shirt in the night. Sleep had him in its dark fist like some kind of precious possession clutched to a dead pharaoh's chest.

Taking a fresh pair of boxers from an underwear drawer that hadn't been raided, I headed for the bathroom.

I took off my clothes while urinating, dropping everything on the floor. It didn't matter; the suit was ruined.

There was a soap dish screwed into the sea green tile wall next to the bathtub shower. In it was a bright red bar of soap—one of the many little mementos left by Jeffrey the squatter. It smelled like cinnamon and had an oily feel, but I turned on the shower and used the soap: *Waste not, want not.*

When the water hit me I remembered Antigone standing outside the stall while I showered, a lifetime ago. Antigone, and the erection she summoned, reminded me of Bonnie. She had actually been in my house, kissed me to sleep as my mother used to do when I was too young to worry about losing love.

After the shower I went to the bedroom again. When I raised the window shade Evander groaned and winced behind closed eyes.

"Time to get up," I said, taking a square-cut blue shirt and black slacks from my closet.

It came to me that Jeffrey must have been expecting my return. All of his clothes, and most of the rest of his belongings, were in a battered leather suitcase on the floor. He knew that somebody would come one day to kick him out, and he wanted to be ready to jump. He would have cleared that hurdle if it wasn't for Mouse.

I dressed in the kitchen, something I'd never done before. While pulling up my pants I heard Evander's heavy footfalls take him to the toilet. The door slammed but that didn't bother me. Blood and money, torture and imprisonment stalked that boy—and he wasn't half the way home yet.

When I heard the water of the bathtub shower being turned on I was reminded of something. I went to the small room that the side door opened on and looked in the hamper. Therein was a striped cloth laundry bag that I might have need for before the day was done.

Downing my third bottle of Mama Jo's elixir I sat and waited patiently: a wounded soldier left at the side of the road by an advancing army that could not afford to be held back by invalids.

When the heat was flowing toward my feet and hands, Evander stumped in and sat across from me. He looked better for the night's rest. The swelling on his face and head had gone down, and his eyes were neither frightened nor pained.

"Hungry?" I asked.

"Like I got a hollow leg for a stomach."

"Your mama used to say that?"

"One'a her boyfriends . . . Sebastian Shore."

I thought about asking if Timbale had had a lot of boyfriends, but even with the lack of inhibition caused by the medicine, I had the civility to curb my curiosity.

"We could go to a place I know," I said instead. "I need to get out and stretch my legs."

"I should go home and get some clothes," he replied. "This shirt like to fall off me, and if I don't curl my toes I'd walk right outta these shoes."

"Domaque is just about the biggest, strongest man I ever met," I said on the heels of grunted laughter. "He could pick up a big man and hold him over his head. I've seen him do it."

"So all this room is for muscle?"

"Damn right."

"You know some strange people, Mr. Rawlins."

"First we'll go eat," I said. "And then we'll head out to a store to buy you some clothes."

"Why can't I go home?"

"Blood, money, dope smugglers," I said, listing them on the index, middle, and ring fingers of my right hand. "Take your pick."

"That's over."

"Did anybody you been with get a look at your wallet in the last week?" I asked him.

"I don't have a driver's license," he said. "And I don't carry my library card with me, 'cause I lose it sometimes."

"Did you ever say your last name?"

"Maybe, but Mama ain't been listed since somebody used her name to buy furniture on credit."

"Did you ever mention where you lived?"

You could tell by Evander's frown that he was an intelligent young man. He didn't like what I was saying, but he understood.

"Maybe I did," he said. "I don't remember. You think they might come after me?"

"I think they'll be lookin'."

"So what then?"

"First breakfast, then clothes, and finally we'll go talk to Esther—and Angeline."

There was a pancake house up on Fairfax just above Wilshire in those days. We put away some stacks and bacon and then we made it down to the Midtown Shopping Center, a mile or so past La Brea on Pico.

After spending an inordinate amount of time studying different garments, Evander finally decided on a bright yellow shirt with orange stitching along the seams, dark red pants, and buff brown, round-toed shoes. He donned these clothes and discarded what he wore in the store. The salesman just took the tags and I paid in cash.

In the car, on the way back to my neighborhood, I was curious.

"Does your mother usually buy your clothes for you, Evander?"

"Not since I was sixteen."

"And have you always bought loud colors like bright cars crashing at high speed?"

"No."

"Then why now?"

"I don't know. I mean, I guess it's the acid. I can't even, like, see soft colors."

"Uh-huh."

We drove for a while in silence and then I had another question. For this one I pulled to the curb a few blocks from the Corey residence.

"You know I'm trying to help you, right, son?"

"I guess so."

"You don't know me and you've been through some strange shit, but I need you to tell me something before we go to see this girl and her mother."

"What's that?"

"Do you know what Esther's mother and stepfather do for a living?"

"Not exactly, but I know that they're, like, crooks—criminals."

"Then you can understand that when you start talking about blood and maybe-stolen money, Angeline and Ashton don't seem like a coincidence." I was looking hard at the boy but he didn't wilt.

"They don't have nuthin' to do with it. I didn't go over to see Esther until after and I told her what happened but she wouldn't tell."

"L.A. High has a pretty big graduating class," I said. "How come you two are such good friends?"

"Because'a Mr. Alexander," he said without hesitation.

"How could he have anything to do with it? You don't hardly know Ray."

"But evah since he give me that toy gun and I found that envelope, I thought he might be my father. I thought he was my father and I heard people talkin' about him, about how he was a crook like Esther's mother and them. I asked her if she knew him and what it was like havin' a mother or a father like that. We used to talk about it on the bleachers sometimes."

"That's when she became your girlfriend?"

"No," he said somberly. "She never told me how

she felt till I came ovah her house aftah takin' that acid."

Like kismet gone slumming, I thought.

Angeline and Ashton lived in a converted duplex on the sixteen hundred block of Elsmere Drive. I knew the address—everybody that had anything to do with the life did. We parked in front of the duplex, went through the waist-high iron gateway of the burnt-sienna stucco building, and ascended the spiral stairs to the second floor. Angeline had walled up the first floor entrances to her home, some kind of security precaution that wasn't quite logical.

She was waiting for us at the entryway, outside the front door.

Angeline was a Negro woman by the American standards of blood and pedigree, but she wasn't what you would call black. Her skin was the color of dull steel with a hint of red just under the surface. Her salt-and-walnut hair was sparse and soft. And she hadn't achieved five feet in height even at the acme of her youth. Angeline was thin, with small, hard hands and big knuckles. Her lips sneered naturally and there was no sympathy in her watery brown eyes.

"Easy Rawlins," she said in mild surprise. "I heard you was dead."

"Yeah. You know Evander here, right, Angeline?"

"Mr. Noon." She said the words with absolutely no greeting in her tone.

"Ma'am."

"'Scuse me, Mama," a female voice said, and then a young woman—Esther Corey, I assumed—went around her tiny tyrant of a mother to stand next to Evander on the enclosed second-floor deck.

Esther was ocher in color and her face was round like a perfect autumn moon. Her short dress hugged her like the motive leaf of some man-eating plant. She wasn't fat but what the old folks used to call big-boned, with large, upstanding breasts and thighs that looked like they were made for a piano mover's trade.

"I think Evander left something with Esther," I offered the elder Corey.

"Ain't nuthin' on this property belong to nobody except the people that live here."

From the corner of my eye I could see Esther taking Evander's hand. They made a good couple; she was an inch taller and he a bit broader.

"You know I don't hold anything against you, Angeline," I said. "I've never been on the wrong end of a deal with you, your late husband, or Ashton. But I was hired by Mouse to help Evander. And you know I would surely hate to get between you and him."

"I'm not afraid'a Raymond Alexander," she said. "I ain't runnin' from no mortal man or woman."

"Common sense doesn't take fear, Ms. Corey."

"Let me make myself clear," she said. "I will kill you and this boy too if you go against me, Easy."

"Brutus killed Caesar," I said, a preacher on his movable pulpit, "and look what happened to him."

It would have been different if Ashton was there. If he was at the house I would have accepted her decree and used the telephone to complete our business. But I wasn't worried about him, because if Ashton was there he would have met us at the door.

Angeline glowered at me and her natural snarl turned feral.

"Esther," she said.

"Yes, Mama?"

"Do you have anything belongs to this young man?"

"He aksed me to hold a key for him."

"Then give him his key back."

"I already did," the brave and buxom child said. "It was his in the first place. All I was doin' was hangin' on to it."

When Angeline turned her savage gaze upon Esther, I worried that I might have to stop her from killing her own child. But the snarl turned, miraculously, into a smile!

"You mean you just handed it to him right under my nose?"

"Yes, Mama. It's his and he's mine."

Still smiling, Angeline shook her head, turned her back on us, and returned to the depths of her side-street fortress. A moment later Esther gave Evander a deep soul kiss and then went after her mother, closing the door behind.

That boy had some strong luck. Not good or bad, just strong. Like inheriting a battleship at the beginning of a war or earning a winner-take-all chance to fight Muhammad Ali by lottery.

There were three downtown bus stations large enough to contain lockers: Greyhound, Trailways, and the Proctor Street bus depot, which was on Grand. The number on the eye of the key read 33ab. The Greyhound station didn't have that numbering system; neither did Trailways. The Proctor Street bus depot, which served independent group travel concerns and general leasing, was our last stop.

The depot was a dilapidated, barnlike building with wood floors that were neither sealed nor waxed; if they ever got swept it was no more than once every other week. The eleven ten-foot-long splintery wooden benches, provided for waiting passengers, were set too close for comfort.

Two large, middle-aged black women were

sitting side by side on the far end of the frontmost backless pew. They had six or seven suitcases piled in front of them. Both women held their purses to their breasts like newborns that needed protection from a dangerous world.

In the far corner of the dowdy room stood a young white guy wearing blue jeans and a white T-shirt. I say white because that's what I'm supposed to call the sallow-skinned, pock-faced, rail-thin predator. He was staring at those women with hunger for those purses. He reasoned, as I did, that someone clutching anything the way they did their handbags had to be hiding treasure inside.

On the back bench sat an ancient human being clad all in faded rags who was leaning sideways, maybe asleep. This person could have been either a man or a woman. The race was also a thing of speculation, but the napper's place in the world was definite: He or she had been descending for decades and was very near toppling over.

Beyond the makeshift bleachers was a single window in the wall where ticket sales and group rates were negotiated.

A copper-colored man sat on the other side of the whitewashed plasterboard wall, gazing out through the aperture, considering something that had nothing to do with buses, winos, nervous women at the depot hours before their bus was to leave, or anything else that concerned his daily bread.

Evander and I walked up to the window. Looking at the man closely I had no inkling of his origins. He could have been anything from Choctaw to Mongolian, American Negro to Polish-with-a-tan.

"Hey," I said.

"How can I help you, sir?" he said, surprising me with his courtesy.

"Where's your lockers?"

"We don't have lockers here. The bulk of our fares are onetimers, you know, and so if we provided that service mostly derelicts would use it to store their stuff."

"That's still money," I suggested.

"The smell would drive our customers away."

I wasn't sure about the ticket clerk's conclusions, but it was his bus station, not mine.

"Look here, man," I said, taking on a verbal persona that wasn't exactly me—or at least, it wasn't before the accident. "You see this boy?"

The copper man turned his gaze on Evander.

"Five days ago he took LSD for the first time," I continued.

This sparked interest in the dark, hooded eyes.

"He was supposed to pick up something for my sister, but he met this hippie chick just got to town and she put it on his tongue with hers. Three days later he comes in and we ask where's the suitcase he was supposed to get and he says that he thinks he put it in a bus station locker where he met the hippie girl. He thinks! So now we been to every bus station downtown and there ain't no locker fit his key."

"Can I see it?" the shining, dreamy clerk asked.

I held the key out in my palm and he leaned over to get a good look at it. His posture suggested that he was peering over glasses but he wasn't wearing any.

"That LSD must be some strong stuff," he said to Evander.

Evander shrugged his big yellow shoulders.

"You were in the train station, son," the clerk said. "The train, not the bus."

"The train?" That was the real me looking at the kid who was so drugged out that his memory was more supposition than fact. I shook my head and then said to the clerk, "Thank you very much, sir. You've really helped."

"Anything else I can do?"

"Yeah. You see those two ladies sittin' on the bench?"

"Yes."

"You see that skinny boy in the corner?"

I didn't have to say any more.

The copper man nodded as he picked up the phone.

"I'll call the police right now," he said.

The train station was a step up in class. Big and grand, it was full of passengers of all types and ages. The main hall had dark red, cream, and green tile floors that were mopped nightly. There were businessmen and first-class ladies, working-class couples, students, hippies, and every color under the sun. The wooden benches in the waiting area had backrests and were built-in and shiny.

The lockers were off to the side, and 33ab was in a secluded corner. A young white woman in a mauve dress suit was standing at a nearby mid-level square locker door putting in an alligator bag and taking out a red velvet satchel. When she was gone I had Evander stand in such a way as to block me from the casual glance. Only then did I use the key. . . .

The wadded bloody burlap sacks wrapped up in the graying white sheets contained more money than I had ever seen in one place. It was no wonder that Evander wanted to forget where he put it; that kind of money was likely to get a black man killed.

I closed the locker door and tapped Evander on the shoulder.

"You think you can remember where I parked the car?" I asked.

"Uh-huh."

"You sure now?"

"Yeah," he said impatiently. "I ain't trippin' no more."

"Here's the car keys. The square one works on the trunk. Go get the laundry bag and come right back. And don't kiss no hippie girls on the way."

The aisle was wide enough for travelers to attend the light gray lockers from either side without bumping elbows. The floor in this area was plain concrete painted battleship green. I moved across and down from Evander's locker and stood there trying not to look suspicious.

I would have succeeded if it wasn't for the woman in mauve.

I suppose she saw in me what I saw in the white drug addict at the Proctor Street station. She brought with her a Negro station employee in a uniform that might have meant security. She pointed at me from the mouth of the aisle. The man squared his shoulders and walked my way. He was shorter than I, and slimmer. This didn't give me much of an advantage, because the last thing I wanted was a fight.

"Excuse me," he said, looking at my chin.

"What?" I didn't want to seem too friendly, because your run-of-the-mill sneak thief usually puts on jocular airs to hide his intentions.

"What are you doing here?"

"What do you mean, what am I doin'? This is a public station, idn't it?"

"You heard what I said, man."

He was a lighter brown than I, but our skin tones were similar. His features could have been Ethiopian, with a slender nose and high cheek-bones. He was pumping himself up because I promised to be an uphill climb.

"That white woman bring you over here?" I asked.

"What are you doing here?"

"I came with my nephew," I said, relenting with a lie. "We got to the locker and I remembered that I left my key in the car. My hip hasn't been right since I fell three stories from my construction job, and so the one with the stronger legs went for the key. If you don't believe me just ask the lady. She saw me with him. What am I gonna do? Come in here to steal her shit and then just stand around with my thumb up my ass?"

"No need to go cursin' at me now," the train station man said.

"No need to come ovah here actin' like I'm a thief just 'cause some white lady told you I look like one. As a matter of fact . . . where can I make a complaint about this shit?"

"Don't you go worryin' about complainin'," he said. "Just get your stuff and go."

He walked back to the lady in mauve and slowly guided her away from that area of lockers.

All of this made me wonder what she had in those bags. But that was a mystery I was not signed on to solve.

A few minutes later Evander came back. I wasted no time shoveling the bloody sheet and its contents into the laundry bag.

Walking out of there, with all that money slung over my shoulder, I felt like every eye in the place was on me.

31

Evander and I drove down to 117th Street near Hooper to the Alcott Court Presidio Arms apartments. This was a little horseshoe of workingmen and workingwomen's rental units that faced inward upon a swept-clean and barren concrete courtyard decorated only with a granite fountain, gone dry before World War II. The apartments were just large enough for one man or two younger women or a mother with an infant child. The separating walls were thick enough to dull the sounds of TVs and radios, domestic squabbles or cries of passion.

The Presidio Arms was a nice place before the riots. A white woman—I never knew her name— had owned it, and a black woman, Winifred Wolverton, managed the units. But after the conflagration they were bought by an ex-bootlegger from Galveston named Nan Mann. Nan was a freckle-faced bronze-colored woman who, when a permanent tenant moved out, would turn the unit into a day-rate room. Prostitutes, transients, and out-of-town musicians made up the majority of her day-raters, and so, in short order, the regular tenants found different accommodations.

The police didn't bother Nan, because she paid on the first and fifteenth of every month and maintained the peace with the help of an ex-GI named Luce who kept any and all disputes from going too far.

"The police have not had to come once to Presidio since I bought it," Nan often bragged.

That's why I brought Evander, and his loot, there; the police were the last people we needed to see.

The horseshoe was made up of twelve units, A through L. Nan lived in A and Luce in L. The rate was three dollars a night, and so it was usually pretty near capacity.

Evander, once missing and still yet to be delivered, and I showed up at the screen-door entrance to unit A a little before two in the afternoon.

I knocked and called, "Nan?"

After a minute or so the short and stooped onetime moonshiner shuffled into sight behind the haze of the doorway.

"Easy Rawlins," she said in her deceptively high voice. "I heard you was dead."

"Yeah. You got a room?"

"One room or two?" she asked, looking at Evander.

"One."

That raised her eyebrows, but Nan was about money—not morals.

"Four fifty," she said.

"Price went up fifty percent?"

"No. It's just when it's two men I charge more. The wear and tear, you know."

There was all kinds of innuendo in Nan's words, but I didn't care. She could have charged me twenty dollars and I would have gladly paid.

"J open?" I asked. I wanted to be as far away from Nan's prying eyes as I could be without sharing a wall with Luce; he was an angry Korean War veteran who thought the whole world owed him something.

"It is for you."

I brought out a five-dollar bill and we walked down to the unit I requested. Nan handed me a copper key. I forked over the five but didn't receive any change. Nan liked to be tipped for her services, especially when discretion was an unspoken element of the rental agreement.

There were two wooden chairs, a folding card table, and a queen-size bed set on box springs for furniture. A fat man would not have fit comfortably in the toilet, and the kitchen wasn't much larger. The Presidio Arms was the only place I'd ever been that had one-burner gas stoves.

But the window had bars and a shade, the overhead lamp was fitted with two one-hundred-and-fifty-watt bulbs, and the front door was substantial, with a chain for extra security. That's all we needed.

I split the money into two more or less equal piles and, sitting across the table from each other, Evander and I started counting.

Just shy of an hour later we came up with the sum of $214,461, more money than any recent graduate from L.A. High had ever held in his hands.

"This is one fuck of a lot of money, Evander."

"Yes, sir, it is." There was awe in his voice from the immensity of our calculations.

"It's also a fuck of a lot of blood." He had no answer to that, so I added, "Enough that if only one man shed it, he's probably a dead man now."

"I don't want this money, and I don't remember what happened. Why can't I just leave it with you and go on home?"

I just stared at him.

"What you lookin' at?"

"You love your sisters, Evander?"

"Of course I do."

"You want people like them drug dealers takin' them out in the woods, or maybe you want them at your funeral when the men lookin' for you catch up?"

"You don't know they're after me."

"Not you, boy, this money—and maybe, just maybe, revenge for all this blood. I hope you don't think two hundred thousand dollars is just forgotten." I kept my voice to a whisper. Wisely Evander followed suit.

"When you woke up in that motel, was there a knife or a gun in there with you?"

"No, sir."

"You're sure?"

"Yes, sir."

I was glaring at him. He'd been high for days after taking the LSD. Maybe he'd overlooked the weapon or dropped it after committing the crime. Maybe he was lying. . . .

Under the indictment of my stare Evander clasped his hands and then yanked them apart. He stood up and went to the kitchen, then came back, sat down, and got right up again.

He went to the door and I said, "Where you think you goin', boy?"

"I don't know," he said nervously.

"Come here and sit down."

He obeyed, almost meekly.

He and I, as different as we were in age and temperament, had been reared in the same atmosphere: the ether of perpetual vulnerability and subsequent lifelong fear. Black people in America at that time, and all the way back to our first conveyance, the slave ship, had received common traits. For the so-called white man these attributes were merely hair texture, skin color, and other physical characteristics. But our true inheritance was the fear of being noticed, and worry about everything from rain collapsing the walls around us to a casual glance that might lead to lynching. We—almost every black man, woman, and child in America—inherited anxieties like others received red hair or blue eyes.

"I got to go out and figure what to do," I said. "Here . . ." I handed him one of Mama Jo's tar balls. "Eat this and rest. You're gonna need your strength later on."

"Where you goin'?"

"First I'm gonna put the money somewhere safe. Then I'm going to try and find out what happened to this Maurice guy."

"Maybe I should go with you."

"And I'd like to bring you," I lied. "But you don't remember what happened. As far as we know there might be a warrant out for you. That's a lotta blood and a lotta money. Suppose you robbed a bank? We don't know."

I liked Evander because he was smart enough to make sense out of the abstractions of language. Many young people hear you say the pot is hot but they still have to touch it. Evander chewed on the tar ball.

Half an hour later he was sound asleep. I put the money back in the laundry bag and threw the sheet and burlap sack in the bathtub with hot water and soap flakes that some previous tenant had left behind.

Before long I was nosing my red Barracuda toward downtown, to a building on Wilshire where I hoped to get help from an old friend and a new one.

32

It was close to four thirty when I reached the first-floor entrance of the forty-four-floor office building that housed Proxy Nine. The architecture was very modern, with lots of steel and glass, white stone, and a high ceiling. This was the main office of the international French insurance company, and no expense had been spared.

Before being allowed through to the elevators you had to pass a minor inquisition at a counter behind which labored at least a dozen young clerks, receptionists, and other, less definable preprofessionals. That day a young man with almost alabaster white skin, coarse red hair, and pale blue eyes was my corporate magistrate.

"Yes?" he said.

The fact that he didn't say *sir* reminded me that I was black and hadn't worn a jacket and tie—all while toting a tan-and-black-striped laundry bag.

"Jackson Blue," I said.

"Excuse me?"

"Mr. Jackson Blue. Tell him that it's Mr. Rawlins calling on him."

The young man was my height and gave the

appearance of physical fitness gained from tennis or maybe golf. He hesitated and then asked, "Do you have an appointment?"

A pretty young woman with black hair and pale eyes looked up from a nearby table where she was typing on a state-of-the-art IBM Selectric typewriter.

"If I said no would you turn me away?" I asked, knowing that I was wasting my time.

"I can't let you in without an appointment."

"What if you called Mr. Blue and he said, 'Sure, send him up'?"

The young man, nameless as far as I was concerned, raised his right hand and gestured somewhere behind me. I didn't need to look to know what was coming. I might have taken a glance if I wanted to see how many, but that was of no concern either.

The young woman was now talking on the phone. I wondered if she was calling for additional backup. I imagined that she and the redhead were lovers and her attentiveness was instinct for her man.

The feeling rising in my breast was at once familiar and alien, not unlike my identification with Evander's fears. Along with anxiety and fear my people had inherited spite and rage for the centuries of oppression that we were reminded of almost every day of our lives. To experience the malice of generations in a moment is a taste so bitter that it could make an otherwise healthy man retch.

I saw this emotion in my imagined reflection in the young man's blue eyes, but I didn't feel a thing. I had died and there was nothing that anyone could do to match the experience of my semiresurrection.

"Yes, Mr. Graham?" a man asked.

There were two of him, tall and in gray uniforms, hatless but armed. Both of them were white men, though that didn't matter; enough Negroes protected the property of men like the receptionist Graham.

"I was trying to explain to this gentleman," the redhead said, "that you can't go in without an appointment."

"Okay, guy," one of the two said.

"*Pardon?*" French is a lovely language. It was the black-haired young woman. "Monsieur Rawlins, *non?*"

"*Oui,*" I replied, and she smiled.

"*Parlez-vous francais?*"

"*Pas vraiment, un peu.*"

She smiled at my feeble attempt and said, "Monsieur Blue's secretary, Crystal, *non?* She says that 'e is in the building but not in 'is office. She says to bring you up."

"What are you saying?" the talking security guard asked.

This question was also on Graham's face.

222

"If someone asks to see somebody you should call," the young woman said to Graham. "It is not for us to question them like Nazis."

This last word told a whole story. There was a generation of French men and women who understood, however briefly, what it was to be treated like a dog in your own home.

"So he can go up?" the guard asked Graham.

"I . . . I guess so."

"Come," the young Frenchwoman said to me.

"It is so beautiful in California," she said as we waited for the executive elevator half a block or so away from the front desk. "Too bad people like Loring Graham cannot count their blessings instead of trying to be bosses all the time."

The silvery doors slid open.

One thing I liked about Proxy Nine was the interior of the elevators; they were utilitarian, floored with linoleum and encased by walls of dull chrome.

"What's your name?" I asked as she pushed the button for the thirty-first floor.

"Asiette," she said. Her light eyes were violet— strikingly so.

"Beautiful name."

"*Merci*." Her annunciation contained a pert curtsy.

"Do you know Jackson?"

"We are supposed to call no matter 'oo comes," she replied.

"Yes, you said that, but do you know him?"

She grinned and I felt like part of the family.

"*Oui*," she admitted. "Monsieur Blue comes down to the employee cafeteria a few times each week and sits with us. Most of our officers 'ave never seen the basement—except for Monsieur Villard, but that is different. 'E really is the boss.

"But because I 'ear you say 'Jackson Blue' I look and I see that you are 'ere and I think maybe Loring should just call but 'e does not and so I do."

She was wearing a close-fitting black-and-white herringbone skirt that came down to her knees and a thin, dark blue woolen sweater, proof against the air-conditioning. I smiled because she was dressed the way her mother did when she was the same age.

"Something is funny?" she asked.

"No, just thinking about Paris during the war."

"You were there?"

I nodded. "The people were so happy to have us. I really felt like a hero."

"I was in Dijon then, too young to remember."

"You are a child of that country, though."

The elevator doors opened and I gestured for Asiette to go first.

"*Merci, mais non*," she said. "They didn't ask me to come, only to make sure that you got 'ere. Do you know where you are going?"

"Yeah. Pleasure to meet you, Asiette," I said,

and we shook hands before the doors closed on her smile.

I looked at the elevator for a few seconds before turning. I had been raised to be wary of change in the world. *The more things change, the more they stay the same,* people had always told me. But maybe that wasn't so.

I stopped at the threshold of Jackson's secretary's door and said, "Knock, knock."

"Mr. Rawlins," the elder white woman said. Crystal was gray-haired, wearing a rose-colored dress suit. Her accent was mildly English. This might have been her birthright or her education. Either way it took me another step away from America. "Come in, come in. Mr. Blue is with the technicians working on some computer matter. I don't pretend to understand what they do. If it was up to me I'd do everything with pencil and paper, maybe a typewriter now and then. I mean, what's the big hurry?"

"I completely agree. Can I have a seat?"

"Please."

There was a burgundy sofa set across from her mahogany desk. I set my laundry bag on the floor and sat back comfortably. It was as good a place as any to wait. Crystal's office was big enough for most vice presidents, certainly larger than my little detective's room down on Central.

I sat back and she said, "Nice weather outside?"

"A little hot."

She nodded and went back to whatever project she was working on before I got there. That was fine by me. I needed a moment to think about why I was there. Talking to Jackson was always a pleasure. He was a genius, the smartest man I ever met. He could see patterns connecting the sunshine and a child's laughter with nucleic acids and the theory of relativity.

Jackson's province at P9 was its worldwide computer system. He was also a confidant to Jean-Paul Villard, president and CEO of the insurance giant. The amount of money I had in that laundry bag wouldn't mean much to somebody like Jean-Paul. I needed a pair of eyes that would be unimpressed by Evander's lucre.

"Easy?" Jackson was standing in the hallway outside Crystal's door looking at me with the most frightened eyes I had seen since before my untimely demise.

He wore a medium gray suit, bright white shirt, and a burgundy-and-blue tie topped off with spectacles that I knew were just clear glass. Jackson worked hard to give the appearance of a nonthreatening black man. The craziest thing about his charade was that it seemed to work.

"What is it, Jackson?" I asked with only a hint of the exasperation I felt.

I realized one day that Blue and I were friends simply because I knew him so well. I understood

226

him better than his girlfriend or his mother. Jackson's fears were more profound than the greatest intelligence. I often felt that he had to be as smart as he was just to keep his head above the waters of continual and needless anxiety.

"Say," he commanded, " 'forgive me my sins,' and then say, 'lived.' " He was so frightened that he sputtered a little.

"Forgive me my sins. Lived."

When I pronounced this nonsense he relaxed— some. After a minute he came into the receptionist's chamber. Crystal and I watched him peering at me as if he expected the words I said to cause spontaneous combustion.

When I didn't burst into flame he knitted his eyebrows in concentration and then, finally, made his decision.

"Come on in, Easy. . . . Yeah. Come on."

Jackson's office was immense, wider than five tall men laid down head to foot and longer than ten. Wilt Chamberlain couldn't have touched the ceiling on his best jump. One wall was a library's worth of bookshelves, filled to over-flowing, and the opposite wall was replete with oil paintings of famous jazz musicians who had, at one time or another, been to France. The Oriental carpet was royal blue, almost metallic gold, and bloodred. Half the way through the room, before his ebony wood desk and the picture window beyond, sat two canary yellow sofas facing each other over a big glass box used as a coffee table.

In contrast to his workspace, Jackson was skinny, tar black, and shorter than most women he ever dated.

"I understand the 'forgive me my sins,' " I said, sitting next to my friend on a yellow cushion. "I guess that's something Lucifer, or his minions, can't say, but why *lived?*"

"That's like a backwards signature."

"Devil . . ."

"You got it, brother. The devil spelled backwards is *lived.*"

I laughed heartily and slapped Jackson's shoulder. He was still wary of me, but that was a natural state for him with almost everyone.

"I got a problem, Jackson. Mouse hired me to find this kid named Evander Noon. . . ."

"Timbale's son."

"How'd you know . . . Oh, right, Raymond got you to hire her. . . . But she won't talk to him, so how did she know to apply for the job?"

"Lissa MacDaniels," Jackson proclaimed.

"That's her friend?"

"Yeah. Mouse had me hire Lissa, and then Lissa told Timbale about the security job."

"So you know about Evander?" I asked.

"Only that he's her son. I never met the woman."

"Mouse went through all that just to get her a job?"

"Yep."

"Did he tell you why?"

Jackson shook his head. "I'idn't ask. You know doin' a favor for Mouse is like money in the bank, like your own personal block'a gold in Fort Knox. And as you well know—you don't look a gift horse in the mouth."

"Jackson, I need to talk to Jean-Paul."

Without hesitation the skinny little man jumped up and walked back toward his broad black desk. I followed and gazed out of his window while he worked the dial on his phone.

The farthest mountains south and east of the city were snow-capped, and the sky was as blue as it gets.

"Jean-Paul?" Jackson said. "I got Easy ovah here, man. He said he needs to talk to you. . . . Huh? No, I don't know what he wants, but you know he almost died, so it's got to be serious. And I was thinkin' that he might be able to help us wit' that thing I was tellin' you about. . . . Yeah, yeah . . . Okay. See you in a minute then."

Jackson looked up at me with conspiracy in his eyes. That look said, *For a dead man you sure can get into mischief.*

33

Still looking at me, Jackson got up from behind his desk.

"Let's get comfortable, Easy," he said. "You know I don't like bein' stuck behind a desk; makes me feel like I'm my own worst enemy sittin' in that chair."

Back on the yellow sofa Jackson kicked off his black shoes, revealing blue, green, and yellow argyle socks. He pulled these dressy feet up under him, settling into half lotus, his back resting against the window-ward armrest of the office couch.

He took off his useless glasses to scrutinize me.

"I'm not a ghost, Jackson, just a very lucky man who survived a hellacious car crash."

"Then why you ain't in bed?" he asked, flinching a little at his own question.

"Like a shark."

"Got to keep movin'," he agreed tentatively. "You wanna drink?"

"You know I don't drink."

"They said you went off that cliff drunk. Now you back on the wagon?"

"Either that or the bottom of the hill."

That got Jackson to smile.

"And you just come by to say hi to me and JP?" he asked.

"Evander's in trouble and I promised Ray that I'd dig him out."

"Uh-huh."

The light knocking on the half-open office door announced Jean-Paul Villard. The Frenchman was olive-skinned with dark, dark brown eyes, almost black. The little mustache he'd sported the last time we met had been shaved off. His hair was longish compared to the crew cuts of his corporate American counterparts. If the police asked me to describe him I would have said that he was about five-nine, welterweight and wiry.

That day Jean-Paul was wearing a black suit designed for a slight build. His shirt was slate gray with no tie, open at the neck.

Seeing the understated French CEO I understood what my old friend and I were doing—or, more accurately, what Jackson was doing. The whole act, from half lotus to his honest questions, was a holding pattern until his boss arrived. Jackson was born to be another man in another country, where his worth would have been realized from the start. When Jean-Paul hired him at P9, Jackson felt not only friendship but a kind of patriotism for the man and his company. Black men of our day were never told, *The sky's the limit.* Our limits were more like the inner lid of a coffin. Our potential was purely physical and necessarily short-lived. We could aspire to Joe Louis but never Henry Ford.

"Come on in, JP," Jackson hailed.

Villard closed the door and approached us, an irresistibly charming grin on his lips.

"Easy," he said, holding out a hand.

I rose and shook his hand, smiled and nodded. "Jean-Paul."

"Sit, sit, my friend," he said.

Jean-Paul perched on the glass box table between Jackson and me.

"I am so 'appy that you are not dead, Easy," he said.

We'd only met once, but the French business-man was very friendly toward black Americans, especially veterans of World War II. He'd first met them at the liberation of Paris and he, like Asiette, was contemptuous at the particular nature of racism in the United States.

"How's Pretty doing?" I asked.

Pretty Smart was a beautiful young black woman who had fallen for Jean-Paul, or at least his wealth, when he and Jackson helped me smoke out one of her boyfriends who was the subject of a complex investigation.

"Coming along," he said. "She does not understand that a Frenchman and the Negro American woman are so very much alike. I mean . . ." He moved his head from side to side. "I mean, she understands, but it makes her uncomfortable.

"But, Easy, what is it you need from me?"

Instead of talking I dumped the money from the laundry bag onto the glass table.

Jackson Blue, in spite of all his success in love and in business, was amazed by the immensity of the pile.

"*L'argent*," Jean-Paul said, unimpressed. "What does this mean?"

I told both men the story of Evander and his misadventures as far as I understood them. I skipped over the fact that the luckless boy's mother worked for P9. That bit of information didn't seem salient for JP.

"I need to put this money somewhere until I figure out what it and the blood mean," I said. "You're the richest man I know, and so I thought maybe you would have a secure place to store it until I put the rest of the pieces together."

The Frenchman was looking into my eyes. From the age of sixteen he had been a part of the resistance in Paris; this service lasted over the entire occupation. Villard was a man who studied other men.

"Yeah?" I said in response to his stare.

"You trust me?"

It was the only question worth asking, and so I smiled.

"I don't know you hardly at all, Mr. Villard, and in part that's why I came here. This money is no threat to you, and what do you care about a little pile of cash when you own this whole building?"

There was knowledge in my answer, understanding of myself in relation to the man sitting across from me. We both knew that knowledge is the deepest kind of trust.

"I could put it in my private safe if you want," he offered.

"I want."

Jean-Paul smiled without showing his teeth and cut a glance at Jackson, who still had his feet folded under his thighs. This brief, wordless exchange told me a great deal about the relationship between the two men. There was intimacy, conspiracy, and friendship there, but also the hierarchy of roles.

Jackson let out a quick breath and said, "Easy," and I knew that my particular therapy for the reversal of death and dying was about to be expanded.

"You ever know a guy named Charles Rumor?" Jackson asked.

"Sneak thief, cheat, and liar," I said. "An ex-girlfriend of his once told me that the only true thing he ever uttered was his snoring when he was asleep, and not always then."

"That's him."

"I knew Charles back in Galveston before the war," I said.

"He up here now. We used to run together before I got straight."

"Yeah?"

"Uh-huh. Mostly it was a floating blackjack game, but we also used to go do target practice in the San Bernardino Mountains. He had this collection of pistols and liked to shoot beer cans and bottles, stuff like that."

"Hm," I grunted, just to keep the patter going.

Jean-Paul had clasped his hands together and was looking down at the floor.

"Anyway, that's it; at least, that's all I thought it was. Had to be seven or eight years ago. You know men like shootin', Easy. I'd pop them bottles and cans off a wood railin' up there. When I hit six I'd reload and shoot again. When we were finished I just dropped the piece in a bag and we'd drive back to visit these two sisters he knew."

"Jackson," I said to underscore the stupidity of his actions.

"I know, Easy. I know. I know I'm a fool. I mean, what has Rumor evah done that wasn't only for him? But I didn't work it out until three weeks ago."

"And why then?"

"A white dude name'a Huggins called me one day here at work. He said that he could make me ten thousand dollars for just one afternoon of my time. I told him to get lost, but then he said that I'd get paid ten percent up front just to listen. I didn't see anything wrong with it. If he aksed me to do sumpin' against P9 I'da just said no and taken a thousand for the time. So I goes down to meet 'im at this little bar on Temple. It was pretty fancy, a white place, and they didn't wanna let me in, even though I was dressed in a business suit an' everything. But when I mentioned Mr. Huggins the waters parted and I was shown to a private room in the back.

"There was this big blousy dude in a brick red suit introduced himself as Theodore Huggins. He was with another man that he called Johnny Portia. This dude looked just like his name, sporty and sharp. His suit was as dark as green can get, and his smile coulda been used for a dentist's ad.

"Huggins works for Portia, and Portia is a vice president of TexOk."

"The oil company?" I asked.

Jean-Paul looked up.

"Yeah, man," Jackson said. "Portia told me to look up in the old newspapers back in 'sixty-four when a cop broke in on some burglars and one of the crooks shot him in the leg. He told me that the gun used in that shooting had my fingerprints on it, that he had got that gun from Charles Rumor. He said he would give it to the cops if I didn't sign an investment note for twenty-three million dollars to a company that works for TexOk's experimental drillin' up in Alaska."

"But you work in computers," I argued, as if I was at the table with Portia and Huggins.

"I 'ave allowed Jackson some power as an officer of the company," Jean-Paul said. " 'E would be an asset for business because people underestimate 'im, and that is always good in negotiations."

"So you made it that just one man can make a loan like that?" I asked Jean-Paul.

"Of course not. There must be three officers signing the document. This Portia must 'ave two of my men in 'is pocket."

"So you could've done this?" I said to Jackson.

"Yeah, I *could*. Of course, then I'd be on the run. But if the cops got hold'a that gun that I know only I touched with bullets that I loaded it with, that's attempted murder, twenty-five years minimum—if the cops don't kill me first."

"And how," I asked, "does Portia make money on this investment?"

"At first I didn't get it, Easy," Jackson said. "But when I looked into it I found out that Portia's sister's husband owns the exploratory company. Jean-Paul found out that the place they're lookin' at probably won't pan out, so the company goes bankrupt and they put a good half'a the money aside."

"So you came to Jean-Paul?" I said.

"I woulda come to you, Easy, but you were in a coma and Portia give me a deadline."

"What was the plan before me?"

"We were looking for countries where Jackson could go that did not 'ave extradition treaties with America," Jean-Paul said.

"Makes sense. So now what?"

"I haven't been able to find Rumor," Jackson said. "You know I been off the streets too long. Nobody is where they were when I was at large. But you could find him, Easy."

"That's all?"

"*Non*," Jean-Paul said. "The president of TexOk is a man named Merkan. 'E will not believe this of his top man, not without proof. I want this proof . . . without paying for it, of course. I also want to find out who it is in my company that would betray me. I cannot allow people to do to me like this."

"And you'll hold my money?"

"I would if you 'elped us or not."

I gazed into the Frenchman's eyes. There was nothing for me to consider. "Okay, then. Let me try and come up with somethin'."

Jean-Paul gave a satisfied nod and Jackson grinned like a coyote.

"I don't care if you are Mama Jo's zombie, Easy," Jackson said. "I'm gonna shake your hand."

I stuck out my hand to test Jackson's mettle. He

licked his lips and, with obvious gumption, he grabbed on. I smiled and held his eyes with mine.

"That's a good thing, Jackson," I said. "Because you know you got to get out there with me to make sure we get it right."

34

Jean-Paul was stuffing money back into the laundry bag when Jackson and I left Proxy Nine. I offered to help, but he said that he liked doing manual jobs, said that he used to have to cook his own food and then bus the table back when he was in the underground looking for Nazis to maim, blow up, and kill.

I was glad to leave the CEO to it, because Mama Jo's Gator's Blood was thinning out in my veins.

We reached my Genesee house at a little after six p.m. I said that I was going to take a nap and told Jackson to call Raymond.

"Tell him we need to find Charles Rumor and that he should drop by at midnight."

"Okay, Easy. You want me to wake you up when he gets here?"

"No. Let me wake up on my own."

"What should I tell Jewelle I'm doin'?"

"Anything but the truth, Jackson. Anything but that. And one more thing," I said.

"What's that, Easy?"

I stared at him, wondering what his question meant. My mind had begun its now familiar slow spiral downward.

"Um, uh, oh, yeah . . . call over to the Presidio Arms and tell Nan . . . I mean, ask Nan Mann to tell the man in J that I'll be there in the morning."

"Done."

I couldn't have uttered another word. Staggering to my bedroom I fell a thousand miles into sleep so complete that it felt . . . final. During the next five or six hours I had monumental dreams, but luckily, when I awoke they receded into the void of unconsciousness.

My alarm clock said 12:07. I smiled at the timing and rose up from the shroud of sleep.

Mouse had only recently arrived. He and Jackson were sitting at the dinette table drinking beers and laughing. Mouse was a great storyteller, mainly because he spoke the whole truth.

I stumped past the men to the back pantry, where I grabbed the bottle of Gator's Blood.

Swallowing the stuff in a single gulp, I returned to the kitchen with the empty bottle in my hand.

"Gator's Blood," Mouse said with a grin. "Jo forced that foul shit down my gullet for eight days after I got shot that time."

"Did it work?" I asked.

"I'm here, ain't I?"

Jackson was looking back and forth between us.

His expression contained equal parts fear and awe.

"You find Chuck?" I asked Mouse.

"Oh, yeah. I know a guy know a girl know a guy who knew where he was at. Before I came here I checked it out. He's there."

The warmth was returning to my limbs. A feeling of nascent hilarity rose in my chest.

"You armed, Ray?" I asked.

"For Mr. Bear and his brothers."

"Good."

Out at the car Raymond said, "Why'ont you let me drive, Easy?"

"Why?" I was almost angry.

"That shit'a Mama Jo's make you lose control sometimes, especially when it's been in your system for a few days. I should know."

I piled into the backseat of the Barracuda while Mouse drove and Jackson explained the point of bracing Rumor. He didn't mention the fact that he was an officer of the company or that he had partial power to loan out millions; there was no need to let a man like Mouse know where he could wangle that kind of money.

"Damn," Raymond said. "He got a whole sack full'a guns with fingerprints not his on 'em? That shit is some long-range plannin' right there."

"Yeah," Jackson agreed. "Plannin' to damn me."

"Why didn't you call me in the first place,

Blue?" Raymond asked. He almost sounded hurt.

"I . . . I guess I should have. But you know, Ray, I didn't wanna, wanna . . ."

Mouse laughed and said, "Don't worry, man. You got me now."

Charles Rumor lived on the sixth floor of an apartment building that had one unit per floor.

"There's a indoor stairway up in front," Mouse said. "And a fire escape door out the back. You go up the front way and ring the bell, but gimme eleven minutes before you do."

When he was gone I asked Jackson for a cigarette. He handed a Kool over the seat and lit a match.

After my third drag he said, "I went into the bedroom to ask you a question, Ease. It was only about a minute after you went in there. But you were dead to the world."

"The aftermath of the accident. I get really tired."

"I know, but . . ."

"But what?"

"Easy, you looked like you really was dead, man. I mean, most'a the time when people are at rest that's what it is—rest. But your mouth was hangin' open and slack just like my uncle George when he died in his bed."

"Is there some point to this, Jackson?" I didn't like the menthol taste but kept on smoking.

"What does it feel like, man? What does it feel like to come back from sumpin' like that?"

I took in a lungful of smoke and held it. The question tickled me. It brought me to a place I had not considered before—at least, not directly.

"It was like," I said. "No . . . It *is* like there's no yesterday and no tomorrow, like time comes together right where I'm standing. It's . . . it's magnificent, almost too beautiful to bear."

"Damn," Jackson said, and I felt I had imparted some kind of vital knowledge that I didn't even understand.

"We better be goin', Blue," I said. "It wouldn't be good to keep Ray waitin'."

We went through the unlocked entrance of the dirt-streaked salmon-colored building. The walk up to the top floor winded Jackson, but I was running on superior fuel. When we got to Rumor's door I knocked loudly, like a cop might do.

I could see at the crack of the door when the light came on. The two little shadows that appeared indicated that someone was standing there, looking through the peephole.

I knocked again and the shadows went away. Maybe three minutes went by and the door came open. Charles Rumor was standing there with mortal fear in his eyes. Gun in hand, Raymond loomed behind with a big smile on his face.

Rumor's apartment was a study in contradictions.

He had a fancy sofa. The multicolored upholstering was made from and stitched in raw silk. In front of this sat a fruit crate for a coffee table flanked by three brown metal folding chairs for any overflow of guests. A fancy Nikon camera was on the pitted pine floor, and the walls were all bare. One wall had been recently painted bright orange, but the other three were base white and stained.

A door opened and Mouse swung around, his pistol up and ready to fire. The young woman who came through gasped and brought her hands to her mouth.

"Hello," Raymond said instead of shooting. "What's your name?"

"Fiona."

"Nice name. Pretty girl. Do me a favor, honey. Sit down in one'a them chairs there and we'll be through with our business in a minute."

Fiona *was* pretty. Maybe seventeen and dark-skinned. Her hairdo was a flip fashioned after Diana Ross of the Supremes. She wore a man's threadbare white T-shirt, that's all. You could see the darkness of her skin through the thinning weave of cotton.

For his part, Rumor had on jeans and a green T-shirt. He was in such a rush to get out the back that he hadn't put on shoes. He was a buttery brown color, handsome except for his eyes, which seemed untrustworthy and a little jaundiced.

"You know why we're here, man," I said.

"Can I sit down?" he asked.

"No."

"I ain't done nuthin' to you, Easy. Not to Mr. Alexander neither."

"Cough it up," I said.

"What?"

Mouse leveled his long-barreled pistol at Chuck's forehead.

"Oh, no," Fiona said.

"I . . . I give it to . . . to the white man," Rumor suggested. "Um, he bought it."

"No," I said. "No. You wouldn't give him the gun, because it's too valuable, and he didn't buy it, because you could have been lying about Jackson's fingerprints."

Mouse grinned to show his appreciation of my logic.

I turned to see what Jackson thought. He was so scared that he had his back up against the recently painted wall.

"Now, Charles," I commanded. "Because you know, and I do too, that it's either the gun or your life."

"Oh, my God," Fiona said.

"Sh," Mouse told her.

Charles's handsome face disappeared behind the fear bubbling up from his soul. He actually shivered and panted.

"We got to go, man," I warned.

He went to the big fancy sofa and pulled off the

center cushion, then ripped out the tan nylon netting that covered the frame. He reached inside and came out with an army surplus duffel bag.

"That's it!" Jackson said. "That's it. That's the bag with the guns."

"Step aside, Charlie," Mouse said. He moved in and grabbed the sack, handing it to Jackson. Squatting down next to the crate, Blue took out revolvers one at a time until he came upon a .22 target pistol. It had a fake pearl handle.

"This is it," he said.

"Take it," Charles told us. "Take it and go."

Fiona was mumbling a prayer to God.

I took the gun from Jackson, cracked it open, and saw that three shells had been fired. I clacked the chamber back into place and aimed at Charles's left thigh. He bent over and fell trying to avoid being shot.

"I'm just gonna shoot you in the leg, man," someone said with my voice. "That way you will have paid for shootin' that cop and framin' Jackson with one wound. But if you move I might hit you someplace vital."

Rumor froze with a terrified grimace on his face. I shifted the gun muzzle, fully intending to fire.

Mouse laid a hand on my wrist.

"Somebody gonna hear a shot in the dead'a night, Easy," he said. "And you know that gun is too hot to be caught with."

My breath was coming fast.

"You could stab him," Mouse offered.

"Please, no," Rumor said.

"Please," his teenage girlfriend echoed.

The rage subsided in me, but Charles didn't know that.

"If you answer one question and don't lie," I said.

"Anything, man. Anything."

"How'd Portia and his man Huggins get to you?"

"I don't know no Portia, but . . . but . . . but this cop named Brady come here with a big white dude in a gray suit so rumpled it looked like it haven't never been ironed. Brady had my police file. Five, six years ago me and Jackson got busted nine times on gamblin'. . . . You remembah, Jackson . . . when we run that floatin' blackjack game?"

"That's true, Easy," Jackson said willingly. He hated the sight of blood. "You remember I told you that."

"Brady left us alone and the big white dude, his name were Huggins, wanted sumpin' on Jackson. I used the pistol when a cop almost busted me one time when I was stealin'. I always wear gloves on a job, so I had the right shit."

I was still staring.

"They didn't pay me right off, but I told 'em that if I didn't get five thousand in a week I'd give the gun to Jackson. I told 'em if they wanted to buy it, it would cost twice that." His rheumy eyes were pleading with me.

"Why didn't you go to Jackson and try to get paid twice?"

"Because'a you."

"Me?"

"Everybody knows you and Jackson's tight. On the one hand a man had five thousand dollars; on the other side there was you. I was gonna go down to Houston with the five grand, but I waited too long."

I was still pointing the gun at his leg. It came to me that part of my mind was still considering the karmic shot.

"Let's get outta here," I said to my friends.

In the Barracuda, now sitting in the passenger's seat, I was smoking again. This time Jackson was driving.

"I told you, Easy," Mouse said after a few miles. He was using a blue oil rag from the trunk to wipe down the pistols and their bullets.

"Told me what?"

"That that Gator's Blood will mess wit' yo' mind."

35

We dropped off Mouse and the seven revolvers at EttaMae's in Watts proper.

"I'll get Peter to help me pick up the Caddy tomorrow," Mouse promised from the curb, "after we use the smelter at Primo's to get rid'a these here."

"Peter Rhone still live here?" Jackson asked.

"Yep, he sure does. He Etta's French maid and my man Friday."

We were getting off the Santa Monica Freeway at Fairfax when Jackson said, "I never thought I'd see this day."

"What you talkin' 'bout, Blue?" I had been staring off into the night lights of my adopted city, thinking about how far I'd come and how little progress I'd made.

"The day when Raymond Alexander had to tell Easy Rawlins to hold back."

I chuckled. The humor brought back the things Charles said to stave off my wrath. This led to another train of thought.

"Does Jean-Paul have a contact with the police like Portia does?"

"Um . . ."

"Come on, Jackson. I just saved your ass, man."

"Yeah," he said reluctantly, "but we couldn't use 'im. A fingerprint on a pistol woulda been too much for a cover-up."

We got to Genesee at a little past three.

"I want you to call Jean-Paul," I said to Jackson while handing him a bottle of beer.

"Now?"

I nodded. "Tell him that I wanna meet with his police contact down at the far end of the Santa Monica Pier at eight a.m."

"It's late, Easy," Jackson whined.

"And I don't need it gettin' any later."

After sharing the particulars of what I needed from his boss, I told Jackson that he could sleep in my bed or on the couch.

"What you gonna do?"

"Go out for a drive. I'll be back to take you to work by ten."

I drove up to our Bel-Air squat and waited until almost six. Sitting in the car, concealed by the deep driveway, I smoked a few menthols that I'd borrowed from Jackson and planned how to execute the rest of Jean-Paul's revenge.

It felt good plotting, the way a spider must feel when spreading his web.

When the sky was light but the sun not yet risen,

I pressed the button on the outer gate of the mansion.

It took a few minutes for someone to answer.

"Yes?" a soft but masculine voice said on the intercom speaker.

"It's me, Juice."

The gate swung slowly inward and I drove my gaudy red car toward the family I loved.

Jesus answered the door with the caramel-colored Essie sitting in the crook of his left arm.

The baby smiled, holding her hand out to me. I kissed her fingers and she giggled, pulling the hand quickly away.

"I think your little girl is telling me I need a shave."

"How are you, Dad?"

"Keepin' on, son. Keepin' on."

"You want some coffee?"

"Maybe a quick one. I got to be down in Santa Monica by eight."

He boiled water and made me a cup of instant in the kitchen. We stood at the counter while the baby cooed and pawed his chin, a look of infinite wonder on her face.

"How's everything?" I asked.

"Fine," he replied. "Are you still drinking?"

"Not much for small talk, huh?"

"Are you?"

"Not a drop."

When Jesus smiled it was like a little blessing or an unexpected moment of charity from a stranger. I sipped my coffee. Jesus held his daughter with intimacy and understanding that had no words and needed none. He and I had been together for many years. At the beginning he never spoke at all, and when he finally found his tongue, he was very conservative with its use.

We stood there for seven or eight minutes in deep silence.

"Where's Feather's bedroom?" I said at last.

"Across the hall from yours," he said. "She wanted to be close in case you needed her."

Feather's room was the color of a half-rainy day, dominated by mild blues and soft grays. She had a short cherrywood bookshelf and a maple writing desk, both set upon a swept pine floor. There was a casement window, the doors of which opened out onto greenery so deep that it might have been a forest.

Her head was on a sea green pillow, and her bare leg stuck out from under the ash gray blanket. When I pulled the cover over her leg she woke up.

"Hi, Daddy."

"Hey, babe," I hailed, sitting down at her side.

"How are you?"

"Happy to see your sleepy head."

She grinned and sat up, holding the blue sheet

up to her neck in the mature gesture of a much older woman.

"I miss you, Daddy."

"I'm right here."

"Are you finished with Uncle Ray's case?"

"Not yet. I'm going down to Santa Monica in a little while to work out the last few kinks."

"Then will you come home?"

"Yes."

"And can we move back to Genesee?"

"Don't you like it here?"

"It's nice, but all my friends live down near school."

Thinking about Jeffrey, I asked, "Would you mind if we moved somewhere around there?"

"How come?" But before I could answer, she said, "It doesn't matter. If we're close to Louis Pastcur that's all I care about."

"Then it's done," I said. "I have to get going. I just came over to kiss you good morning because I wasn't here to kiss you good night."

Feather proffered her light brown cheek and I kissed it.

"Ooh, Daddy! You need to shave."

Changed, showered, shaved, and armed, I was sitting on a bench at the far end of the Santa Monica Pier at 7:47 in the morning. My only company was two old fishermen, one white and the other Mexican, or Mexican American, or maybe he was from some other colony of the conquistadores. Nine curious seagulls hovered around the old friends, hoping to get at the bait fish they were using.

"Mr. Rawlins?" a man said.

He was neither tall nor short: a white man with prematurely salt-and-pepper hair, slender, wearing dark blue trousers and a checkered red-and-black dress shirt. The shirttails were tucked in but he wore no belt. His eyes were slate gray. I've always been partial to gray eyes—they remind me of the cat my mother once owned.

My visitor was carrying a large brown paper bag by twined brown paper handles.

"Yes?" I said.

"Tim Richards," he replied, lowering into the empty space next to me.

"Really?"

He smiled and gave a little chuckle out from behind closed lips.

"I don't care what your name is, man," I said. "Did you bring me what I want?"

He reached into the bag and came out with a single sheet of white typing paper.

"There are quite a few guys with that first name, but I finally decided that it had to be Maurice Potter that you were referring to. He's mostly a pimp, but he's been busted for lots of stuff, including the kind of crimes that you told Villard about." He handed me the sheet. "That's the address we have for him. It's up in Cheviot Hills. That's the Jew Beverly Hills."

"Yeah," I said. "I know where it is."

The man calling himself Richards cocked his head, looking at me quizzically.

"What is it with Villard and Negroes?" he asked. "I mean, he's got that little black dude with him half the time, and now he's helping you."

"If you don't like black people and you don't like Jews, the real question is, what are you doing here with me at eight in the morning?"

"I don't dislike anybody, Mr. Rawlins." The cop's voice was as cold as his eyes. "I just call a spade a spade."

He was baiting me, and Mama Jo's medicine wanted to rise to the hook. But I inhaled deeply, putting that urge down.

"You needed a whole shoppin' bag for one sheet'a paper?" I asked.

"Oh, yeah. I got something else in here, something JP thought you might be interested in."

He pulled out a manila folder. It contained well over a hundred sheets of various kinds and colors of paper. It was the thickness of a small town's white pages.

When I got it in my hands I saw a familiar name on the filing tab—EZEKIEL PORTERHOUSE RAWLINS.

There were reports filed on me that went all the way back to the late forties. Other than Mouse it

255

contained briefs on my friends Odell, John, EttaMae, Jackson, Primo, and a dozen or more others. There were all kinds of crimes I had been a suspect in—some of them I actually committed.

I must have spent five minutes engrossed in the life that the LAPD attributed to me.

"Damn," I said at last. "You got one'a these on Ray Alexander?"

"I'd need a helper to bring down the file cabinet we got on him."

"I guess you need this back, huh?" I asked.

"No. You can keep it."

"Won't it be missed?"

"If they go lookin' for it they'll just think it got lost."

"They're that careless about their files at the LAPD?"

"Look at the last page."

I turned the tome over and opened it from the back. The final page of the damning document was mostly blank except for the sentence: SUBJECT DECEASED DUE TO A SINGLE-VEHICLE ACCIDENT ON PCH. INVESTIGATION CLOSED.

I was so engrossed in those twelve words that I didn't notice the man who called himself Tim Richards rising from the bench.

"Keep your nose clean and they'll never know you're out here," he advised.

He walked away, leaving me with my epitaph in my lap.

36

Every morning was a new experience since coming out from the semicoma. That day I was feeling pretty spry, even though the effects of Jo's medicine had waned. I didn't need rest, and I had information that could possibly lead to an end of Evander Noon's problem—one way or another.

Carrying the city-authorized biography, I went to a phone booth that overlooked the Pacific Ocean, smoked the last menthol, and thought about how lucky a man could be to sit in a glass box set at the edge of a vastness like that.

It was five minutes before I dropped the dime and dialed a number.

"Hello?" Jackson Blue said on the fourth ring.

"Hey, Jackson, I wake you up?"

"No, man, I was readin' your copy of *Cotton Comes to Harlem.*"

"You never read it before?"

"Course I did, when it came out two years ago. But you know I got to be readin' if nuthin's goin' on. Got to or else I'd go crazy."

I smiled to myself at Jackson's impotent self-awareness.

"I want you to call Huggins and tell him you're ready to sign the loan papers," I said.

"Why?"

"Get Jean-Paul to set us up in a suite with a connecting room in a hotel downtown. Tell Huggins to bring the papers and Portia and to meet us in the suite. Let's make it tonight about eight . . . no, no, nine."

"What if somebody says no?"

"They won't."

"But what if they do?"

"Find a place where you, me, JP, and anybody else he wants to bring can meet at seven thirty."

"But, Easy—"

"Can't talk now, Jackson; I'm on a schedule. Call Etta's and give the information to Peter Rhone. If he's not there try Primo's garage. And I'm sorry, Blue, but you're gonna have to make it to work on your own."

The address the cop gave me was on Crest View Drive, a street that followed a hill up to the highest point of the solidly upper-middle-class community. The houses were mostly large and prosperous-looking, like architectural versions of fat burghers at a Dutch theater before the blemish of the world wars.

Maurice's two-story house had a magnificent weeping willow dominating the front yard.

I parked pretty far up in the driveway and walked briskly to the front door, trying to look as if I belonged there. I was wearing work jeans and the kind of rough cotton shirt that a gardener or a day worker might have. Of course, I was a black man in 1967, so anybody looking at me in that neighborhood would look again.

I didn't care. I didn't have patience for people's suspicions. There was a job to do.

I knocked and rang and knocked again. The front door was on a raised porch partially concealed by a trellis that had a vine of sweetheart golden roses covering it. To the left of the heavy oak door were three large windows that were completely hidden from view.

I tried the knob but the door, of course, was locked.

Then I wondered how much noise the breaking of one of those three-by-three-foot panes would make. I spent way too long thinking about breakage.

Why don't you just try to open it? I said to myself.

The window didn't come open, but it jostled more than a snug lock should have allowed. I grabbed the two handles and pulled hard. The wood along the frame had rotted, and so the lock tore out from its pulpy mooring.

I donned the cloth gloves that I always carried while working and climbed through the window.

The first room was set up for dining. There was a long wooden table, dark brown and shiny, surrounded by eight equally dark chairs that had plush, bright vermilion-cushioned seats like so many panting tongues. Leading from the dining area was a doorway with no door that brought me to a boothlike space that had no purpose except the transition from here to there.

"Hello?" I called.

No answer.

Through the booth I came into a living room. The colors here were gay pastels with lots of padding. There was an extra-long sofa and four chairs, upholstered cousins of the couch. On one wall hung three framed prints of chubby Renoir nudes: one bathing, one drying off after bathing, and another bending over to test the temperature of the lake. There was a glass-and-cast-iron coffee table with huge tomes that contained photographs and paintings of nudes. Thick, creamy carpeting muffled my footsteps, but I didn't go far. . . .

There was an interloper in this soft landscape: a chrome-and-purple-vinyl kitchen chair with arms held a dead man in dark green trousers, bare feet, and a bloodstained wife-beater T-shirt. His wrists and ankles were bound to chromium arms and legs. The dead man had a receding hairline. He'd been wounded in the left shoulder and bandaged up before this last bit of torture did him in. His head was thrown back and there was a neat little bullet hole in the temple above his right eye. Probably a .22, I thought, with a steel-jacketed shell. One of his eyes was open, bloodshot, and brown. His lips had formed a rictus to which there was not even the hint of humor.

The skin was cool to the touch. His fingers curled toward their palms like a bird's talons. There were cigarette burns and bloody marks on his chest and face. I wondered how loudly he had screamed and then noticed a stiffened wad of white cloth on the floor next to him. This, I imagined, was the rag that had been shoved into his mouth at the worst moments.

He might have been handsome. It was hard to tell through his death mask.

His wallet identified him as Maurice Potter. He was forty-seven, my age, and weighed one hundred and seventy-one pounds at the time his driver's license was issued. He had seven hundred and thirty-three dollars, not counting change, and two credit cards.

I sat on the edge of the coffee table and studied the man that had died. There was no real reason for this amateur examination except that death had been much on my mind of late.

Potter had stubble on his chin. He seemed like a fastidious man, and I wondered if the facial hair had grown out since his demise.

It was while having these thoughts that I noticed the heavy, dark blue trunk set in a far corner, behind two squat stuffed chairs.

I made a quick reconnaissance of the house; there were two bedrooms, a yellow kitchen, an office the size of a workingwoman's dream closet. All the rooms had been violently and yet meticulously searched.

On my way out I went back through the dying room, gave Maurice a parting look, and then stopped.

That blue trunk.

It was banded in metal, heavy, and completely out of place in the soft-colored sitting room—like Maurice himself, it was an eyesore.

I observed that the creamy carpeting around the trunk was a bit darker and yellowy. Upon closer inspection I realized that the dark area was wetness. There were no plants, overturned glasses, leaks from the ceiling or walls, just wetness all around the front of the blue trunk.

I felt my heart throbbing in my chest. It wasn't beating fast but preparing to. I hadn't been afraid in a very long time, and so these biological preparations amused me.

I crouched down, flipped the two latches holding the lid of the trunk in place, and stood as I lifted the top.

Inside was a naked white girl, maybe eighteen, maybe not quite. She was in a fetal position. Her stringy blond hair was well on the way to getting matted. Her eyes were shut. For a moment I thought that she too was dead. I was trying to make sense of the dead man lashed to a chair while a dead girl lay hidden a few feet away when she blinked at me.

She stared up, squinting at the light and a little confused. Who could blame her?

"Are you okay, miss?" I asked.

She sat up, covering her small breasts with crossed arms. I took off my shirt, helped her to stand, and wrapped the rough cloth around her shoulders. I still had a T-shirt on.

"Where is he?" she asked in a voice that vibrated with fear.

"Maurice?"

She nodded.

"He's dead," I said, indicating the corpse with a slight movement of my head.

When the girl saw Maurice a smile flickered across her lips and then she began to cry.

37

The girl smelled bad but I didn't mind. The odor reminded me of how I smelled just a few days before.

"How long have you been in there?" I asked after ten or twelve minutes of shivering and sporadic crying.

I'd ushered her into the kitchen, where she

downed three big glasses of water between sobs and tremors.

"I don't know . . . maybe a week, maybe more. He . . . he made me stay there for hours and told me I had to hold it for the bathroom. He only gave me three minutes in the toilet and then he'd put me back in the trunk. That's when he'd give me a jar of water and two cookies to have in the dark."

"Why?" I asked. "Was he mad about something?"

"I didn't even know him. We met at the bus station. I only just got into town and he started talking to me near the gate. He was nice. He bought me lunch and said he owned a restaurant. He offered me a job. I thought I was lucky. We came to his house because he said he had the waitress uniforms here.

"Then he . . . he slapped me around, ripped off my clothes, and . . . and . . . and he made me get in the trunk. He said that when he got through with me I would do anything he wanted.

"But then, two days ago, I think, maybe three or four, he came in and he was shot in the shoulder. He handcuffed me to the chair and made me help him put on some bandages. He kept saying, 'Damn niggers this' and 'Damn niggers that.' I was so scared. I begged him to let me go, but he punched me and threw me back in."

I noticed a blue-and-red bruise on the left side of her jaw.

"Then what?" I asked.

"I was hungry and I had to go, but he wouldn't let me out. He told me not to make any noise or he'd kill me. I knew he would, so I just laid there and prayed. I never prayed before. Even in church I'd just lower my head but I didn't say the words in my head. . . ."

"Did you hear what happened to him?"

"It was another man's voice," she said, looking up from the floor. Her eyes were blue and red, her skin pink with a hint of gray. "He was very angry and he hit Maurice. He kept hitting him and Maurice was begging him to stop. But he didn't stop. . . ."

The flickering evil grin worked its way back into her face. At her early age she had already experienced hate deeper than I would ever know.

"What did the man ask Maurice?"

"He kept asking, where was the nigger? He kept saying that, over and over."

"And did he open the trunk?"

She nodded and looked down again. "When I heard him I turned my head away and pretended that I was unconscious or dead or something. I thought he'd kill me but he didn't."

"Why not?"

"I don't know. I just heard the top open and felt the light on my eyelids. Then he closed it up again and I didn't hear anything else."

I sat back and watched the white slave in the

mustard work shirt. Her hands were balled into useless fists, and a kind of tuneless humming came from deep in her throat.

"Did you have a suitcase when Maurice got you?"

She nodded and said, "He put it in the backseat of his car."

"Where's that?"

"In the garage."

I stared at the girl for a long time. She twisted her shoulders to get away from the scrutiny.

"What's your name?" I asked, mostly to relieve the pressure.

"Sue."

"Where did you come from, Sue?"

"Flagstaff . . . in Arizona."

"Can you go back there?"

She shook her head miserably, and I wondered if what she was running from was worse than even Maurice.

"Did the man who beat on Maurice say any names that you remember?"

"He said something about a guy named Giles," she said. "Just before he opened the trunk he said, 'This is for Giles,' and there was this sound like my brother's cap gun."

"Did you see the man through a crack or something?"

She shook her head.

"How old are you, Sue?"

"Sixteen. I'll be seventeen in September. What are you going to do with me?"

She looked up again for that question.

I brought my palms to chest level and shook my head. "After what you've been through I will do whatever it is you want."

Sue's brows knitted as she tried to comprehend what I was saying.

"I want to get away from here," she said.

"Okay. Where to?"

I might as well have asked her to recite the Old Testament backward. She shook her head and slumped forward.

"Listen, Sue," I said. "You just went through some shit I can't even imagine. That dude deserves to be dead. That man didn't kill him 'cause of what he did to you, but there is some justice in the world. You need to go someplace where you can be safe and where maybe you know somebody, somebody you trust."

"I have a . . . a cousin named Ginger. We were close when we were kids."

"Where is she?"

"Sacramento."

"You should call her."

Sue stood up with sudden resolve and moved toward the black wall phone next to the counter.

"Not from here," I said, touching her arm.

She skittered away from my hand and asked, "Why not?"

"Because there's a dead man in this house and the police might check out who was called over the last few days."

Sue stared at me, looking for some kind of duplicity in my words. When she couldn't find any she wilted back into the chair and sighed in desolation.

"It's okay, girl," I said. "You're going to go upstairs and take a shower; then we're gonna go down to the train station, call Ginger, and buy you a ticket to as close to her as you can get."

While the girl was upstairs in the bathroom I went out the back door, across a neglected concrete patio strewn with leaves and streaked with dried mud, over a patch of shaggy grasses, and into the garage. I'd retrieved the car keys from the dead man's pockets, but the doors were unlocked. He drove a late-model forest green Cadillac convertible.

There was no suitcase in the car, but there was a straw bag set on a raw pine shelf at the back of the garage. Her white plastic purse was on top of it. I smiled at the trusting nature of careless youth. It occurred to me that if anyone ever treated Feather like Maurice had done to Sue, I would kill him without even a moment's consideration.

The purse supported Sue's story. Her last name was Hellinger and she lived until recently on North Post Road in Flagstaff, Arizona. I carried the small valise and purse back to the kitchen. Sue had half a pack of Winston cigarettes in her cheap purse. I was on my third one when she came downstairs from her ablutions.

Her hair was combed and the smell was gone. The odd thing was that cleaning herself up allowed me to see how plain her face was. Suffering, I concluded, sometimes accents and beautifies its victim.

The girl took the bag into the bathroom and changed. While she was in there I found a straw hat in Maurice's bedroom closet. This I put on with the brim tipped over my face. Then I led the girl out to my borrowed Barracuda and drove within the speed limit while my heart was racing far up ahead.

"He was gonna make me into a whore, wasn't he?" Sue Hellinger said when we were half the way downtown.

"That's what it sounds like," I said. "But it's kind of crazy. I mean, why not find somebody who wants to do the work?"

My mind was all over the place. Between my official death and Evander, Jackson Blue's comparatively simple problem, and the immensity of Sue's suffering, I felt like a flea trying to wrangle an elephant.

"He would come and sit on the trunk sometimes and talk to me," Sue said. When I had no comment she went on. "He sounded calm but it was crazy. He said it made him feel good when he was asleep at night to know that he had a girl locked in a box downstairs."

She said many other things after that. None of which I wish to repeat or remember.

It took two hours to contact Sue's cousin. She lived in a rented house with three other girls. After many tries we got Ginger's work number and finally reached her after her lunch break. With coaching from me Sue explained that she got into trouble without giving any specifics. Ginger was a true friend and told her to come right up; a train would get in by midnight. We bought the ticket and waited near the track door.

"Should I tell Ginger what happened?" she asked.

"You'll have a whole lifetime to ponder that question."

"I mean," she said, "you don't want me to tell about you, right?"

"What's my name?" I asked her.

"Um . . . I don't know."

"See? You could tell her all about what you know about me and the killer, because you don't know a thing. And there's no reason to go to the police, because Maurice is already dead."

This assessment, for some reason, brought tears to the teenager's eyes.

"Don't worry, girl," I said with my hands down by my sides. "You're gonna live through this. You're gonna be okay."

By then it was time for her to board her train. I hailed a redcap. He was an older Negro with kind eyes and a slight limp. I tipped him five dollars and told him to help her all the way to a seat.

I had already given Sue the money from Maurice's wallet. She smiled for me and turned to follow the redcap. As I watched them walk away I had the sudden impression that I was a dead man saying good-bye to a ghost.

By the time I got back to the illegal hotel I was flagging—not exhausted or shattered, as I had been before my last bouts of sleep, just very, very tired.

Unit J was empty, and so I told myself that I had to go out and find Evander. Nan Mann would have seen him leave. Luce might even have noted the direction. It was early afternoon. I laid my head down on the unmade bed, in the little cell that passed for a room, taking a few minutes to close my eyes before going out looking for my troubled ward.

When I woke up, maybe four hours later, Evander was perched on a chair at the side of the bed. Our positions brought back my first memories after the accident. I was once again an invalid, and Evander flipped back and forth between being Mouse and Lynne Hua sitting vigil over me.

Inhalation promoted me from invalid to merely exhausted.

The young man that Mouse called Little Green was deep in thought. His fists were under his chin, he was leaning forward like Rodin's *Thinker*, and his eyes were cast down but looking inward.

"Evander."

"You awake?" he asked, not looking up.

The mechanics of raising my torso from a prone to a seated posture seemed infinitely complex. But I managed it, making the grunting sounds that old people do when they have to bend down—or crank themselves back up again.

"Where'd you go?" I asked.

"Tulip Café," he said.

"What's that?"

"It's a soul food place. Miss Mann told me that I could get somethin' to eat there."

"Good?"

"I called my mama." Full stop.

"Yeah?"

"I told her what Mr. Alexander told me to." Stop.

"And?"

"I told her that Mr. Alexander told me that he knew who my father was, and that if she didn't tell me, then he would." Stop.

Evander's halting story didn't bother me, because I knew his lineage had nothing to do with me and my problems.

"She said," Evander continued unexpectedly, "that Mr. Alexander should know who my father was. He should know because my father was a man named Frank Green and Mr. Alexander murdered him."

It was nineteen years before that a white gangster named DeWitt Albright hired me to find a white woman who preferred the company of black men—Daphne Monet. But Daphne only looked white, and used her looks to pass as something she was not in the American notion of race. She was a Negro woman but her skin was white. Her half brother, Frank Green, however, was the color of a starless night. Frank was a gangster too, and he was bound and determined to kill me for even thinking about his sister.

Frank was hunting me but Mouse found him first. And even though Raymond did the deed, I was the reason he killed Little Green's father.

"Did you know my father?" Evander asked from a far-removed place in time.

"Back in those days L.A. was a much smaller

place," I said. "There were two million fewer people in Southern California. I knew almost every black face back then. And if I didn't know 'em I knew somebody who did."

"Did you know Frank Green?"

"Not personally, but I knew who he was."

"Did Mr. Alexander kill him?" Evander sat up straight to ask this question.

"Your father," I said, "if Frank Green really was your father, was a killer, a terror with knife or gun. I know of six people he slaughtered. Not murdered, not killed, but butchered like beef cows. Ray's a bad man too. If they crossed each other one or both were destined to die. On that side of the tracks killing was just another part of life."

"If it's true then I have to kill him," Evander said to his hands.

"Maybe," I agreed. "Maybe he did and maybe you do. But let's follow it down first. Did your mother actually see Ray kill Frank?"

"I don't know," the young man said.

"First you got to make sure you know what you're saying is true, because you only have two and a half possibilities if it is. The most likely outcome is that you try and kill Ray, but he gets you first. After that there's the slim chance that you kill him and then one of his friends'll hunt you down and kill you, that is unless you get arrested and the judge sends you to the gas chamber."

Evander, Little Green, was concentrating on my

words. I thought my logic was getting through to him when he asked, "Did you go to college, Mr. Rawlins?"

"No. But I been to school."

"I was gonna go to college."

"Why didn't you?"

"Because Mama needed help and I was just . . . I don't know . . . I just wasn't ready to take myself seriously like that."

I lifted up on my left side and pulled the car keys out of my pocket.

"I got a bottle of Mama Jo's medicine in my trunk," I said. "Car's parked right out on the street. Go get it for me, will you, son?"

Evander went and I wondered if I was the reason that the lost boy wasn't ready to live his life. Could I have saved his father? Should I have died so that the next generation would live? I thought about how Mouse had taken care of the boy and his family for nearly two decades after killing Frank Green. Mouse and I had been friends since our teen years, and I was still finding new sides to him.

When Evander returned I gulped down the sweet and foul brew, and then lay back to consider what to do about so many different and conflicting troubles.

"I found Maurice," I said some while later. I had a multitiered plan in place. I might not have been able to articulate every step, but you don't have to be able to forge a pistol in order to shoot a man dead.

"Did he know what happened?" Little Green asked.

"I'm sure he did, but he didn't tell me, because he was dead."

"Dead? How?"

"Somebody shot him in the shoulder, but he survived that. Then somebody tortured, beat, and then shot him in the head trying to get to you."

"Me? What for?"

"That money, of course."

"Where is the money?"

"In a safe place."

"I been thinkin' 'bout it, Mr. Rawlins. That's my money and I want it."

"We don't know whose money it is," I said. "One thing for sure: There's blood on it. If you take one you got to take the other. But in the meanwhile we can't put it under the bed or in the trunk of my car. The money is safe and it will stay that way until we figure out who killed Maurice and dissuade them from doing the same thing to you and yours."

Evander frowned again. He was worried about his mother and sisters. That was good. I wanted to keep him focused on right now so I could work some magic around later on.

39

"Where we going to, Mr. Rawlins?" Evander asked as we drove away from Alcott Court. The mostly cleaned burlap sacks and sheets were in my trunk, destined to be burned in the days that followed.

"To drop by a friend's office," I said, "Jewelle MacDonald."

"How come?"

"I own some apartment buildings around the city. Her office is the managing agency. If any unit is free she can set you up in one to wait until I figure out how to make sure those men will leave you alone."

"How you gonna do that?"

"Maybe a little conversation," I speculated. "You might have to return some or all of that money."

"But I need that money for my mama."

"What you and your mother need is for you not to get killed."

"It's gonna be my own apartment?" he asked, his mind as flighty and intense as the humming-birds Feather's dog, Frenchie, chased around the backyard.

"For a few days."

"Will it have a telephone?"

I laughed at that. "We'll see. But at any rate, I'll give you a few dollars for food and phone calls in case you need to talk to some girl."

"It ain't like that, Mr. Rawlins."

"As you get older, Evander, you come to learn that it's always like that—if you're nine or ninety."

At that time Jewelle's rental management operation was on Avalon. Evander and I walked into the storefront office: two men traveling under a whole sky of troubled clouds. A wide counter formed a small foyerlike area as you entered the long room. This counter blocked entrance into the greater part of the office, where there were six desks set up for agents who helped people find places to live.

A young colored woman with curly blond hair and thick red lips stood pouting behind the counter. Two men and one woman were working at three of the desks.

I remember that there was a burly-looking fly hovering near the wall to my right. It was humming peacefully, almost as if it was flying in its sleep.

"May I help you?" the receptionist asked, insincerely, I thought.

"Easy Rawlins," I said.

"Nobody here with that name."

"That's my name. You manage my properties."

"Say what?" She was amber-skinned and quite pretty. But the sneer on her face told of an unattractive life that she'd survived, just barely.

"Can I speak to the office manager?" I asked.

"Easy, you said?"

"Yes."

We watched her turn from the blockade and wander to the very back of the room, where a slim, dark-skinned man sat behind a blond desk. He wore a black suit, white shirt, and powder blue tie. He was prim and also discontent, the male counterpart to the receptionist's scornful visage.

He asked the young woman to repeat my request and then, with great reluctance, he stood and walked to the front. The young woman followed him.

"Yes?" he said. "Can I help you?" He was in his forties, but the weight of those years had yet to settle on him.

"Easy Rawlins."

"Do you have proof?" He accented the question by shifting his left shoulder and holding out his left palm.

The Gator's Blood told me to sock him, but I reached for my wallet instead.

He studied the driver's license like it was a ten-page rental agreement and then handed it back.

"What do you want?" he asked.

"I need to put up my friend Evander here in an apartment for a few days, maybe a week," I said.

"And?" the prissy real estate agent asked.

"I'd like you to make that happen."

"Sorry," he said.

"About what?"

"I'm busy. You can't expect to walk in here and have us do something just like that. We represent over eighteen hundred units."

"And twenty-seven of them are mine."

He answered that statement with a twist of his lips. This reminded me of the gestural disdain cultivated by churchgoers I'd known.

"May I speak to Miss MacDonald, please?" I asked.

"I don't know where she is."

"I do," I said. "May I use a phone?"

Our eyes met and he gleaned something from the tone in my voice. He wasn't sure what that something was, but it leavened his demeanor from scorn to suspicion.

Reaching under the counter, he came out with a big black telephone that was probably older than the disdainful receptionist.

"I'll have to dial," he said. "We don't allow toll calls."

"Sure," I agreed. "Tell the switchboard operator that it's Easy Rawlins for Jewelle MacDonald. She'll transfer the call to Jewelle wherever she is. You can talk to her yourself."

I recited the number and he dialed with equal parts precision and wariness.

We waited while a phone in some other part of town rang.

"Yes," the thus far nameless office manager said. "I'd like to speak to Jewelle MacDonald. What? . . . Oh, it's for . . ." He looked at me.

"Easy Rawlins," I said.

"Easy Rawlins," he repeated. "Yes, yes, I'll hold."

The man looked at me with different eyes. I was a sudden surprise in a landscape he felt that he knew inside and out.

After a few moments he said, "Yes, yes, Miss MacDonald? This is Clive Chester at the Avalon office. No, no, he's here. I was just dialing for him. Sure, right away."

He handed me the phone like a baton at an intermediary leg of the relay race.

"Jewelle?"

"Easy," she said with great relief in her mature voice. I always thought of Jewelle as a child. It was a constant surprise when I was reminded that she had turned into a powerful businesswoman. "Jackson told me that you had come out of that coma. He said some crazy stuff about voodoo, but I told him he was nuts. I'm so happy to hear your voice."

"How you doin', girl?"

"Great. Business is good and I'm building a little empire around me and Blue. Are you okay?"

"You know me, got to keep on movin'."

"What do you need to help you on your way?"

"Can you direct Mr. Chester here to find and open a unit in one of my places or elsewhere and to install my friend Evander in it today?"

"Of course," she said. "Is that all?"

"Yeah."

"Did Clive give you a problem?"

"In his defense I must tell you that me and the boy look like we just got back from trench warfare."

"Okay, Easy." She giggled, sounding once more like the child I'd once known. "Give Mr. Chester the phone and I will make it happen."

It was a pleasure to watch the office manager sputter and try to explain himself. In the end he just started nodding and grunting his agreement.

When the call was over he cradled the phone and said, "I'll just clear up some things here and then drive the young man over to our Colby Street apartments. There aren't any units available in your places, and Colby is partly furnished."

"Will you also get your people to put in a phone for him to use and then give that number to Jewelle's secretary for the answering service?"

"She didn't mention anything about a phone."

"Okay," I said. "Let's call her back."

I held out my hand for the phone again. Clive Chester did not move. He was looking for a place where he didn't have to seem like he was losing

282

the contest. But he was losing, had already lost.

"We can manage a phone connection. The jack's already in the apartment, and there's a phone company number we can call. . . ."

I left Evander on the sidewalk outside the real estate office.

"We will answer all of your questions," I said to the boy. "Everything from the money to your father's death. I promise you that. But keep your head down until I tell you it's safe. And if you call Esther, remind her, if she doesn't already know, not to tell her mother where you're staying."

Three blocks away I stopped at a phone booth and called EttaMae Harris's home.

"Hello?" she said on the eighth or ninth ring.

"Hey, Etta, how you doin'?"

"Easy Rawlins, oh, Lord, am I glad to hear your voice. You know Raymond brought me up to your place after the accident. It broke my heart to see you like that, baby. I been prayin' for you."

"Thanks, Etta. I hear you sent LaMarque down Texas for the summer."

"Got him on my brother's farm. You know he needs to get some country in his bones. He got mixed up with the gangs around here and I had to send him away or Raymond was gonna start a war. You know he don't have the patience of a rabid dog."

"Yes, ma'am. Holdin' Mouse back is like trying to put your arms around a tornado."

"It's good to hear your voice, Easy. What do you need?"

"Peter."

"Yes, Mr. Rawlins?" Etta's manservant said after a short wait.

"Jackson call you, Pete?"

"They're at the Biltmore downtown," he said, "suite twenty-one thirty-five. You're supposed to meet him at seven thirty at a restaurant called Angelo's. He said you knew where that was."

Angelo's was *the* place for Italian cuisine in Los Angeles at that time. The pasta was cooked al dente and the sauces had the full body provided by garlic, red wine, and extra-virgin olive oil. His wife, Angela, baked the bread every morning.

I found Jackson and Jean-Paul sitting with a square-shouldered, square-faced man wearing Brooks Brothers gray. When I entered the semisecluded booth at the back of the restaurant, the stranger rose first.

His glasses frames were rose-gold in color, and his blue-gray eyes reminded me of Clive

Chester's—wary of the new. Once again I was an unknown quantity in a previously known universe.

"Monsieur Merkan," Jean-Paul said, also rising. "This is the man I was telling you about."

"Easy Rawlins," I said, extending a hand.

"You're the one making these accusations?" he said, not taking the proffered hand.

"I'm the one setting up the proof," I corrected. "Jackson here is the one who made the allegation."

The flesh around Merkan's left eye quivered.

"Shall we 'ave a seat?" Jean-Paul suggested.

"I want to tell you right off that I don't believe a word of this," Merkan said as soon as we were settled. "John Portia and Theodore Huggins have been with my company for nearly twenty years. Johnny's engaged to my niece."

Angelo came to our table at that moment.

"Easy," he hailed.

I stood to hug the Italian-born restaurateur. He was a roly-poly man with coarse mustache hairs, an antifascist who had a great love of his native land. Bonnie and I had met him one evening on a date at his place. I started talking about my experiences in Italy during the war and won his favor.

"What do you wish for dinner?"

"Just keep it comin'," I said.

He nodded and said to my guests, "You are all welcome here."

He went away, and a slender young short-haired waiter came to serve us red wine.

When the waiter had gone I said to Merkan, "If you don't believe it then why did you come?"

"Are you questioning me?" Merkan asked.

"Are you calling Jackson a liar?"

My insolence enraged the captain of industry, but I didn't mind; I had learned in the war, by bitter experience, that all of us, in spite of any constitution or theory of government, were equal, and equally vulnerable to one another.

"What right does either one of you have to impugn the integrity of senior officers of one of the largest companies in America?" he stated.

"Jean-Paul," I said.

"Yes, Easy?"

"Maybe we should call the police in on this. I know a cop would probably come out. Mr. Merkan can go home to his bags of money and wait for the news of his officers' arrest."

"Henri?" Jean-Paul said to Merkan.

"What?" Merkan snapped.

"It is either you or the police. I believe these men, my men. I want to see what is 'appening."

Merkan didn't like Negroes; he most certainly had never been on eye-to-eye terms with one. He probably didn't like the French either. But there we were.

"Fine," he said. "But when I prove to you that

this little shit here is lying, I expect you to can his ass."

Jackson held up his wineglass, giving a wordless toast. Jean-Paul smiled broadly.

The hotel suite was well-appointed, composed of colors that were muted and austere, gathering light from the chandelier and lamps and magnifying it with oddly subdued intensity.

Jackson and I were sitting in the living room area. He was sipping cognac while I drank Coke from a six-and-a-half-ounce bottle modeled, it seemed, after the figure of Jayne Mansfield.

"I got three microphones hidden around the room, Easy," he'd told me before we entered. "JP and Merkan will be able to hear everything in the connecting suite."

"So what do you think about *Cotton Comes to Harlem* now, Jackson?" I asked to keep up his courage while not letting anything important come out with the white men listening in.

Merkan had been joined by two white security men outside the restaurant. They wore suits of a slightly inferior cut to their master's and carried pistols in shoulder holsters.

"I think that Himes is equal to Ellison," Jackson opined.

"You compare *Cotton* to *Invisible Man*?"

"Not just that," Jackson countered. "Chester got

thirteen other books and still countin'. Ellison is good, but you know the word *masterpiece* comes from paintin'."

"So?"

"There ain't nevah been an artist in history evah painted just one paintin' and had it called a masterpiece. You got to do a lot of work, get experience before you can say somethin' like that. I like Ralph's book, but I think it's Chester get down to where the shit stinks. Ellison made a window that the white man could look inta, but it's Chester made a door so we had a way out the burnin' house."

At that moment I forgot about TexOk and fingerprints, about a boy who wanted to kill the man that had gotten me to save his life. Jackson had the ability to set a fire in my mind. He was forever thinking, and a thinking man is always in trouble—especially if his skin doesn't fit into the color scheme of the dominant culture.

The bell to the suite chose that moment to ring.

Jackson made to rise but I gestured for him to stay where he was.

I went to the door and opened it.

There were five men there to greet me. The man up front and two directly behind him were muscle. I expected that. If Jackson really had shot a cop, which I'm sure Charles Rumor had claimed, Johnny and Theodore would have been fools to come unprotected.

The three white men in cut-rate business suits were probably off-duty cops, or maybe they were ex-cops or underemployed security guards. Their stances indicated that they expected trouble.

I smiled and stepped backward.

"Come in, gentlemen," I said in greeting.

The two backup guards pressed past me and checked out the rooms. They searched the toilets, bedroom, and utility kitchen—went through all the closets. Nothing. The door to the connecting suite was locked. There was really no reason to be suspicious of that.

Finally the principals came in.

Theodore Huggins was once again wearing the brick red suit and blush pink shirt that Jackson had described. He was tall and blousy. Rumor and Jackson were right: He did look like an animate pile of rubble. Even his grayish complexion reminded me of the mortar used to pave factory walls and chimneys.

Huggins's hair was close-cropped, black with a few stubbles of white. Johnny Portia had longish, Elvis Presley–like black hair and wore a dark green suit that was tailored to his compact form. He carried a sleek black briefcase with his left hand.

One of the two bodyguards whispered something to the one that lagged behind. This man in turn whispered to Huggins, who replied, "Okay, Turner, have your men wait outside. We'll only be a few minutes."

Huggins then turned to me, saying, "You too."

"Not hardly," I replied. "Jackson is skittish, and he paid me fifty dollars to sit by his side."

"That's right," Jackson said. "Porterhouse here is the best friend money can buy."

And so it was the five of us, there to do business in a particularly American fashion.

The layout of the room was a cream blue-footed sofa surrounded by three similarly upholstered chairs. The coffee table was frosted oak with dragon feet for legs. Jackson and Johnny sat side by side on the sofa while us others took the chairs.

Portia put the black briefcase on the table, opened it, and took out a contract sheaf. Underneath this document lay a few bound stacks of money.

"You have to sign each page," the TexOk officer said. He handed Jackson a fancy-looking pen.

Jackson looked to me and I shrugged.

My mind was already past that room. I was wondering about dead men and their legacies, young men and their desire for fathers and revenge. I wondered what Mouse would do if he was Merkan. That thought made me grin.

"I been thinkin' about this, Mr. Portia," Jackson said, as we had planned. "I mean, once I do this I'm out. JP'll fire me. He might try and put me in jail."

"I will send you to spend the rest of your life in prison," Portia promised.

"I know that. But here you want my signature and I don't even have the gun."

"I have no reason to burn you unless you betray me," the VP said.

Betrayal, I repeated silently. It was an odd concept for this criminal.

"But if I got to run I'll need more money," Jackson argued.

"Ten thousand is all I'm giving," Johnny said. He was in charge and reveling in the power.

"How much did you pay the other two?" Jackson asked. "I'm the senior officer."

"You're just a monkey dressed up in business-man's clothes."

Turner, the gunsel, glanced at me. He was younger but I was larger. Wherever he came from, he had learned that black men don't appreciate being talked to in that manner.

I looked back with no aggression in my eyes. If I had been Mouse, all three white men would have been in jeopardy by then.

That was when the connecting door came open.

Jean-Paul and Merkan followed their gunmen in. Turner leaped to his feet, but the two security guards already had their weapons out.

"Henry?" Portia said. He was too shocked to stand. "What are you doing here?"

Instead of answering Merkan went to the coffee table and picked up the papers.

"You don't understand, Henry. This man came to me. It was his idea."

Merkan looked from Huggins to Portia and back again. He took a deep breath and held it. Then he handed the documents to Jean-Paul, who immediately scanned the papers for the other two signatures.

"Go home, John," Merkan said. "You too, Theo. Go home. I'll have your offices packed up and sent to you by the end of the week."

"Henry," Johnny Portia said.

"Go."

"You're going to be sorry for this, Blue," Johnny told my friend.

Jackson cowered even though he knew that he was safe.

After our guests were gone, Jackson, JP, and I sat in the sumptuous living room. Jackson's face was glistening from sweat. It took all of the courage he could muster to face his blackmailers. I realized that over the years he had developed some semblance of personal bravery.

"'Ow can we repay you, Easy?" Jean-Paul asked.

"Hold that money and let me sleep in this suite tonight."

"That is all you want?"

"It's all I need," I said.

Jackson and his boss left soon after that. I curled up on the sofa because I didn't have the strength to make it to the bed.

41

"Sir?"

I was on a dusty road in Louisiana, the sound of war and suffering faint, and getting fainter, behind me. I was bone tired, but that didn't matter, because I had escaped the conflagrations of a lifetime. Survived? Maybe not, but survival is overrated, as a man I once called friend often said.

"Sir?"

There was the mild scent of brine in the air. The ocean. Anthropologists, Jackson Blue told me, say that all human life began in Africa, but life itself had started one day when lightning struck the deep blue sea. That's where I was headed, away from everyone else that was hating and bleeding and dying because they didn't know any better.

"Sir, are you all right?"

My eyelids were stuck together by the teary secretions of sleep. I managed to get them partly open to see the short white woman in a blue housekeeper's uniform.

"Hello," I said, blinking at burning eyes.

She looked concerned, as if she didn't really want me to awaken. Maybe she thought I was dead.

"Are you all right?" she asked again.

"I think so."

"What are you doing here?"

The question confused me. The bewilderment must have shown in my face, because the slightly stout, middle-aged brunette added, "In this room."

"I was working," I said, "for the man who paid for it. Jean-Paul Villard, CEO of Proxy Nine."

It was her turn to be mystified. She understood all of the words but not coming from me.

"There's a phone on the table over there, darling," I said. "Call the front desk and have them check with Jean-Paul if you want."

I got up from the sofa and walked deliberately to the bathroom. By the time I'd showered the maid was gone. I called downstairs and asked for them to send up a razor and a pack of Camels.

"Yes, sir, Mr. Rawlins," the desk clerk said brightly.

They had called Jean-Paul, and he had paved my dark footsteps with gold.

"Hello?" Peter Rhone said, answering Etta's phone at eight fifty-one.

"Raymond there, Pete?"

"He's asleep, Mr. Rawlins."

294

"I promise you he will be more upset if you don't wake him."

"If you say so."

"Yeah?" Mouse said into my ear nearly ten minutes later.

"We got to talk, Ray."

"Now?"

"It's important and it's business. Your business, not mine."

"All right. What is it?"

"Down at my office," I said, "in an hour and a half."

"Whatever you say, brother man. I'll be there."

My car was valet parked by the hotel. Jean-Paul had made sure that everything was paid for. He'd also explained, probably to the manager of the hotel, that I was to be treated like they would treat him.

In America money could buy anything, even pretend dignity.

I downed another bottle of Mama Jo's elixir and pointed my car back toward the slum.

The word slum and the word slump are only separated by one hunchbacked letter, Jackson Blue had once said. *That's a hopeful sign.*

I had asked him why he thought so.

Because, Easy, a slump is just a temporary

kinda thing. The fact that you in a slump means you gonna come out of it sooner or later.

My energy increased with the drive, my optimism too. There was change on the wind and hope in the air.

42

My office was on the third floor of a block-long building between 76th Place and 77th Street. It was on a floor of various businesses owned by blacks and whites. There was a locksmith, a notary public, a seamstress from Eastern Europe, and a Negro lawyer who had whiter skin than most white men I knew. There was a theater company at the end of the hall, the Afro-American Mobile Theater Group, that had a room the size of a janitor's broom closet where they rehearsed their civil rights plays seven nights a week.

The sign on my blue pine door still read, EASY RAWLINS—RESEARCH AND DELIVERY. That was the title I used before I had a valid PI's license.

Mouse was blocking the sign. He wore a pink suit and a lime green dress shirt with a slender violet tie and a short-brimmed straw hat that had been woven by a master. There was no bulge or other evidence that he was armed, but that didn't fool me.

"You plannin' to go to some cotillion after our meeting?" I asked him as I worked the brass Sargent key in the lock of my door.

"Felt good to be alive this mornin', Easy. Thought I'd put on something bright and happy."

I just laughed and pushed the door open.

It was a midsize office, big enough for the extralarge desk that sat near the far window looking down on Central, and a blue sofa for the nights I might not make it home. I made my way behind the desk and took a seat. Mouse looked at the three visitors' chairs and then at the closed door behind him. He moved the rightmost chair against the far corner in front of a little recess formed by the outcropping of a structural beam.

Most men worried about sitting with their backs to a door, but that was usually just self-inflation and pretense. Mouse, however, truly was a man with enemies.

"What's up, Easy?" he asked, leaning his chair back into the recess.

"Frank Green."

Mouse grinned and shook his head.

"I used to have a girlfriend," he said. "A woman who was a minister in a storefront Baptist church. She told me that she wanted to save my soul. I figured that was as close to God as I was ever likely to get.

"Anyway, Reverend Antonia used to tell me that whatever goes around comes around. I thought

297

that was just some Holy Roller hocus-pocus, but then here comes Evander, and damn if that fine young minister didn't know her words."

"He's Frank Green's son?"

"Frank was a wild man, Easy. He make me seem like some kinda angel. Back when you had all them problems with him and DeWitt Albright, he had falled in love with a fourteen-year-old girl."

"Timbale?"

Mouse nodded. "Grabbed her right off the street and locked her in a room in his house. Made her into his woman like he was some kinda wild animal ruttin' after a mate. Then I killed him and Timbale went home. When they found out she was pregnant they kicked her out, and I been givin' her two hundred dollars a month evah since."

"Why?"

"Because I killed Evander's father and her parents wouldn't stand up for what was right."

"Evander thinks he should kill you," I said. "He feels that that's his duty."

"I understand that. I murdered his father. What else he gonna do?"

"Ray."

"What?"

"Evander could no more kill a man like you than a fly could topple a lion."

"So? It only matter that he try."

"And if he does that?"

Raymond tilted his head to the side. "He'll die like a man."

"No."

"No? What else could he do?"

"Not him, man, you," I said.

"Me? What can I do?"

"I want you to deny killing Frank Green. If Evander asks you I want you to tell him that you didn't do it."

The consternation on Mouse's face was almost comical. He pulled his chin in and raised his hands in a confused gesture.

I understood. He felt respect *and* responsibility for the boy. Mouse had killed his own step-father and biological father at different times, in different conflicts. This was a way of life for him.

I wondered how I could explain that it was more important to keep Evander alive than to duel with him in order to show respect for his manhood. It was going to be a difficult discussion and possibly even dangerous.

It was almost a relief when the heavy thud came against my office door.

It wasn't a knock but a strike meant to break the door in. There were a couple of extra bolts that engaged whenever I closed the door, so it took two more blows for them to break in. By that time Mouse was on his feet, plastered into the recess with that terrible long-barreled .41 in his hand, pointed, for the moment, at the ceiling.

For my part I grabbed the receiver of the telephone. There were two reasons for this: First, I thought that if the intruder had heard voices, the phone would be a good explanation for what he'd heard, and second, I wanted his attention on me and what I was doing.

Three big white men rushed in. They all wore cheap suits in dark hues: green and blue and gray.

Fear hit my heart like an electric jolt, and suddenly I was alive again for the first time since going over that cliff. It was a miracle that I had no time to contemplate.

I wasn't worried for myself. It was these foolish men with their numbers and confidence, their last mistake if I, the living Easy Rawlins, didn't think fast.

"Where is he?" the man on my right said.

"Who?"

"Evander."

Just mentioning that name brought the white hoodlum closer to death.

"Who's that?"

"Don't try to shit us, brother man," he said. "We talked to a girl named Vixie. She told us that she brought him out to a place in the woods up north."

"I don't know what you're talking about," I said. "I never go anywhere near the country."

Incredibly the men hadn't looked behind them. If they did Mouse would kill them. If they drew on me Mouse would kill them. If they mentioned Evander's last name he'd do the same.

"Vixie took us to a house we know, and this guy named Yancy told us all about you. Black dick name of Easy Rawlins who went around asking people where this Evander was."

The options for a living solution were diminishing. Mouse was slowly bringing the muzzle of the pistol down in line with the middle man's head.

The good thing about my telephone is that I'm a restless talker. I like to wander around the room, looking out the window and then back to see who might be in the hall while I talked. That meant the curled wire to the receiver was very long. I threw the thing with all my might at the guy on the right. It hit him in the forehead, dead center.

It was my next action that surprised me. I climbed up on the desk and jumped at the guy in the middle. While I wrestled him backward, Mouse clocked the guy to the left with the heavy barrel of his gun. The man I'd jumped pushed me against the desk and was reaching for his gun when Mouse struck him.

I turned toward the guy I hit with the phone and hit him with an upthrust elbow to the chin. His head hit the wall and when he bounced back I elbowed him again.

The fight was over just that quickly. The men were down if not completely out. They floundered like stunned fish out of water while Mouse went from one to another, relieving them of their weapons and tapping them more or less lightly if they seemed about to rise.

Since getting my PI's ticket I kept various law enforcement paraphernalia in my file cabinet. Mouse and I handcuffed the dazed men wrist to wrist in a circle with their backs facing one another. That way they had no real ability to escape.

"Damn, Easy," Mouse said when this operation was complete. "You gonna make me into a mothahfuckin' saint."

"You go on, man. Leave the stooges with me."

Mouse shrugged his pink shoulders and made his exit. On the way out he stepped on one man's hand. The intruder yelled and Raymond slapped him with his pistol, as if to prove that his sainthood was only a temporary aberration.

I placed chairs over the chains that held them. The weight kept them on the floor and unbalanced. I also produced a pistol, which calmed their desire to complain.

Then I called the one policeman I trusted, Melvin Suggs, and told him that I had a surprise.

43

Detective Melvin Suggs had taken up permanent residence at the 77th Street precinct, and so he and four uniformed police were at my office in less than ten minutes.

In that time the guy I'd hit with the telephone, who wore the green suit, told me, "Nigger, if you want to live you better take off these cuffs and let us go. You have no idea who you're messin' with."

"I'd like to, man," I said. "I really would, but I'm already scared. And if I undid those cuffs who's to say you wouldn't try to get even with me for hittin' on you like I did?"

"You got the gun."

"And the police are coming. I have never seen nor have I heard of a black man shooting a white man and not going to prison. Only during the war, and even there you had to be careful. I knew one guy got tried for attempted manslaughter when a German officer blamed him for shooting him when he said that he was unarmed and trying to surrender."

The man in the green suit tried to rise and I pushed him down with my foot. He was a large specimen, younger, taller, and bulkier than I. The

303

fact that I had saved his life only served to earn his eternal ire.

"Easy." The voice came from my destroyed doorway.

Melvin Suggs was four inches shorter than I, about five-nine, with beautiful fawn-colored eyes and thick, gnarled hands. His body was bulky too. I was used to seeing him in shabby suits and wrinkled shirts with at least three or four grease spots here and there. But that day his tan suit was pressed and his white shirt bright enough to be new. His usually dull shoes were shined, and he might have even lost a pound or two.

"What's her name?" were my first words in the delicate situation.

Melvin stared at me while his uniformed minions piled into the room around him.

"What's going on here, Rawlins?" a sergeant, I'd forgotten his name, said.

"Office invasion," I replied. "These men broke down my door and accosted me. I'm pretty sure they meant me physical harm."

Suggs looked at the trapped white men.

"And you subdued the three of them all by yourself?" the sergeant asked.

"I was with a friend. He and I caught 'em off guard. I guess they weren't expecting any kind of resistance."

"Who was the friend?"

"Guy named Navrochet," I said. That was one of

Raymond's stepfather's sons who got it in mind to revenge himself on my friend. He'd been dead for a very long time.

"Where is he?"

"There was a church meeting that he couldn't miss. Deacon, you know."

"What church?"

"I forget the name, but it's the big pink Baptist one on Hooper."

The uniforms didn't like me, but I had too much juice with their superiors for them to treat me like they did the rest of my brothers. It wasn't that I was loved by the upper echelons of the LAPD; it's just that I was useful when they needed a window on the communities of color.

"This man attacked us," the green suit protested. "He pulled a gun on us and beat us with five of his friends."

I could see that at least two of the officers were inclined to consider this alternative explanation.

"Really, Keith?" Suggs said. "You think that I'm gonna believe that Haman Rose's top lieutenant was bushwhacked by a black man? Did he break down his own door too?"

"You know this man, Lieutenant?" the sergeant asked.

"This is Keith Handel. He works for the Mickey Cohen of West L.A., Haman Rose."

"I disarmed them, Melvin," I said. "Their guns are on the desk."

305

"He attacked us!" one of the other goons shouted.

"And how did that happen? You got lost on your way to the beach and then he just decided to beat on you," Melvin asked, "and then he called the cops for a joke?"

"Yeah," the seated felon said, looking as stupid as he felt.

"Andrews," Suggs said.

"Yes, Lieutenant?" replied the sergeant.

"Take these men down to the precinct. Book them on assault, breaking and entering, illegal possession of firearms, and throw in extortion for good measure."

"After we search the premises, sir?"

"Search for what?"

"We're here," Andrews said as if this was self-explanatory.

"Mr. Rawlins is the victim here, not a suspect."

"But, Lieutenant."

"Easy, when can you come down to press charges?" Melvin asked me, effectively cutting off any debate with his man.

"I got some business right now, but tomorrow will be fine."

"Take these men in," Suggs said to Andrews. "I'll be around a little later to sign the preliminary paperwork."

Two of the cops had taken up positions at the entrance to keep gawkers away from my gaping doorway. They came in and helped the three thugs to their feet.

"You got the keys to these cuffs?" one cop asked me.

I patted my pocket and then looked dumb.

"I guess Navrochet took it with him. Sorry about that."

It was a stumbly exit for the cops and their daisy chain of prisoners. The thugs complained while the people watching them from the various offices laughed.

My full resurrection was less than an hour old and I'd already made enemies who would remember me, and my address, for the rest of their lives.

"I heard that you were dead, Easy," Melvin Suggs said after the parade had departed.

"Yeah."

He wandered over to a visitor's chair and I sat in one too.

The Gator's Blood had changed in its effect; instead of feeling wild I felt a sense of powerful optimism.

"What do you have to do with Haman Rose?"

"I've heard his name before, but I have no idea who he is."

"He's based in West L.A. and Santa Monica, like I said," the rough-hewn, lovely-eyed cop told me. "He supplies drug dealers and leases numbers operations."

"Prostitution?" I asked.

"No. That's a labor-intensive industry. He doesn't like to have too many people in his employ."

Suggs had an abrasive disposition but we got along. He was tolerated by his bosses because he was so intelligent. This intelligence forced him to see the validity of many of my arguments.

"Either somebody died and left you a fortune or you're in love, Mel," I said. It felt good to be of the world, talking as if I belonged among people.

"You're not worried about Rose?"

"It's like you said, Lieutenant."

"What?"

"I'm already dead."

"A man like Rose wouldn't hesitate to put a bullet in the back of a corpse's skull."

I shrugged and shook my head.

"What's this got to do with prostitutes?" the cop asked.

I smiled at my only real friend on the force. He was a good man but he was still a cop.

"I really don't know what any of this has to do with me, Lieutenant. Four days ago I was in a coma. A friend took me out from my deathbed and we went up to the Sunset Strip to meet this girl he knew, a prostitute named Mary."

"How biblical. Did she oil your feet?"

"Something like that."

"You're not going to tell me anything?"

"Not a thing."

Suggs scowled at me a moment and then grinned. "My girl's name is Mary too."

"Where'd you meet her?"

"I busted her for buying a new Chanel dress with runny hundred-dollar bills."

We both went silent over that confession. It was a monumental revelation for a man like Suggs to make to a man like me—or to anyone else, for that matter.

"Did she get off?"

Suggs got to his feet and stared.

"You have yourself a good life, Easy Rawlins."

"You call me if you want to keep havin' yours," I replied.

I stood up and we shook hands as equals. He left my office headed sprightly for whatever Alamo or *Titanic* he was bound to.

I called Martin Martins and was lucky to find him in.

"Hey, Mr. Rawlins," he said. "I fixed the locks and put bars on all the windows. You could still break in if you really tried, but it won't be no cakewalk. I left the keys in the light fixture above the front door."

"That's great, Marty," I said. "I need one more favor."

"Name it."

I told him about my office door. He didn't ask how it got knocked in or why.

"I'll be right over. It'll just be a jury-rigged job, but it'll beat any new door just off the assembly line. I'll drop the key in your mailbox downstairs."

I levered the door into place so that it looked like it was closed; with the exception of some fresh splinters along the hinges the illusion was pretty good.

After that I got into my loaner red car and headed for the western part of town.

On the way I had more on my mind than it could hold at any given moment.

To begin with, I felt alive again. There was sensation in my fingers and toes. The breeze from the open window on my skin was somehow related to the here and now, not some weird flow from a nearby afterlife.

I was alive, and with life came a laundry list of worries. First there was Evander, a fatherless boy who wanted to kill my best friend because of a lifetime of brooding over the absence of his father. And then there was the shoulder wound on the dead man I found tortured in his very own chamber of horror. I doubted that Maurice Potter could have bled as much blood as I'd found on those burlap sacks and that money. He might have done, but he wouldn't have been able to drive home afterward. There was a lot of money and now there were gangsters to go along with it—gangsters that knew my name.

Flickering between these troubles was the image of Bonnie Shay. My near self-destruction had brought her almost back to me.

I reached the temporary Rawlins mansion by early afternoon. Jesus was making a variety of tamales along with dirty rice and collard greens. Benita was perched on a high stool near her man with Essie drowsing on her lap.

I could see Feather outside on a pool chair through the window wall.

"Hey, boy," I said.

"Dad."

"Mr. Rawlins," Benita added.

Essie cooed and I gave her my finger to grab.

"Thanks for staying here all this time," I said to the new parents.

"It's okay," Benita said. "But you know me and Juice got to get back soon."

Benita was often the mouthpiece for the couple.

"We need to put our house together," she added. "And we have friends that can look after Essie now that Antigone ain't here for you."

"I thought Nurse Fowler said that she was going to keep coming for a while," I said.

311

"Doctor told her that if you were out and about you didn't need her. Today was her last day."

"I was just making these tamales for you and Feather," Jesus added. "I know you both like them, and I didn't know if you were going to have the time to cook."

There's something wonderful about domestic life: not much struggle and hardly anything to think about. It's like being in love and asleep at the same time, blissfully floating.

"Go on home, you two," I said. "I'll take Feather where she'll be safe."

At poolside I pulled a plastic yellow chair next to Feather. Frenchie, the little yellow dog, looked at me for a moment, remembering, I think, the days that I was his enemy. But he trotted right up to me and sniffed my shoes in greeting.

"Hey, baby," I said to the daughter of my heart.

"Oh," she said, "hi."

"I'm sorry for all this. I mean, I didn't plan it; it's just that I knew I had to get a jump start or I might have died."

"I know."

"Then what's wrong?"

Even though she was lean and endowed with a cutting intelligence, Feather's visage was often soft and contemplative. Her stare was like a large unidentifiable object submerged just far enough underwater to keep its true nature hidden.

"What?" I asked.

"I still want to know about my mother," she said with gravity. "Juice told me that all he remembered was the day that you brought me to the house and told him that he had a new sister."

My other worries, seemingly of their own volition, climbed quietly over into the backseat of my headlong life.

"Well?" Feather asked.

"Well what?"

"Did you know my mother? Are you my father?"

"No," I said. "I never knew your mother. I never met her. She was already dead and you had no place to go, and so I brought you home with me."

"I want to know what happened."

There was a long moment of silence inside my mind. In that hush was the memory of a white mother slaughtered to protect her family from shame, killed by her own father and disowned by a mother who was so distraught that she'd been institutionalized afterward.

"Daddy?"

"It's a hard story, baby, but I know it all. I got to keep my mind clear until I finish this thing with Uncle Ray, but I promise you that I will tell you just as soon as this mess is over."

"You promise?" It was her child's voice.

"Cross my heart and yours too."

She jumped out of her chair and dropped onto

my lap. There was some vestigial pain from the car accident, but Jo's medicine had done more than mask the symptoms—I was on the mend.

An hour later Feather and I were pulling up into the driveway of Royal Crest not far from Olympic. The green-and-white house had a wide porch and rare double doors for an entrance.

Feather and I walked up the six porch stairs, but Bonnie opened the doors wide before we could ring the bell. She was wearing a white dress that had drapelike creases from the waistline to her calves.

"Hello," she said, kissing Feather twice in the European fashion.

She hesitated half a second before kissing my lips.

Looking over her shoulder in the middle of the peck, I saw why.

Joguye Cham, Ashanti royalty personified, was standing in the living room gazing bitterly upon our intimacy. We had never met, but I had seen his photograph more than once in the *Los Angeles Times* and *Examiner*.

"Joguye!" Feather said as she ran to the tall, slender, night-dark man.

He embraced my daughter. Why shouldn't he? It was his influence and wealth that had saved her life.

"Come in," Bonnie was saying to me.

The sunken living room was decorated with real African art and furniture. Horn and hide, feather and foreign wood made up the room, which smelled of frankincense.

Joguye and I were introduced. I don't remember shaking hands.

The discomfort in the room was made clear by the fact that no one sat down.

I asked Bonnie if Feather could stay with her a few days until my business was through.

After agreeing, Bonnie started talking about a new route that would take her to the South Pacific twice a month. Feather expressed interest. Bonnie said that they could go together in August. . . .

"So you want your woman back after sending her away like a dog," Joguye said.

"Cham!" Bonnie complained.

"That's about the size of it, brother," I heard myself say. "I been down so many dead ends that I didn't know a throughway when I saw it."

"Feather is not your daughter."

He knew this because Bonnie had to tell his doctors that a blood test from me wouldn't help their treatments.

"Not by blood," I halfway agreed.

"I am building a new nation, a world that would embrace both of them," Joguye said, and for a moment I saw the zealot that lived inside his body.

"And all I got to offer," I replied, "is a hard road that you have to crawl on as often as not."

"My people are warriors," he said.

"And mine are sick of war."

Feather moved half a step away from Joguye.

Bonnie came up and took me by the arm.

Joguye blinked. I think that this might have been tears for him. He nodded once and walked around us toward the door.

"Cham," Bonnie called.

But he just kept on going, out the door and into the street.

"I'm sorry," I said to Bonnie.

"It's not you, Easy. Humiliation is a cultural stigma for most African men. Their pride is magnificent, and also an Achilles' heel."

Bonnie made us hot dogs with French mustard and sourdough bread. After a while we were all laughing and happy. Joguye was no more than a shadow cast from a tree outside, through a window that protected us from wind and rain.

The front door of Terry Aldrich's mansion was ajar. This worried me, but I decided to leave the pistol nestled under the belt on the left side of my waist. The foyer was crowded with shoes and coats, duffel bags and two or three suitcases. It was an upscale hippie crash pad, and an open door might have been just as much policy as the sign of a crime.

I heard sounds to the left and followed a corridor of small doorways to an unfurnished room almost large enough to be called a hall.

Ten or twelve young people dressed in gaudy rags sat in the riches of that home. Terry was one of them. Ruby was sitting on his lap. Coco/Helen sat apart from the group on the marble ledge of a dead fireplace.

Two fat joints were being passed around. A woman was softly playing a large guitar in Spanish style with great speed and articulation. There were two black members of the temporary tribe: a man and a woman, both of whom wore brightly colored and beaded headbands, though they didn't sit together.

"Easy!" Ruby shouted.

She jumped out of Terry's lap, ran to me, and kissed my lips wetly.

"Come on in," Terry hailed, waving me over.

I managed to lever myself down on the marble floor next to Terry. Ruby got back on his lap and took me by the hand. This gesture, more than anything else at the time, showed me the heart of hippie logic and philosophy. All the old rules about gender and race, class and relationship had been temporarily jettisoned for the hope that people could come together like any other social animal. We could sniff butts and rub noses, share our warmth and howl at the moon together without spoken agreements, contracts, or laws. There might have been a hierarchy, but this was a shifting thing, and the herd was more important than any temporary leader.

Somebody offered me a joint but I just passed it on.

"You a narc?" a redheaded, broad-shouldered young man asked. This accusation, strangely, carried no ire.

"No. I just need to stay straight to make sure I don't get my head shot off."

"Nobody's gonna shoot you here, man," said a young woman with hair so fair that it didn't seem human.

"This is just a stop on my way," I replied. "Terry?"

Terry took a hit off the joint I passed on, and so it was a moment before he could exhale and then catch enough breath to talk.

"Yes, Easy?"

"Can I get you and Ruby and Coco to go somewhere where we can talk privately?"

"Sure, brother. Come on, girls."

"Women," Coco corrected.

"Women," the ugly young man said with a grin and an awkward, stoned nod.

There was a redwood picnic table in the overgrown backyard. Grasshoppers leaped and bumblebees hummed around us. There were green hummingbirds making the rounds of passion fruit vines. A cool breeze that passed one way and then another moved like an invisible snake weaving its way between and beyond us.

Ruby and Terry were high, very much so. Coco seemed as she had before.

"What can I do for you, Easy?" Terry said, placing both hands palms down on the table before him like a king at his judgment table.

"Three men broke into my office today," I said. "I think they meant me harm. One of them was a guy named Keith Handel. He said that he found out about me from people in your house."

"Bummer," Terry replied.

"Is it true?"

Terry paused, staring at me with both distraction and intent. He nodded to himself and then said, "Yancy was moving his stuff out and Vixie came over with Keith. That was yesterday, I think. I don't know what they talked about."

"How do you know Handel?"

"He works for this dealer, Haman Rose. I buy a kilo from Haman almost every week, you know, to keep my friends high."

"And Keith delivers?"

"No, no . . ." Terry drifted off then, looking at something in the sky.

"Terry."

"What, man?"

"How does Haman deliver?"

"He doesn't. Ruby or somebody else goes down to this Laundromat in Venice and picks it up for me. I let whoever it is that goes drive my Jaguar."

"Yeah," Ruby said with a dumb grin. "You just go in and act like you dropped off some laundry and they give you a cloth bag full'a dope."

"What about the police?"

"They got a deal with Haman," Coco said.

"You know him too?"

"Everybody up around here knows Haman. He supplies a lot of the grass and hash. Keith Handel makes sure people don't get ripped off."

"Oh."

"Handel had been looking for this guy Maurice," Coco said. "He was lookin' for Maurice and Evander. Vixie musta told him Evander's name."

"Yeah," Ruby said. "Vixie told me that Keith was looking for me, but then she told him what he wanted to know."

"He was asking everybody where could he find Evander," Coco added. "I told him I didn't know anything."

"Me too," Ruby added, "but Yancy had already told him your name."

"Have you been out to Mama Jo's?" Coco asked me.

"Not since we were there."

"I'd like to see her again."

"I'll tell her that," I said to Coco, and then to Terry, "When do you make your pickups from Rose?"

"Anytime. I'm one of his special customers."

"You mind if I go down with Ruby to pick up a key?"

"No problem. You wanna drive my Jag?"

"Yeah," Ruby said greedily.

"I'll drive," I said.

I stood up and then stopped, because King Terry looked as if he was about to utter some royal decree.

"You wanna talk to Vixie?" he asked me.

"Where is she?"

"She was sitting in the big room with us. Why don't you stay here and I'll bring her back."

Terry went to find the informer. Ruby went to change clothes, and Coco said that she was going upstairs to the roof. And so I was left there in the mansion's backyard. It was lovely and sumptuous, a shaggy retreat for the wealthy and their children.

It occurred to me that before my encounter with mortality I believed that wealth could somehow save me. This illusion had been dispelled by experience. I knew that all I owned was my body and its mind, and that was a tenuous bargain that would be scratched off in time.

"Here you go, Easy," Terry said, coming out of the back door.

Accompanying him was a sharp-featured, small-eyed redhead that I'd only glimpsed in the pot-smoking circle. She wore a black shift and had a reluctant frown on her face.

"Vixie?" I asked.

"What?" she said petulantly.

"The men you told about my man Easy here attacked him," Terry said. "He needs to know why they're after him."

"He already knows," she said, not looking in my direction. "He ripped off Keith Handel."

"What makes you think that?" I asked.

My tone made her look at me.

"He said so," she said.

"What did he say, exactly?"

"That you and Maurice stole his money."

"What about Evander?"

The question seemed to confuse her.

"Him too," she said, uncertainly.

"Him too what?"

"He said that Maurice and a black guy . . . you . . . I don't remember exactly. But he was lookin' for you because you were looking for Evander."

"Did you take Evander up to Caller's Creek?"

"Yeah. So what?"

"Did he tell you about blood on some money?"

"He was tripping," she said defensively. "Why did you leave him up there when you knew those men would have killed him?"

"I . . . I didn't know."

322

"You knew they tied him to a tree. You asked him where was the key to the bus locker and then left him with those animals. Why didn't you tell the cops?"

"I'm only sixteen. They would have sent me home or to juvy."

"You could have told me," Terry said. "I would have called the police to save him."

"What did Keith tell you about Evander?"

"That him and Maurice ripped him and Giles off?"

"Who's Giles?"

"He works for Rose too," Terry said. "And you don't have to worry about Haskell and his friends."

"Why?"

"They got busted tryin' to move the dope out of their camp when there was a fire the other day."

I wanted to say something else to Vixie. I wanted to make her understand, or at least to feel the kind of pain and danger she brought down on others. I wanted to hurt her.

So instead I shook Terry's hand and walked away from the false security of his wealth.

46

I took Ruby down to the beach in the Barracuda. She was wearing jeans shorts and a peacock blue halter. Her bare feet were up on the dashboard and her thin brown hair blew into the backseat from the window wind.

I noticed that her feet were white and clean.

"Do you ever wear shoes?" I asked her.

"If it gets cold or if I know I'm going someplace that has broken glass or a lotta rocks. Otherwise no. I like going barefoot. The only time I hate it is when you step on a cigarette butt. It's that burn that comes outta nowhere and won't go away."

"How often do you wash your feet?"

"I do it pretty much every day, and then there's Edgar."

"What is?"

"I know this guy named Edgar who lives down on Venice. He's married, you know, but he's kinda crazy about me," she said. "Well, maybe not about me, but people like me, and I don't think he's weird."

"And what's that got to do with your feet?"

"Edgar works at this parking lot over on Pico, and I go there and he washes my feet."

"Just washes them?"

"Yeah. He gets all excited about feet, and I don't like it when they get too dirty. He tries to pay me but I only take money if I need it for something. I tell Edgar that we're there for each other and he doesn't have to feel like it's for sale."

"What's he like?" I don't know why I asked. Maybe I suspected that there was more to the story.

"He's fat with curly hair and short fingers. Sometimes he cries when he's washing them. It's like some really important thing but really not about me at all."

I was quiet for a long while after that. Ruby was a truth that I didn't need to know. I wasn't afraid of or repulsed by her, but she was so loose in her approach to life that she flung doors open that wanted to stay closed.

"He's married and has three kids," Ruby said after a few minutes had passed. "I always call before I hitch down there. I asked him if he wanted to ball me one time but he said, 'No, ma'am, I couldn't do that.' I really like it that he calls me ma'am and then washes between my toes."

"We might have to lie to Haman Rose," I said.

"Why?"

"That guy Maurice used Evander somehow to steal money that I think belongs to Haman. Haman wants to hurt Evander, and I'd rather he didn't, and so I want to feel him out without letting on that I know Evander. You know how to lie, right?"

Ruby scrunched up her long face as if this notion was some long-ago memory.

"The best kind of lying," I continued, "is by limiting the truth."

"What does that mean?"

"Answer anything he says without letting on about me and my interest in Evander."

The hippie's eyebrows knitted as she gazed at me the way someone might look at a strange creature in a zoo. Then she nodded and smiled as if she had worked out my species.

"But what if he already knows?" she asked.

"Yeah," I said. Keith Handel knew, but Keith was still in jail—I hoped. "Even if he does, you don't have to. You just say that I know Terry, and Terry sent us both down there."

The Laundromat was on Lincoln Boulevard a few blocks south of Venice. It was a broad and shallow front with twenty or so coin-operated washers and maybe half that many dryers. On the right side as you entered was a waist-high counter behind which stood an Asian woman (I thought she might have been Vietnamese but wasn't sure) who worked folding clothes that customers dropped off to get washed and folded for fifty cents a pound.

"Hi, Loo," Ruby said to the short, rum-colored woman.

The laundress nodded but didn't smile.

"We need to talk to Mr. Rose."

"Busy," Loo said.

"But Mr. Terry said that we had to talk to him."

"Not here."

"If Haman wants to keep doing business with us he better get unbusy and come on out here," I said with some feeling.

Loo looked up at me.

Her right eye was dead in its socket with a jagged white scar starting at the temple and slashing down in the direction of the bridge of her nose. Her other eye worked but it seemed flat and largely unobservant, like a specialized organ designed for one purpose, detecting danger.

"You wait here," she said to me.

With that Loo put down the orange rayon sweater she was folding and went through what I can only describe as a fold in the wall beside the table she was working on.

"That was kind of rough, wasn't it, Easy?" Ruby said when the laundress had gone.

"I believe that she has lived through worse."

"But people should be nice to each other," she argued.

"I'm nice. It's just that my kind of nice comes from a place where people like it rough."

This admission elicited a smile from my protector.

I liked her too.

A few minutes later two white men in ill-fitting leisure suits came out from the wall like new characters in a dull and yet unpredictable play. The shirtlike jackets both had four buttons down the front. One suit was tan and the other almost black. The men were different heights; the short one on my left sported a mouse-brown mustache and the other one wore sunglasses. The man with the sunglasses and light-colored suit had a bandage on his left hand that seemed to go up pretty high on the forearm.

"Who are you?" the mustache asked.

"Name's Joppy," I said, "Joppy Shag."

The words rolled off my tongue easily. I remember thinking that I should have told Ruby that name before we entered the laundry. Joppy Shag had been a bartender and a good friend before he betrayed me and was subsequently murdered by Mouse. Joppy had died within days, maybe only hours, of Frank Green's demise.

"What do you want?" Sunglass Man asked.

Loo worked her way around the two men back into the room, then started folding again.

"I'm here representing Terry Aldrich," I said.

"So? He knows the procedure." That was Sunglass Man again.

"He did," I said. "And then Maurice Potter rolls up to Terry's and says that Terry gets a ten percent discount on three keys that he will deliver. He took the money but never delivered the dope."

The thugs looked at each other, and Mustache went back through the fold in the wall.

This departure acted as a kind of punctuation, a semicolon or a dash, in our conversation. Sunglass Man stared from behind his dark lenses while Loo folded and Ruby moved close enough that her shoulder was touching my left triceps from behind.

I noticed that there was some swelling and discoloration around the left eye of Sunglass Man. He'd been banged up pretty bad. I didn't think much about it at the time, because guys like him, and guys like me, often got dings and bruises from a day's labor.

Mustache came back in less than two minutes and said, "You two come on back."

The aperture in the wall was about half the width of a normal door. It went in two feet, stopped at a wall, turned left and then right and then left again, bringing us into a large room that had no particular purpose other than to hold two desks, half a dozen wood chairs, and a console radio, television, and record-player combo.

The television was set on a boxing match with the volume turned off. The record playing was Connie Stevens, and the radio was whispering news in hushed counterpoint to her sweet voice.

Behind the smaller desk sat a wide man in a dark purple suit with a black cashmere long coat draped across his broad shoulders. His face was birdlike but not delicate or fine; it was more like the visage of some ancient predator bird that ran down dire wolves in the times before man made his presence felt.

"What's this shit Bobby and Mitchell tell me?" Haman Rose said.

I answered, "Maurice Potter collected three hundred and fifty dollars from Terry promising to deliver product from you and then he just disappears."

"Terry knows that that's not how it works," Haman said. His gaze was both suspicious and contemplative.

"Terry had no reason to question Maurice. He said he was representing you."

"Was he with a nigger?" Sunglass Man asked.

"No," I said. "The cracker was alone."

Ruby giggled.

"And your name is?" Haman asked.

"Mr. Shag."

That got a smile out of the gangster boss.

"Well, Shag," he said. "All I can tell your boss is that Maurice wasn't working for me. He attacked my man Mitchell here and his friend too. We've been looking all over town for him."

Sunglass Man was Mitchell. His bruise and wound were making more sense.

"When did Potter tell Terry this lie?" Haman asked.

"A week ago," I said. "That's why Terry sent me with Ruby. He's runnin' low on product and wanted to know what's what."

"And there wasn't a colored brother with him?" Haman asked.

"Not that I know of. What was his name?"

"You think a man attackin' me's gonna tell his name?" Mitchell asked. He was belligerent.

"I don't know what happened, man," I said. "All I know is that Terry asked me to come down here and see where his shit is at."

"We're looking for Maurice," Haman said. "But he didn't work for me and so I can't help Terry."

"How much is this Maurice guy worth to you?" I asked.

"Why?"

"I could look for him if it meant a few dollars. I mean, I know a lot of black people who run around up on the Strip. Maybe I know the man was with Maurice."

"You find me Maurice Potter and I will put twenty-five hundred dollars in your pocket."

"I've seen Potter before," I said, "up at Lula's whorehouse behind the Shangri-La club. Can you tell me what the black man looked like?"

"Like a nigger," Mitchell said.

"You mean exactly like me?"

"He was younger and shorter," the henchman admitted, "a kid really. He had some heft too."

"Dark like me?"

"A little lighter."

"High voice or raspy?"

"He didn't say a word. His eyes were crazy, though. All over the place, and he looked scared."

"Is he the one beat on you?" I asked.

"You think you're funny?" Mitchell took a step toward me. His friends watched with some interest.

"I was just wonderin' if he was a bad dude or what," I said, getting into the rhythm of my persona.

"Maurice had the gun," Mitchell said. "Nigger just grabbed up the—"

"So that's all you need," Haman said, interrupting Mitch before he could talk about the money.

"Not much to go on," I said, "but I could look if you wanted."

That was a crucial moment. I was like a foreign soldier offering to become a spy for the enemy. They had no reason to believe me or trust me, but, then again, if I was a part of the robbery why would I be there?

"You know this man, Ruby?" Haman asked.

"Yes. He's been hangin' around Terry's lately."

"Do you know Maurice?"

"I've seen him. He's the one that always wears all green, right?"

"You ever seen Shag here with Maurice?"

Ruby turned to stare at me, thinking hard. This,

of course, made me wonder what I really knew about her.

Then she said, "I never saw them together."

"Did Terry send you?"

"He said we could take his Jag but instead we came in a red Barracuda."

This unimportant detail seemed to satisfy the headman.

"Okay, Shag," he said. "You go tell Terry that I can't help it that he threw his money away. Tell him that either me or Keith has to say the rules have changed. I don't have any dope for him today but he can send somebody down tomorrow.

"And if you find Maurice or his partner I will make it worth your while."

There were other questions I could have asked, but we had come to the end of our tête-à-tête. Haman Rose was a dangerous man: Ruby and I were in a precarious position as long as we were with him. He had given me a trove of unintentional information and all I had to do was push it just a little, but not in that room and not then.

"I'll be in touch," I said. "I surely will."

47

"You wanna pull into some parking lot and ball me in the backseat?" Ruby asked a few blocks from the Laundromat.

"What?"

"I'm all excited," she said. "I wanna get it."

She was sitting on her knees in the seat looking at me.

"I'm old enough to be your father, girl."

"You were the same age the other night at Terry's."

"And I thought you and Terry were a thing now." I don't know why I argued; maybe it was my way of biding time on the bigger issues in my life.

"So? People don't own each other. He doesn't care what I do."

"I'll get you up to his place and you can get together with him."

"You don't want me?"

"I want you in all kinds of ways, Ruby," I said with both feeling and honesty. "I do. But I got a job to do, and maybe there's a woman I love who I want to be with."

"That Bonnie?"

I nodded, thinking that she had paid closer attention to my words than I thought.

"What does she have to do with me?" Ruby asked.

I laughed at the brazen honesty of the hippie girl.

"Will you please let me off this hook, child?" I asked. "I'm an old man who almost died a couple of months ago, and right now I'm just trying to do a simple job."

She smiled and turned around in her seat.

"Sometimes I just don't understand men," she said to the world at large.

"What fun would there be in that?" I reached out and squeezed her hand. This seemed to satisfy her need temporarily. That was the least I could do. After all, Ruby had been instrumental in getting me over the hump of my slapdash investigation.

Ruby gave me another wet kiss before jumping out of the car at Terry's mansion. I watched her running on those young haunches, thinking that I was alive again but not exactly the same man. I would miss the old Easy Rawlins. He was running into the yard behind Ruby, looking for that sweet oblivion that all young men, white and black, thought could save them from the greater darkness that dogged their heels.

I arrived at the 77th Street precinct at a little past eight. The good thing about the police is that they're open twenty-four hours a day. It often seemed to me that the constabulary was a modern-day church—always there . . . waiting for your confession.

"Yeah?" the desk sergeant asked when I approached his desk.

I had a valid carry license but left my gun in the car. The police in L.A. were a skittish lot. Even the sight of a pistol on a black man's person might call down a hail of gunfire.

"I'd like a powwow with Melvin Suggs if you don't mind, Sergeant." I might have even smiled.

"Rawlins, right?"

"Yes, sir." I was feeling very Southern and civilized, the way that the ex-slave-owning, Jim Crow–enforcing white Southerners liked to pretend to be. I was a new man with a new life and three-quarters of a pack of Camels in his breast pocket. But the world I lived in had not yet registered the changes in itself or in me.

The wait was nearly forty-five minutes.

I was expecting Suggs to come from the swinging doors behind the desk sergeant's post, but instead he came through the front door wearing a burnt orange–colored suit and shiny black shoes. His pressed shirt wasn't even white; it was lemon with little cherry dots here and there.

"This way," he grunted as he rushed past me through the swinging doors.

336

We climbed three stairs and turned right through a door marked EXIT. This brought us to a stairwell that went up and down and to a door that probably went outside. I followed as Suggs rushed up the stairs all the way to the fourth floor.

There we crossed a large room filled with booking desks, alleged felons, and their captors.

It's a strange thing to see a powerful man's hands chained behind him, almost poetic in a brutal sort of way. Maybe those fists had beaten some hapless pedestrian to the ground, or the fingers had choked the life out of a woman that he loved so much he couldn't let go; but now those fists and fingers were like bunches of dark plantains hanging down around the crack of his butt, helpless in every way possible.

Melvin led me to a desolate corner of the booking floor where there was a brown door painted on in black letters that read, "off-limits"; no caps, no punctuation. Through this door and up half a flight we came to a solitary and dusty office, dimly lit through a window by an outside security light. Suggs ushered me in, shut the door, turned on the desk lamp, and then collapsed into his squeaky-wheeled chair.

I took my seat across the desk from him and lit up a Camel.

"I thought you'd be here at work," I said. "I didn't mean for them to get you out of bed."

"Do I look like I was in bed?" he asked. "I told

the desk to call me if you came in. I'm interested in this Rose thing."

"You still got them here?" I asked.

"Transferred downtown. They'll be out by eleven in the morning unless you decide to come in, with your friend, and make a complaint."

"My friend's shy."

"Yeah."

That might have been the end of our talk, but we both wanted something, maybe some things.

"You sure that Handel works for Rose?" I asked.

"For the past eight years," Suggs replied. "Why?"

"I don't know. I just heard that he might be working on his own, that's all."

"Hm," Suggs said, sitting back. "Yeah . . . that fits."

"Fits what?"

"Handel didn't call the Rose lawyer, and the guys he had with him were from Vegas. Neither one had ever been busted in L.A."

"Yeah," I said to myself. "That's what I thought." Because Rose didn't ask about Easy Rawlins. It seemed that he would have wanted to know about another black man that he'd sent Handel to brace.

"What you got on Rose?" Suggs asked. Then he yawned.

"First I need to know some things."

"Like what?"

"I know that Haman has two guys around him named Bobby and Mitchell, and you say this other guy is Keith Handel. Is there anybody else he's got?"

Suggs pulled a thick and dusty folder out of the desk and opened it up in front of him. He paged back and forth for at least three minutes.

"He's had quite a few cohorts over the years. He works for a downtown mobster named Lofty, Aaron 'Lofty' Purdy from Cincinnati. It says here that there's a Giles Lehman that he's tight with. Giles and Keith are his underbosses; at least, that's what the organized crime unit calls 'em. I say that they're just midsize thugs in a broke-nose jungle."

"You got an address on Lehman?"

"Why?"

"I'd like to strike a deal with him," I said.

"What kind of deal?"

"That's my business."

"I need more than that, Rawlins."

"Do you have in that folder that Haman Rose runs a Laundromat down near Venice and Lincoln and sells grass in laundry bags?"

"No."

"How about that he pays the cops down there to leave him and his business alone?"

Suggs had become subverbal, shaking his head and looking like he just licked a lemon.

"This is fact?" he asked.

"I don't know. It's just what I heard along the way."

"Okay," Suggs half agreed. "So if I sting this place I get Lehman too."

"I need to talk to Lehman first."

"Why?"

"From what I hear Giles Lehman and I have a lot in common."

"I'm still the law, Easy. I can't let you just go out and do whatever you want."

"I know that, Melvin, I do. That's why I'm giving you this. But if you're gonna want any more help I need that address."

It only took six or seven minutes for him to pass me the numbers.

G. Lehman lived on Renvert Street in Culver City.

The Gator's Blood felt like it was permanently in my system by then. I didn't even need to drink it anymore. I was tired but it didn't feel like I was about to die. It wasn't the first time that the blue sofa in my office stood in for a bed. I napped the night away, dreaming about a man on a raft sailing between two islands, both of which were in flames.

I woke up four or five times but always, when I fell asleep again, I was somewhere in relation to that man and his hapless voyage. He wasn't worried, this intrepid sailor. He knew that sooner or later, when the flames died down, the combatants would also be dead. All he had to do was keep from landing too soon and paradise would be his.

Giles Lehman's apartment occupied the middle floor of a turquoise-colored triplex in the center of the city-suburban block. I made my way up the inner stairwell somewhere around eight the next morning. I used the brass knocker to announce myself to a dead man.

That was the most logical conclusion. The only man missing was Lehman, Giles. The blood on those burlap sacks said that somebody had died. And Giles was the only man not around.

Knocking was a useless gesture, I knew, but there was a certain decorum that had been drilled into me since childhood. I would knock before breaking and entering; that's just what a civilized man was supposed to do. The knocker hammering against the cheap, wood-veneered frame door made a hollow sound.

I was counting to twelve out of deference. When I reached nine she pulled the door open, the smell of alcohol reaching me on her first breath.

"Who the fuck are you?" She was a synthetic

341

blonde, and lovely at one time, maybe even recently. Taller than most women and shorter than I, she wavered, unsteady from a nightlong bender, holding on to the doorknob and sneering.

"I'm looking for Giles," I said, half in truth. "I owe him some money and he said I could come by in the morning as long as it was after seven."

Details—give someone enough of them and it sounded like you were telling the truth. Add to that the possibility of money and even racial differences began to lose importance.

The woman was fortyish and grief-stricken. She'd been crying in her drinks and alone in a way that was contradictory to clear thinking. She stared at me, slowly culling through the words and the meanings they held in her jumbled and pickled brain.

"What's your name?" she asked after a lot of teetering and squeezing of eyelids.

"Sam," I said. "Sam Sellers. Did Giles tell you about me?"

"I . . . I don't remember. How much money do you owe him?"

"I'm sorry, ma'am, but I don't know you. Is this even Mr. Lehman's apartment?"

She grinned and was maybe trying to look sexy. She got lost in this role for a moment or so and then said, "My name is Shawnie. Shawnie Lehman."

She held up her left hand, which had a gold band on the ring finger.

"That just means you're married," I said. "It could be to some other man."

She invited me in, letting go of the knob and waving at the same time. All that motion was too much for her inebriated coordination, and Shawnie Lehman tumbled into my arms.

"Oops," she said, pressing against my chest to keep from dropping to the floor.

I got an arm around her waist and carried her to the sofa in the sun-bright sitting room that lay behind her. I put her on a walnut-footed coral couch that was shorter than its modern-day heirs. I sat in a plain white chair at the side. The floor was made from a golden-hued wood that I could not identify. It was a pleasant room, with a painting of flowers in a vase on the wall and a vase filled with dying roses on a stand between two large windows.

"Sam?" she said.

"Yes?"

"That's your name?"

"Yes, it is."

"Who sent you here? That pimp?"

"What pimp?"

"What do you want?" She was near tears.

"Are you okay, ma'am?"

"No. No, I'm not. Giles isn't here. He's not coming back either."

"He left you?" I felt like an ass misleading her, but what choice did I have?

"I got a bottle of good whiskey in the kitchen, Sam. Why don't you go out there and pour us both a shot?"

"It's kinda early, Mrs. Lehman."

"It's all the same fuckin' day, Sam."

I went through a doorway she gestured toward and found myself in a stubby little kitchen with bright yellow tiles and a table with its own benches built into the wall next to a window that looked out on a plane of red and green roofs.

The less than half-empty Sterling's whiskey bottle said that the spirits were twenty-five years old. I poured her a glass and me one too. I had no intention of imbibing, but she had to believe I was drinking with her if I was going to get what I wanted.

When I came back into the sitting room, a glass in each hand, I was met by a mostly erect Shawnie. She was holding a small-caliber pistol and grinning like someone who just pulled a good prank.

"Okay, now, Stan," she said. "Tell me what the fuck it is you're doing here."

"The name is Sam," I said as I leaned over to put the glasses down on the maple and blue-and-white-tiled coffee table in front of the short sofa.

Between my words and actions I used a backhanded swipe to grab the gun from her fingers.

"Hey!" she complained, "that's mine."

I sat down on the same white chair, flipped out the cylinder of the .25 pistol, removed and pocketed the bullets. Then I handed her the gun and said, "Here, you can have it. I just don't want to get shot."

"You think you're pretty slick, don't you, Stan?"

"Sam."

She slumped down on the couch, picked up a glass, and drained it.

"What do you want?" she asked.

"So many things that you'd think I was Little Lord Fauntleroy on Christmas Eve."

I smiled and Shawnie grabbed hold of the second glass, putting it away like a pro.

"Giles is gone," she said to the empty glass. "Him and Keith and that pimp thought they were so smart. Giles always thought he was some kinda mastermind. Make a big hit and go out to Vegas, that's what he said. Now I called down to the Laundromat and they told me he left town. . . ." Shawnie slammed the shot glass down on the table tiles and it shattered between her fingers. "You know what it means when they tell you someone's left town?"

I nodded and then looked down.

Her hand was bleeding.

I went back to the kitchen, got two hand towels and a glass of water. When I returned she was up again, pointing that pistol at me again—at least, I was pretty sure it was the same gun. The fingers curled around the butt and trigger leaked blood on the golden wood. There might have been ammunition in a hiding place, but I didn't think that she'd had the time or the coordination to reload.

Anyway . . . why should she want to shoot me?

She pulled the trigger on an empty chamber and there I was; a dead man who cheated the call once more.

She kept pulling the trigger as I walked up to her, put down the napkins and glass, and took the gun away again.

This time I sat next to her on the sofa, dampened one cloth, and washed off the bloody fingers. I felt around for glass in the cuts but found none. I wrapped the second towel around the little wounds and closed my fist gently around her hand.

"Hold it like this until the bleeding stops," I said.

"Thank you," she replied in such a way as to ask my understanding of her attempt at murdering me.

"Nuthin' to it," I said.

"I loved that fool," she uttered. Her eyes were the color of okra, striated green and bark with no glint or sparkle.

"Him and Keith were going to rob Haman?"

"And blame it on somebody else," she said. "They had it all planned. They were gonna use this guy named Jammy, a black man like you.

They told Jammy that he was gonna get ten thousand dollars. But really they planned to kill him and Mitch and blame the robbery on a gang of niggers. That way Haman wouldn't know, and me and Giles could move to Vegas in a few months or a year and set ourselves up out there. Giles said that we could buy a house for seventy-five hundred dollars and he could get a job as a dealer and we could have some kids."

It sounded like the kind of plan an underling might hatch, halfway smart. It would take you just far enough to get yourself killed.

"Only Jammy got busted for beating on his wife," Shawnie went on, "and they put him in jail. I thought they was gonna give it up, but when Bobby told me that Giles was gone I knew what happened. I knew it."

She shook her head and then laid it on my shoulder. I might as well have been an angel on a round of house-call confessionals.

A few spots of blood had soaked through the white napkin. Shawnie took a heavy breath that ended in a snore. We sat there for quite a few minutes, her sleeping and me wondering what to do.

I couldn't help Shawnie. She'd lost her brass ring and there was no getting it back. Giles's death was probably the best thing that could have happened to her.

After a long while I moved out from under the

sleeper and laid her as comfortably as I could on the squat divan.

As I passed out the front she called out, "Gilesy?"

I shut the door and went away.

49

On the drive back to my Genesee house I considered the problems that had arisen. The biggest one was, of course, my own resurrection from the mountainside crypt that a fool had earned himself and dumb luck had nixed. I was alive and no longer even in need of Mama Jo's elixir. I was a man again, on the job again, back in the world where nothing ever turned out right but it kept right on turning anyway.

Shawnie wouldn't remember that I'd been there, and even if she did she didn't know anything that could harm me. I was sure that when she sobered up she'd know better than to tell Rose, or anyone else, that she was privy to a plot to rob him of nearly a quarter million dollars.

Evander was almost home free; that is, except for the fact that he wanted to kill the deadliest man I'd ever known and was in love with the daughter of a woman that might give Mouse a run for his money in the dangerous department.

The stolen money was safe.

It struck me as funny and somewhat ridiculous that men died to obtain and protect money. It was like wild rams batting horns over water rights, or Shawnie believing in Giles even though she knew he was wrong.

I drove past Genesee on Pico and took the right on Stanley, parked a few houses down and crossed the street to the back duplex where the Noon family lived.

I climbed the white stairs, remembering the few days before, when every step felt like my last.

The screen door was open again. The off-the-shelf doorbell made its two-tone plea, and footsteps sounded from a place deep in the darker parts of the sunny unit.

When Beatrix Noon appeared, the first thing I noticed was that she had grown nearly two inches since last I'd seen her. Also, the hardness that I'd noted in her face the first time we met was greatly diminished. I thought that maybe she mimicked her mother only when in Timbale's presence.

"Hello, Mr. Rawlins," Beatrix said through the screen. She even smiled.

Looking down I saw that she was wearing high heels around the house. I would have bet that she only did this when her mother wasn't around.

"Hi, Beatrix. Is your mother in?"

"She's at the store." The girl was at ease with herself in the house, probably alone.

"Oh," I said. "When do you expect her?"

"Anytime. You wanna come in?"

"Maybe I should wait outside."

"No," the girl said. "Mama'd be mad if I made her visitors stay outside. Come on in and sit down."

She pulled open the screen door and I followed, pulled along by the gravity of her invitation.

I sat in the same backless sofa as before and she settled opposite me.

"Do they call you Bea?" I asked my host.

She shook her head no, and said, "Evy called and told us that you found him at the beach and brought him back."

"Yeah."

"But he can't come home?"

"With a little luck he'll be here by this time tomorrow."

"Is he in trouble?" Beatrix asked.

I had to remind myself that I was talking to a child. Her seated posture and attitude placed her well beyond her years. This reminded me of Feather, and, in another way, of the young hippies wandering up and down the Sunset Strip. The world was changing fast, and young people had to hurry to keep up with those changes.

"No," I said, answering Beatrix's question. "He just stepped on a couple of toes. You know that brother of yours has got some big feet."

That elicited a smile.

There came the sound of clattering from the back of the apartment.

"Beatrix?" Timbale called. There was the incipient tone of worry in her voice. I imagined that Timbale was always worried about her children—night and day.

"In here, Mom." Beatrix kicked off the heels and pushed them under her chair.

When Timbale entered the little den through the foyer she put on her angry face. Her eyes were searching for impropriety, and I understood why, seeing how as a teenage girl she'd been kidnapped and raped by the monster Frank Green.

"Mr. Rawlins just got here," the dutiful daughter said, rising from her seat. "He said that he'd wait outside, but I told him that you wouldn't like it if I made him do that."

Timbale didn't like my propinquity with her child, but she trusted Beatrix, and so I went unstabbed—for the moment.

"Go down to Brenda's house and get LaTonya," Timbale told her daughter.

"Okay," the girl said. She ran into some other part of the house and, less than half a minute later, she was bounding down the white stone stairs in boys' black-and-white tennis shoes.

"What's this nonsense I hear from Evander?" Timbale asked. She had no intention of sitting down.

"Your boy got himself into some deep shit, Ms.

Noon," I said. "That girl he met gave him some LSD. While he was high a man who needed a patsy fooled him somehow into getting involved in a robbery—"

"Not my boy!" Timbale threatened.

"Sit down, Ms. Noon."

Her eyes were wide and her fists trembling. Timbale wore a shapeless purple dress that had probably been stitched in Mexico, smuggled into Southern California, and sold downtown replete with fake tags.

Timbale sat down where her daughter had rested. Her look told me that I had better watch my words.

"The man who fooled Evander," I continued, heedless of her silent warning, "was in business with two other guys. They were all pulling a fast one on the boss of the other two. Maurice, the guy who tricked Evander, planned to double-cross his friends and leave Evander holding the bag. One man got killed and two others got shot—"

"Oh, no."

"Somehow Evander and the man who tricked him got separated and your son ended up with the money. Maurice was killed by his surviving partner, who is now looking for your son."

Timbale's eyes had narrowed to slits. I would have bet that she could have repeated my explanation word for word.

"Why?"

"It's a lot of money," I explained.

"So? My son is not a thief."

"That's right," I said, pointing a finger at her. "Your son."

"What's that supposed to mean?"

"The man looking for Evander is not the problem. He doesn't know a last name or where to start looking. He never even met Evander, so there's not much for your son to worry about on that account. What the trouble is, is you telling your son that Ray killed Frank Green."

"That's the truth," Timbale sermonized. "The God's honest truth."

"Yeah . . . and right after you told Evander that truth he told me that he intends to kill his father's murderer."

I could see the whole history of Timbale's bad luck in her shocked expression. The last thing she expected was her baby boy going out with a gun in his hand looking for revenge on the baddest man in town.

"No," she said softly, shaking her head in feeble denial.

"Yes," I said. "Yes and yes again. Evander's a man and you just told him that another man slaughtered his father. Now, what's gonna happen when he goes down to the places where Mouse hangs his hat? What's gonna happen when he goes out with a gun among those hard men?"

"I won't let him," Timbale said with devout certainty.

"Like you stopped him from goin' up to the Sunset Strip? Like how he came home when you told him to?"

"Why doesn't he come home now?" the mother wailed.

"He's with a woman and he's runnin' for his life," I said. "And if you don't talk to him and tell him that you have no proof that Raymond killed his father you might as well start shoppin' for pine boxes now, because he won't live out the year."

"What woman?"

"Timbale," I proclaimed, "don't be a fool. Men get with women; you know that. Evander's a man. He's a man and you're sending him on a mission of vengeance. All that anger and rage and years you sat up here nursin' a grudge don't even make no sense. You never saw Raymond kill Frank."

"How do you know that?"

"Because I knew Mouse back then. If he saw a witness, that witness was dead. Tell your boy the truth, that you don't know who killed Frank, and I'll handle Mouse."

Timbale's fragile eyes might have shattered if she blinked hard. Her chest was heaving, and I'm sure her fingernails had cut into the skin of her palms.

"I have the money Evander got away with," I said, suddenly persuasive and kind. "I can have it sent to you at a rate of fifteen hundred dollars a month for the next twelve years. That with your salary and whatever Raymond gives will make it so your kids can have a good life and none of them will need to die."

"After all these years you just want me to let it go?"

"What's worthwhile hangin' on to, Timbale? Frank raping you? Kidnapping you? Getting you pregnant and then livin' the kind of life that kills twenty-three outta twenty-five? You want Evander to seek your revenge? You want Beatrix and LaTonya to cry the rest of their lives? Make sense. It's ovah, honey. You ain't nevah gonna get back what you lost. Only thing you can do is take it out on those kids."

I had never uttered truer words, and Timbale heard me too. She hung her head down, and tears from some other lifetime dripped from her face. She shivered and shook and I knew enough not to try and comfort her. Giving up all that bile and hatred was a private duty, not one that could be shared.

She was still crying when LaTonya and Beatrix returned. The girls were both licking soft-serve ice-cream cones. That must have been part of their ritual, I thought: LaTonya would always be happy to see her older sister coming to take her home because that meant ice cream on the way.

"What's wrong, Mama?" the younger child cried,

running to put her arms around Timbale Noon's head.

Beatrix went to stand in the space between me and her mother. I was proud of both of those children.

"It ain't nuthin', baby," Timbale answered in a cracked voice. "Mr. Rawlins just told me that Evander was coming home and I started to cry."

"But you don't never cry," LaTonya challenged.

"I do when I'm happy, baby." Timbale sat up straight, staring at me. "Evander's coming home and everything is gonna be just fine."

I was thinking that if the four of us in that room were alive twenty years hence, we would all have different memories of that day.

With that thought I got to my feet and walked out of that place of joyful grief.

Driving back to the Genesee house I was feeling almost in synch with myself. I had performed my trials and earned back the life I'd thrown away. I was a new man at the threshold of a different existence.

That man parked in my driveway.

He was almost home.

I slammed the door shut on the borrowed

Barracuda thinking that I might like to keep that car as a reminder of those few days of purgatory.

"Mr. Rawlins," she called, and I knew instantly that there was still some distance for me to travel.

She was getting out from the passenger's side of a gold-colored Lincoln Continental parked across the street. The driver was Ashton Burnet. He came around the car to accompany Angeline Corey on the short span across Genesee toward me.

"Angeline," I greeted her. "Ashton."

"I'm not foolin' with you, Easy Rawlins," she said.

Ashton stood half a step behind her, a dark behemoth risen up out of the hell that so recently tried to pull me down. He was an inch shorter and three inches wider than I, with a reputation for violence that caused most rooms to go silent when he made an entrance. He was wearing a brown suit that paled on his dark skin, and a medium gray, short-brimmed Stetson that struggled to contain his hard head.

"I have always taken you seriously, Ms. Corey," I replied.

"Where's my daughter?"

"I'd be happy to look up the number if you wanted to call."

"I know the number, motherfucker," she said. "She told me that she was with that dopehead and that she wasn't comin' home."

"Evander never took dope on purpose," I told

her. "Somebody fooled him into taking it. He's a good kid. He loves your daughter."

"He just wants her ass, that's what," Angeline said.

"I don't think so."

"Are you contradictin' Angeline?" Ashton asked.

"Yes, I am, Ashton. If somebody's wrong they're wrong."

"He took the dope," Angeline said. "Now he's addicted."

"It's not like heroin, Angeline," I reasoned. "It's not the kind of drug like that."

"All drugs are like that."

"No," I said, "they're not."

"Watch it, Easy," Ashton warned.

"Listen, man," I said to the demon in mortal skin. "I almost died recently, just got out of my sickbed a few days ago. But that's no excuse. I couldn't take you if I was a hundred percent and fifteen years younger, but you know you don't wanna start this war."

Ashton took a step forward, but Angeline held him back with an outstretched arm. I was talking to him but addressing her. She knew that I was a force in our community just as much as she. I had friends like Mouse and the devastating ex–Green Beret, Christmas Black. I even knew police officials that called me mister.

"I'm just tryin' to protect my blood, Easy," Angeline said, trying her hand at reasonability.

"I know that. I know it. But she's more woman than child now. She's got to go with a man that wants her."

"You've seen her, Easy. She 'bout as plain as a brown paper bag, the kinda girl that men shit on and then walk away." Angeline was talking about another young girl, not her daughter.

"When Evander looks at her," I said, "he sees a woman on the same verse as him."

I think it was the subtle biblical reference that appealed to the lady gangster's imagination.

"You mean that?" Angeline asked.

"Why would I help a young man if I didn't believe in him?"

"Is he still in trouble?"

"A little bit, but not nearly the kind of calamity that you and me draw down."

That little morsel of truth got Angeline to smirk.

"Angeline," I said, halfway to pleading. "Esther is grown and as stubborn as you. You could hold her back and keep her down, but sooner or later she's gonna break out. And the later that happens the wilder the ride."

"I just want to keep her from bein' hurt," Angeline said plainly.

"When they were little they fell and lost their loved things," I preached. "They got bullied or came in last. All that was pain and they came to us and we told them that it was okay to feel bad and okay to cry. That's the worst you got with Esther

359

and Evander. He's not a wild child but a young man who thinks the world of your daughter."

I talked and she seemed to listen, but who knows what she heard me saying? Angeline stared at me. Ashton stood behind her, patiently waiting for the word to beat me down.

I had done my best. I wouldn't give up those children. It's always been my opinion that if a man's going to be a fool he should go all the way.

"You tell that boy that I expect to see him and my girl soon," Angeline said.

"I will call him tomorrow."

"All right then," she said, as if it was she who had won the debate.

I watched the woman and her golem cross the street and drive off in that gold luxury car. I could have walked into the house, but instead I went to the trunk of my automobile and brought out the second to the last bottle of Gator's Blood. I wasn't feeling weak anymore, but the mere presence of Ashton Burnet reminded me of how vulnerable my life was.

I put the bottle in the kitchen and called a number that I knew by heart.

"Mofass Real Estate and Construction," a young female voice said.

"Hey, Nesta, this is Easy Rawlins."

"Oh, hi, Mr. Rawlins," the young receptionist

and management trainee said. "Did you want that phone number?"

"I was hoping that you could give me the address where the phone was connected."

"I don't know," Nesta Charles said doubtfully. "Miss MacDonald only told me to give you the phone number."

"I'll wait while you call her, if that's what you need to do."

"Um . . . couldn't you wait till tomorrow morning when she comes in?"

"No, I can't, so either you call her or I do; I really don't care which."

"No, no," she said, more to herself than to me. "Of course I can give you the address."

Colby Street wasn't that far away. I made it there in less than half an hour. It was a broad road with boxy plaster apartment buildings dominating its architecture.

Evander and Esther's unit was on the third floor of a dull red box that had its stairs and hallways on the outside.

I climbed up to apartment 3F and knocked. It was a lazy afternoon, hot but dry. I could see a white haze of gnats roiling under an avocado tree down below in the backyard of the apartment building next door. The bugs couldn't take the bright sun and withering heat. I imagined them congregating there, humming a complaint about the light while praying to the tree for its continued shelter.

"Mr. Rawlins?"

The door had come open and Evander stood there in his jeans and a white T-shirt. He looked stunned but more aware than before.

"Hi, Mr. Rawlins," Esther Corey said, coming up behind her man.

She was wearing a blue cotton dress with nothing underneath. I supposed that they were learning all they could about sex, being free for the first time in a home of their own with no one to distract them.

"Can I come in for a few minutes?" I asked.

The two youths moved apart, allowing me entrée to their motel-like abode. The living room had a long green sofa, two maple chairs, and three round tables set in no particular order. The carpeting was synthetic and thin, the color of dust. The four windows had no drapes or curtains, but the shades were drawn.

"Have a seat, Mr. Rawlins," Esther said.

I took one of the maple chairs so that the kids could touch each other while sitting on the couch.

"We don't have anything to drink except lime Kool-Aid and water," Esther continued as she reached out to take Evander's hand.

For his part he seemed completely happy. What young man wouldn't when he was being loved so hard?

362

"I don't need anything to drink," I said. "I just wanted to tell you that your mother came by my place with Ashton today."

"What . . . what did they want?"

"Angeline was of the opinion that you were a child who could be dragged home. I disabused her of that notion."

"Huh?"

"She wants you to call and drop by with Evander. If you clean up and don't make out on the floor I'm pretty sure that she'll accept you guys living together. But, Evander, I wouldn't go to work in the family business if I were you."

"We're gonna get jobs and go to LACC," the young man said.

"Good. I saw Timbale too. She told me to tell you to call her before she goes to work."

"Okay," Evander said, and then he looked down at my feet.

"Are you gonna tell him?" Esther asked her man.

He shrugged, not making eye contact with either one of us.

"Tell him, Evy," Esther demanded. "Tell him."

Evander Noon looked up at me and said, "I remember what happened."

51

"I was . . . I mean, I went up on the Sunset Strip because this guy Eddie Turkel that I work with was makin' fun'a me for livin' at home and he said that I wouldn't ever do anything different or wild. I told him that I was gonna go up to the Sunset Strip and go to a go-go club. And I did too. I took the bus up there at about eight o'clock and met this white girl named Ruby sellin' flowers out a plastic bucket on Fairfax." Evander said all this in a trancelike delivery. "I saw her and she was nice to me and I kissed her. . . ." He looked guiltily over at Esther, but she just smiled. "I kissed her and . . . and she had a pill or something in her mouth and I swallowed it. We got food and walked around. We dropped by this big fancy house and then went to this place with prostitutes and stuff. She was doin' makeup and I sat on a chair waitin'. And this man, Maurice, came up and asked if I was solo. By that time I was seein' things that weren't there and feeling stuff really deep inside. I told him that I didn't understand and he said let's go and I went. I don't know why I did but I did.

"He took us to the Flamingo Motel on Hollywood Boulevard. There was this cottage out back that he had rented for the night. He told me to put on these dark clothes that were too big. It was a sweatshirt and a trench coat. Then he drove us to somewhere downtown and told me that we were gonna play a joke on someone there. He said that he'd pay me fifty dollars to do that, and I said okay but really I wasn't listenin'. I mean, I heard what he said, but at the same time I kept on seein' things and hearin' things, and it was like everybody and everything was in this play and I was in it too.

"Me and Maurice went into this empty building and then we went into this closet and closed the door mostly, so we could see out but nobody could see in. These two guys came passin' by and Maurice jumped out with this gun and told them to stop, and even though I was high on that acid Ruby gave me I could still tell that those men was scared for their lives. One guy was gettin' ready to hit Maurice but he hit him in the head with his pistol. The men was both carryin' these burlaplike bags and Maurice told me to take them. I was scared then that I might get shot. I didn't know that man. I was so scared that he had to yell at me to grab the bags. As soon as I had them Maurice shot the guy standin' closest to him in the chest. It was really weird, because the guy looked so surprised. The man Maurice shot fell on me and he was bleedin'. Most'a the blood got on the bags, though. And thèn, just like that, in less time than anyone would have to think, the other guy, the one Maurice had hit, pulled out a gun and shot Maurice and Maurice shot him back. I lit outta there with the bags still in my hands. I was holdin' on to them as hard as I could and I ran down the hallway. There was more shots and I thought I heard Maurice shoutin' again but I just kept on runnin'. I ran outta that buildin' and into the street.

"I had them bags and there was monkeys jumpin' all around and the street signs said bad words and my name. I was so scared that Maurice would get mad if I lost his bags, but the blood on 'em was like it was a neon light or somethin', so I took off the trench coat and tied the arms together and the flaps at the back and made another bag for the other two. You could still see a little blood but not that much.

"After that it gets a little confused. I waited at a bus stop, and when the bus came I told the driver that I wanted to go to the Flamingo Motel on Hollywood Boulevard.

"He must'a told me somethin', because I remember gettin' on another bus and another one. People talked to me but I couldn't answer them. When I got to the Flamingo I snuck around to the cottage out back and climbed in through the window.

"After that you know what happened."

I let the story breathe a moment, wondering how

much of it was true. I didn't doubt that Evander believed the tale, but he was on an acid trip.

"When did you remember all this?" I asked.

"It's like . . . it's like I always remembered it, but it was in a part of my head that couldn't get to my mouth. I mean, when I woke up I saw the money and the blood and I was just scared. But . . . but in the back of my mind I knew what happened. I knew it but couldn't tell anybody. That's why I went lookin' for Ruby. I wanted her to tell me so that I could remember."

"And when were you able to speak it?" I asked.

"When Esther took my hands and told me to calm down this morning. I woke up sweatin' and she wanted to know about the nightmare."

"And that was what you just told me?"

He nodded and looked away, ashamed about something.

"You two have to keep this story a secret," I said. "Don't tell your mother, Esther."

"I won't."

"And you, Evander, don't you breathe a word about this. Not a word to anyone—ever."

He nodded again.

"I put the money with a man who will know how to handle it," I said. "I'll ask him to make sure your mother gets a certain sum each month for the next ten years or so. That'll help with you and your sisters."

"What happened to Maurice?" he asked.

"He's dead."

"And the other two?"

"One's dead and the other one is soon to be arrested. I wouldn't worry about them."

I didn't mention Keith Handel. Why bring up problems that might never arise?

"Thank you, Mr. Rawlins," Evander said. "You saved my life."

He held out a hand and I grabbed it, saying, "And you saved mine."

"I want to thank you too," Esther said.

Their gratitude was in its own way payment. It was like in the old days when I traded my skills for favors and friendship.

"I'm sorry I couldn't tell you all this stuff before, Mr. Rawlins."

"That's okay, Evander. It wouldn't have helped anyway."

"Hello?" Bonnie Shay said, answering her phone on the first ring.

"Hey." I was sitting on my TV room couch feeling almost like an ordinary citizen.

Upon hearing my voice she went silent, appreciating the normalcy of us talking on the phone. I did not interrupt that quiet with useless words.

"How are you, Easy?" the island woman asked maybe a minute later.

"Better than ever," I said. "Good."

"Your business with Raymond finished?"

"Just about. Almost done. I went through the whole thing without even getting bruised up or arrested. You know I must be doin' somethin' right."

"It's very nice hearing your voice."

"It's nice hearing my voice talking to you."

That earned us another spate of blissful calm.

"Feather's here," Bonnie said at last. "She wants to talk to you."

"Hi, Daddy," my big girl said a moment later.

"Hey, baby."

"How are you feeling?"

"Really good."

"Frenchie likes you now, huh?" she said.

"A kind of miracle."

"Daddy?"

"Yeah, babe?"

"You can talk to me about my mother when you feel like it, okay?"

"Just as soon as we're settled and a family again."

"I love you, Daddy."

At that moment I fully realized what I had almost lost. An ache filled my chest and I stood up from the sofa.

"Everything's going to be all right, Feather. I promise you that."

Soon after I got off the phone with my almost-again family, it rang.

"Hello?"

"How was your talk with Giles Lehman?" Melvin Suggs asked.

"He wasn't home."

"No?"

"Come on, Melvin," I said. "What kind of trick are you tryin' to play?"

"Whenever somebody asks me about someone and then that someone turns up dead, my mind starts playing tricks."

"Giles is dead?"

"Yes, he is, very much so."

"At his house?"

"In an abandoned building down on skid row. It's a place where people meet to do business off the books."

"When?"

"He bled to death from a gunshot wound three or four days ago."

"Wow. That's something."

"What do you know about it, Easy?"

"Melvin, I was looking for the live Giles just this morning. I had no idea he was dead."

"We busted the Laundromat," Suggs put in.

"Did they know?"

"What do you think?"

370

"I'm sorry, Brother Suggs. But that's what gangsters do, right? They kill each other."

"Walk softly, Easy Rawlins. You might survive this and you might survive that, but once you're in their sights they will keep after you until they get you."

"Is that all you have?" I asked.

He hung up then. Like any intelligent man Suggs knew when the discussion was over.

I dithered around the house for an hour or so cleaning up little messes that the squatter Jeffrey had made. Putting the house back in order, I wondered about my mortality, about moving and thinking while so many others I had known were under the ground, their deeds not even memories to their descendants, any value they accrued either erased or perverted. In the middle of sweeping the kitchen I stopped and downed Mama Jo's second-to-last bottle of medicine. I didn't need it, but it struck me that I'd like to feel one last jolt of power before returning to the day-to-day existence of a workingman in a cracked world.

I went to the TV room to sit down to experience Jo's magic.

The heat from that dose was different than before. It made me feel warm like a sunbather in the noon sun of the hottest day of a heat wave. I passed in and out of conscious awareness, remembering details of a life I'd no right to have endured.

A feeling like the moments before awareness when Lynne Hua sat next to me settled in. I remembered my mother teaching me to laugh and sing, her big soft lap always my refuge from a hard world. I was no longer being tossed about and battered, even though that was the only life I'd ever known.

From outside I could hear the passing of cars, which sounded like gusts of wind. I considered turning on the TV, but the idea of electric sound was too harsh for my mood.

And then there came a soft footfall, a sound so slight it might have been imagined.

In the gray-brown, bulging, cyclopean eye of the TV I saw his form in the doorway behind me and to the left. . . .

I took a fraction of a moment to allow my mind to go blank. Then, with my left hand, I took hold of the cushion next to me and flung it with just enough accuracy. I was up and leaping toward the intruder before the stiff square pillow hit his arm. The .22 pistol fired, sounding no louder than a cap gun.

We were falling in the doorway between the kitchen and living room, the distance to the floor encompassing two entire lifetimes of fighting and struggle.

Keith Handel was still bigger and younger and

stronger than I. The last time we met, his Las Vegas friend pushed me down with only some effort. But this time I was at full power, reliving every fight I had ever been in. There were back-woods juke joints orchestrating my gyrations; the stench of rotting corpses set by the side of the victory road on our drive into Berlin fueled my heart, and there was blood in my mouth, its bitter tang warning me that it was all or nothing right there in my own house.

I strained against my would-be killer with a primordial effort. I wasn't thinking about the attack but relying on the automatic skills driven into my body by three years of warfare and forty-seven years of life on the wrong side of the white man's tracks.

I pressed against Handel with all the power in me, and then all at once my strength was gone. I collapsed on the floor, unable even to raise my arms, incapable of responding to the cramps in my chest and thighs. I was breathing like a Greco-Roman wrestler after his greatest challenge, lost.

Keith Handel, I knew, was gathering his resources, lifting his pistol, readying to shoot me in the back of the head.

Why wasn't I dead? How long did it take to pull a trigger?

Then I remembered that he, Handel, was there to retrieve his loot from the robbery.

He needed me alive, at least for a little while.

After long moments of deep, deep breathing I heaved up on my side, expecting to see the man standing over me with a gun in his hand.

Instead I saw that he was on the floor, on his side too, his back turned to me. I could see both his hands. Neither one held a gun. I wasn't strong enough to get to my feet, so I crawled toward Handel. I grabbed onto his shoulder, turning him over and pushing myself to a sitting position in the same motion.

Keith Handel was dead—strangled by a veteran of the Battle of the Bulge. His eyes were wide-open and his mouth agape.

I sat there next to my attacker feeling like he looked. While I was gasping for air it occurred to me that the only reason he pulled off that shot was because I hit him with that pillow.

I searched but luckily there was no liquor in the house. Jeffrey must've finished off the bottle I kept for guests. If not, I would have drained it, no doubt. But I needed to be sober to figure out the conundrum of the killer's corpse on the floor.

What was I supposed to do?

If I was a white man the answer to the riddle would have been simple. If I was a white man there wouldn't have been a riddle at all. A man breaks into your house with a gun and you fought back and won—that was self-defense in any world. Any world except the home of a black man in an America nourished on the bonemeal of his ancestors.

When I couldn't find any liquor, I poured a glass of water and sat at the table to get my wind back and consider the possibilities. Looking at the tabletop I noticed drops of blood plopping down, spraying tinier droplets around their red centers.

I was bleeding. The bullet Keith Handel fired had grazed my left cheek. I pressed the heel of my palm against the flesh wound. For some reason this had a clearing effect on my mind.

I was a black man in a white world where black men were hated—and worse, feared. Keith Handel, for all his shortcomings, was white. He was dead and I had survived. Where I came from that was a crime in itself.

When the bleeding was stanched I knew what I had to do. Even Melvin Suggs couldn't keep a killing like this from the courts, and once on trial I would be crucified. There was a part of my mind that said this might not be true, that I might be found innocent by a jury of my peers.

This optimism made me laugh; it brought out the rough guffaws of all my dead ancestors back to the slave ships.

"Hello?" EttaMae Harris said at ten minutes past eleven.

"Etta."

"What's wrong, Easy?"

"I need Mouse."

"Hang on."

There was no complaint about the lateness of the call. Etta would never ask me why I would need a man like her husband.

"Hey, Easy, what's up?" Raymond asked on a yawn.

"You got to come over, Ray. I need your help."

"Sit tight, baby, the cavalry on its way."

53

He was at the door by midnight. I let him in and gestured at the corpse.

I had huddled the body into a fetal position so that if we had to take it somewhere it would be the right shape to fit in a trunk.

"That's one'a the dudes from your office," Mouse said as a matter of fact.

"Him and two others got Evander in that jam. It was just a fluke, but trouble still and all."

"How'd he sneak up on you?"

"I figure he picked the back door lock earlier in the day and then snuck through when he knew I'd be in."

"Why was he after you?" Mouse said while squatting down to see my handiwork up close.

"Money, man. The money the guy who fooled Evander stole."

"How much?"

"Over two hundred thousand."

"Damn, I guess that's worth a craps throw with the Grim Reaper."

"Or maybe no."

"Maybe no," Mouse agreed, patting the stiffening corpse on the shoulder.

He bounced to his feet like a much younger man and slapped his hands together.

"What do you suggest we do with him?" I asked.

"Mama Jo the only way to go when a brothah kills a white man."

"Mama Jo?"

"Easy, I hope you don't think you the first colored killed a Caucasian when there weren't no other choice."

"I guess not."

"When that event occurs the best bet is Jo's backyard vat. Here, lemme hold your car keys."

"What for?"

"I'm gonna turn your car around so we can get Slick here into the trunk without bein' seen by pryin' eyes."

On the way out to Compton I told Raymond about my talk with Timbale. I was in a mild state of shock and had to talk about something.

"So she's gonna tell him that she really don't know who killed Frank?" he asked.

"Yep."

"And what if he come up on me and ask me point-blank if I did it?"

"Tell him what you'd tell anybody, Ray."

"You mean I should lie?"

"Either that or we go over his house and kill him right now. And while we're at it we might as well shoot Esther Corey too, because the way they been goin' at it she probably pregnant with his son. And then there's her mama and Ashton Burnet. Might as well go scorched earth and kill everyone."

I was driving and Mouse was facing me, leaning against the door. He rubbed his chin as if he was counting up bullets and then said, "All right, man. I don't like it, not one bit. I don't wanna lie to the boy, but you right about Esther, Angeline, and Ashton. And then Timbale would probably wanna get in on the act too. That much bloodshed is bad for business."

I would have laughed, but I didn't in deference to the dead man in the trunk.

Raymond had me back my red car up between two old eucalyptus trees at the side of Jo's lot.

We went to the hidden front door then and knocked. After a few minutes Jo appeared in a bright blue housecoat and cranberry slippers.

"What is it, Raymond?" she asked.

"We need the backyard vat, Jo."

Her minor vexation vanished in an instant.

"You parked at the back entrance?" she asked.

"Yes, ma'am."

"Okay. Go around to the gate and I'll let you in."

Raymond and I opened the trunk, allowing the dead gangster to be illuminated by moonlight.

What seemed like a stand of bushy vines turned out to be a double-doored gate that Jo pulled open from the inside. This portal revealed a large grassy lot that was surrounded on all sides by trees. I suspected that there was fencing beyond the wood that was invisible to me.

Beside Jo was a deep wheelbarrow. Mouse and I didn't need any direction to pick up the dead man and deposit him in the one-wheeled cart.

"Here now, Easy," Jo said. "Wheel this man ovah to the far corner with me."

There was a magical feel to the big yard. A half-moon shone down, shedding light on big white flowers and light-colored stones placed here and there. We got to a shadowy grotto in the center of a group of trees that I couldn't identify. Jo reached up in the leaves and a weak electric light sparked. Sitting in shadow was a huge oak barrel four times the width of the largest barrel I'd ever seen.

"Can you lift him up?" Jo asked.

I looked around and saw that Mouse had stayed by the gate. Maybe he was guarding the entrance, or maybe the disposal of bodies was the job of the killer in Jo's gospel. Whatever it was I said, "I can sure try."

She lifted the round wooden lid from the top of the four-foot-high barrel. Inside, filling the vat to three-quarters full, was a black liquid that showed sparks here and there that looked like stars if there was no atmosphere to lessen their brilliance. The liquid also seemed to be motile, exhibiting a subtle motion beneath its surface.

"Throw him in," Jo said, and I realized that this was to be my last trial on the journey back to the living world.

I got my arms under the big dead man and then, lifting from my thighs, I wrestled against his weight, which felt like a living thing struggling to get back to the ground. I was breathing hard again. I moved next to the barrel, allowing part of the weight to rest above the center bulge. Then I pressed with all my might, pushing Keith Handel up an inch at a time toward the rim. Twice he began to roll down and twice I lifted him back up again. Maybe three inches from my goal I stopped, knowing that I couldn't budge him one more inch.

That's when Mama Jo got in behind me and pushed, grunting as she did so. Together we got the clay of Keith Handel up and over the edge of the big vat and his body tumbled in, immersed in the dark glittering oil.

I stared after the corpse. It didn't seem to have much of an effect on the liquid. There were a few more sparks and maybe a fraction more of added movement.

"In three days there won't be anything left of the flesh, clothes, hair, bones, or teeth," Jo said. "Even metal erodes in this vat here. It's where dead men come to the very end of their journey."

"What's in there?" I asked.

"Life," she said, like a Baptist minister exhorting the spirit of an entire congregation.

I dropped Mouse off at his home; we didn't say a word on the drive. From there I headed back toward West Los Angeles. On the way I tried to think about my rebirth and the people that were there to bring me that far. But all I could conjure was the image of that cauldron of black liquid fire and a single syllable: "Life."

About the Author

Walter Mosley is the author of more than forty books, including eleven Easy Rawlins mysteries, the first of which, *Devil in a Blue Dress*, was made into an acclaimed film starring Denzel Washington. *Always Outnumbered* was an HBO film starring Laurence Fishburne, adapted from his first Socrates Fortlow novel. A native of Los Angeles and a graduate of Goddard College, Mosley holds an MFA from CCNY and lives in Brooklyn, New York. He is the winner of numerous awards, including an O. Henry Award, a Grammy, and PEN America's Lifetime Achievement Award.

Center Point Large Print
600 Brooks Road / PO Box 1
Thorndike ME 04986-0001 USA

(207) 568-3717

US & Canada:
1 800 929-9108
www.centerpointlargeprint.com